KILLERS BIKERS & FREAKS

A Walt Asher Florida Thriller

ANDREW ALLAN

ISBN-10: 1537037587
ISBN-13: 978-1537037585

THANKS

To you, for reading this book.

To Sally Bosco, for editing this book.

To Lynne Hansen and Jeff Strand, for guidance, encouragement,
and cover art.

To my friends and first draft readers:
Doug McDermott, Noah Belson, Eric Norman, Sean Pfile.

To Leslie, my Bsom, for whom I thank my lucky stars.

To Andrew, Lucy, and Creighton, for providing perfect purpose.

Cheers!

To my parents, Dan & Martie Allan.

The best in the biz.

Also by Andrew Allan

Bodies, Blades & Rituals
(Walt Asher Book 2)

Sell Shock
(A Walt Asher Short Thriller)

Walt's Fault
(A Walt Asher Short Thriller)

The Pimp's Henchman

1

It was late afternoon, golden hour sun cast orange across the pine trees, picture perfect. And, there I was pecking away at a script. Still. Not casually, a tap here, a tap-tap there. Hardcore, up-against-it writing and typing, trying to finish the job in short order. Not because of some cranky client deadline, though I have plenty of those. I just couldn't stand being stuck inside when the conditions were so perfect outside. I needed to be in that river, the Rainbow River - crisp, cool, 72-degrees year-round. My preferred haunt, located just east of Dunnellon, Central Florida.

It taunted me, that river. Glistening, glowing, winking sunlight through my rear office window. Its proposition was clear: Would I like to use the valuable, ever-dwindling minutes of my life afloat and happy, or am I content to sit and type?

That's when the typing stopped. And, I was gone in a blink. Dashing out the back door, across the lawn, my desk chair still spinning by the time I dove into the water. Impulsive, sure. But, I've been known to act fast on a hunch. Sometimes it works, sometimes well...

I broke the water's surface and relaxed my body to let the current take me downstream. It was entirely relaxing. And, a clear reminder of why I do what I do. I make quite a fine living as a freelance infomercial scriptwriter. Yes, those infomercials. "But, wait! There's more!" Yes, those commercials and programs you and your friends laugh about when they play on television in the middle of the night. Sure, they're silly. But, they're also cash cows. And, the more you see them, the more they're working, the more someone is making a ton of money.

And if those guys are making money, I'm making money. And, I like money. But, I don't love it. There's a big difference. I just want enough money to take care of my three kids, keep the ex off my back, and keep the miserable corporate world festering afar in the hot swamp of its deranged greed. Maybe that's just my excuse for a lack of ambition. Some might say I just couldn't hack it. Perhaps. All I know is, happiness is a big part of the life equation. The part those places habitually forget.

I served my time in the grind - Meetings, asshole bosses, dickhead co-workers, and sad, lost people making decisions driven by fear instead of sound ideas. That atmosphere isn't just toxic, it's insane. They'll do fine without me. With infomercials, I set my schedule, work with who I like, balance work with pleasure, and do indeed make just enough. Great work if you can get it.

Problem is, once you get it, you gotta do it. And, here I was happy but slacking. The water felt too good to worry about it. My deadline wasn't until the end of the week. I could always pick up the slack tonight after dinner. Best to enjoy the moment.

The cool water rejuvenated my skin. Long strands of river grass tickled between my toes. I dove under the water and made a grab at some passing fish. They darted away. I surfaced near a knotty cypress knee at the edge of the river. Two baby turtles were perched for their daily sunning. A third baby turtle struggled to get up, so I gave it a push. It immediately drew its head, legs, and tail into its shell, which I steadied on the wood before letting the current take me away.

I set my sights for Ken's place.

"Those guys must have serious juice. Aren't you worried they'll find a way to smack you down, but good?" I said to Ken two weeks back.

He just smiled and shook his head. "Walt, you know the difference between me and ninety-nine percent of the activists out there trying to make a difference?"

"No, what?"

"I have the cash to back it up. And, you can bet I'll put my money where my mouth is," he said. "I could buy off the politicians and flip them to my cause just like the lobbyists did," he said. His tone was more matter of fact than arrogant.

"Good idea. Why don't you?" I said.

"It's still corrupt, even if I do it. Besides, it's more fun to turn their screws in public," he said with a devilish grin.

Ken Kerenz was one of the good guys. A friend, a father, and a man thoroughly dedicated to fixing the world. Although he never disclosed the exact figure, I knew he had made millions selling some bit of software that apparently impacted everyday lives, yours and mine. However much it was, Ken had retired by thirty-six. What a jerk, right? Well, get to know him and, like me, you'll end up being happy for him.

How are you gonna begrudge a guy who spent his days finding every way he can to better our lives? Among other things, he promoted solar energy and off-grid living, worked to strengthen bee colonies, and campaigned against "climate neglect" (his words, not mine.) Maybe not something you care much about. Certainly something you might benefit from. Ken had his convictions.

But, nothing beat Ken's yen for messing with the corrupt politicians, businessmen, and all around scumbags who are convinced they have a god given right to destroy Florida and screw over every Floridian. He didn't just harass them. He shamed them with force. He threw down the gauntlet and dared them to fight back. Naturally, they did, for theirs is a complete contempt. So, Ken would respond in kind and make clear he's no mosquito to simply be swatted away. He liked to ride right up to their high-rise front doors – with protests, lawsuits, newspaper exposes, and more to make his point. In one point-proving instance, he even rented a dump truck and had it deposit three tons of toxic sludge into the water fountain outside the stately Cargon Phosphate Company tower. And, that was after he'd had the CEO's Bentley Continental parked in the fountain.

"If they can pollute our turf we can mess with theirs," he said. I couldn't drum up a suitable counter argument as we walked the humid streets of Downtown Tampa.

Ken did not fuck around. That brought him plenty of enemies. And, I couldn't help thinking they'd be thrilled to hear the news: Ken's dead.

2

All I could see on my approach was two gators ripping a man's body apart. But then they flipped the limp body over and revealed Kens' face. I froze in the water and almost sank, mesmerized. One gator gnawed a leg. The other had its jaws locked around the torso over the shoulder and was dragging Ken into the water. Right towards me.

I swam fast to the riverbank and took a wide approach through the neighbor's yard. When I reached Ken's backyard, I grabbed a paddle off the canoe parked on the dock.

My adrenaline surged and my heart pounded. Jesus, this sucker was huge. I choked up on the paddle handle and moved along the dock until I stood directly over the big beast. I didn't want to mess with it. But, damn...I had to get it off Ken.

I hammered the paddle against its head. The gator roared and chomped and slid further down into the water, dragging Ken with him. I moved further down the dock and hit it several more times. The paddle didn't make much of a dent, but it was becoming an irritation.

The big gator let go and floated back into the water. The smaller gator ripped Ken's leg off. The sound of tearing flesh almost made me vomit. I had to hurry. I leapt off the dock onto the lawn and grabbed Ken's arm. I pulled as hard and fast as I could, dragging his body up the lawn towards the house. Then, I ran back. Gators have a natural fear of humans. But, they'll only back down so much. And, they'll certainly fight for a free meal. Lucky for me, this gator seemed content with just a leg. When I swung the paddle in its direction it slunk back into the river and moved on.

I ran back to the body. He was shredded, mangled, and bloody. I dragged him up to the raised deck so the gators couldn't return for the leftovers. But, it wasn't going to save Ken. He was already gone. All I could do now was make the phone call.

By the time the cops and game officers arrived, the sun had dried me, and I had gotten past the initial shock of Ken's death. From there it was all business, answering their questions, pointing out where I found him with the alligators, and speculating where they might have gone. Ken's wife, Karen, hadn't returned home by the time the clean up crew wheeled what was left of Ken out on a stretcher. I planned on sticking around to give her the news in person.

The Game Officer wandered up wiping his hands.

"Gators don't usually mess with people," I said to game officer who had just walked up.

"Unless they're protecting their young," he said. "But, that's mostly in the Spring when they have a fresh litter."

I looked at him. "Why do you think these two attacked?"

He shrugged, the said, "Couldn't rightly tell you. First time I know of it happening. Sure is a shame."

He shook his head as he wandered off to the front of the house."

A shame indeed. I know I talked Ken up. But, if there was one thing to make you dislike the guy it's how fit and athletic he is. Was. There's no way the gators could have gotten to him unless he didn't see them down low on the river bank.

I could hear the service vehicles driving off. Grey clouds blocked the sun, dimming the natural light. A breeze whispered through the Spanish moss. It rains every afternoon in Florida during the summer. It's a glorious phenomenon that cools the air and tweaks the natural light, making everything easier to see. I looked to the river, focusing on nothing in particular, simply trying to process what had happened.

I turned to the large bungalow house just as the sun re-appeared from behind the clouds. Its light triggered a bright, white glint that caught my eye. Just under the porch deck near the narrow strip of white lattice fencing installed to keep critters from roaming into the crawlspace under the house. I walked over with my eyes locked on the glint. I reached down and picked up a small glass vial.

I sat on the patio deck and studied it. It was three inches long and an inch in diameter. A small label featured three sets of letter pairings.

Code I couldn't decipher. Amber tinged liquid residue inside, like diluted honey. It wasn't sun bleached or dirty, so it couldn't have been there long. I didn't recall any of the crime scene techs injecting anything into Ken's body. Not sure why they would. He wasn't dying. He was *reported dead*. Now, this was weird.

I stood up and scanned the ground for more but found nothing. It was then I heard Ken's wife's car pull into the drive. I tucked the vial in my swimsuit pocket and walked up to the house. Things were about to get ugly.

When I reached the front of the house I saw Sheriff Baker hadn't left. Karen glanced out her car window looking worried as she gathered her belongings. I trotted over to the Sheriff.

"Hey Sheriff, I found this in the backyard. Might be important," I said.

He took the vial and looked at it with skepticism. "What does this have to do with alligators?"

"I don't know. Seems an odd thing to find in the backyard of a family home."

"Your friend dabble in this kind of stuff?" He sniffed it. "Smells like chemicals."

"Not that I know of. But, he's pretty diverse."

A funny look.

"Was, I mean," I said.

He drew a white, discolored handkerchief from his back pocket and wrapped the vial with it. "I'll take it to the office and see what they can find out about it."

"Thanks," I said.

Karen walked our way.

"Walt, what is it?" she said.

The Sheriff lingered by his car. "I'm legally obliged to tell her. But, I can let it slide if you think it best."

This sucked. But, I had to be the one to tell her. "I'll do it."

She walked towards the police car. "Is everything...what's going on?" she said.

"Let's go inside Karen," I said as I took her by the arm.

3

Karen did not take the news well, as expected. I offered to stick around and help out. But, she wanted to absorb the blow in private. She also didn't want anyone there when she told the kids. Understandable. I hugged her goodbye and hit the road. It was a rotten walk back to my place.

After I had poured my preferred drink, a boulevardier, and let it kick in, I called my significant other, Ilsa. She was managing her bars in Gainesville, an hour and a half north of here. She was shocked and dismayed by the sad news. We had spent plenty of good times with Ken. She asked me to give Karen her love, which I agreed to. Ilsa and I had plans to go to Melbourne on the Space Coast this weekend. It was to be the latest of our mandatory every-six-weeks mini vacations. But, she said we should wait. Do our natural grieving and we'll go after Ken's funeral, for which I promised to get the pertinent details.

Losing a friend makes you pull your loved ones closer. And, I was dying to see Ilsa. It had been almost two weeks. Nothing we weren't used to. But, still...long distance relationships are tough and require work. And, these were strange circumstances.

I was about to hang up when a thought nagged me and interrupted my parting salutation.

"What?" she said.

"I found something strange at the house. Ken's house," I said. I paused a moment to collect my thoughts. "A little glass vial. Had copper liquid in it and some abbreviated markings on the label."

"So?"

"Well, I don't know. Just seemed out of place, you know?"

"Not really. I wasn't there," she said. Ilsa could be blunt at times. I blame her stoic Dutch heritage. "Was it for the lawn?'

"No. Looked like it came out of a lab. Maybe medical," I said.

"Was Ken taking anything?"

"Not that I know of. Maybe. He didn't update me on that."

"But, it made you think something's up?"

"Sounds funny. But, yes, that crossed my mind," I said. I felt like a fool for mentioning it. "Anyway, I gave it to the Sheriff. Maybe he'll figure out what it is and if it relates to Ken."

"Hmmm. Well, I am proud of you, lover. You aided a friend in a desperate time and performed a civic duty. You should treat yourself to a cocktail. You've earned it," she said.

"Already there." I held my glass up in toast, took a sip, and smacked my lips.

"Good boy. Now, do what you do best – write and relax. Drink to your fallen friend. Remember your best times."

She had me feeling better already.

"Okay. I don't know why finding that vial struck me. It was like all my sensors went off," I said.

"Forget your suspicions. If something foul is up, you don't want to get involved. I don't want you involved." Her voice was sharper now.

"I'm not..."

"Besides, what would my big, strong infomercial writer do if there were some bad guys? Sell 'em to death?"

Point taken.

"Sounds like I need to get up there and smack your sassy ass back into place," I said.

"Mmmm. Don't tease. Just get me the details for the funeral and be ready to love me when I drive down," she said. Quite a woman.

"Will do," I said.

Click.

Chill, sweet women don't excite me. I need one with kick. She had plenty. And, I found her irresistible.

Between Ilsa and the boulevardier I felt loose enough to sit down and write. Work would be a fine distraction. And, progress on an assignment always made me feel better. But, after just a few pecks on the keyboard, it was no go. I was distracted. Something nagged at me.

Those sensors again.

Questions arose: How could Ken not have seen those Alligators? He was fit and strong. How could he not have gotten away in time? The logical answer: Only if something or someone prevented him from escaping. And, what did the glass vial have to do with anything?

Ilsa wouldn't like it. But, I grabbed my phone and called Tom Brown, an inventor friend. He'd invented a revolutionary new type of can opener for one of the big infomercial marketing companies. I was hired to write the script. We hit it off on set while shooting the commercial. Fast friends. My theory: His ridiculously boring name is a counterpoint to his radically brilliant mind.

"Tom, it's Walt," I said.

"Hey man. It's been so long I figured you stopped talking and vowed only to type."

"Not a bad idea. Computers don't talk back."

"What's doin? New show?"

"No. Personal business. Something weird."

"Okay..."

I had to get the words straight in my mind before speaking. I didn't want to sound crazy to Tom, too.

"All I can say right now is I found a glass vial with some amber liquid in it. The vial had an open tip end. There was no packaging other than a small label with handwritten letter combinations on it. The letters are: LN, BTX, VX."

"Doesn't tell me much."

"I know. But, see what you can dig up on those letter combos."

"How fast you need it?"

"As soon as you can get it. But, not end of the world stuff. Just trying to satisfy my curiosity," I said. I was relieved he didn't say I sounded insane.

"Okay, I'll let you know soon," he said.

"I appreciate it."

I felt good after talking to Tom. It may have been something...or nothing at all. Either way, I had to check. Ken would have done the same for me. Following up was the least I could do for him. I'd love for my suspicions to have been wrong about it.

4

Ken was buried four days later. It was a fine service. But, knowing Ken was dead felt rotten. And, wrong. Karen Kerenz pulled me and Ilsa aside as the mourners started to depart the gravesite.

"Thank you for all your help, Walt," she said.

"Let me know whatever else I can do," I said.

"And, if you need to just get away, please come up to Gainesville. We can make it a girl's weekend.

A small smile from Karen. "We're overdue."

Ilsa noticed Karen's attention drifting. She stepped in and gave her a hug.

Then, I screwed it up.

"Karen...did Ken ever work with chemicals or homemade compounds?" I said.

Ilsa shot back from her embrace with Karen. "Walt..."

"What do you mean?" Karen gave me permission to proceed despite Ilsa's glare. I gave her a 'don't worry' look. She responded with a 'would you please shut the fuck up' look.

"Well, I don't know. Just something he talked to me about once." Weak, Asher. Weak.

"Walt, let Karen get back to her car. The kids are waiting," said Ilsa, stepping over, winding her arm through mine, and pulling me away.

"I'm taking them to my parents in West Palm. I need to get away from the river. It won't be the same without Ken," said Karen.

She looked over to a stretch limousine parked a few yards away. It was one of the last cars remaining at the cemetery. Her kids, two boys – Kelvin, nine, and Kory, six - they were a 'K' family – were taking turns running the interior length of the vehicle. The driver looked like he wanted to snap at them, but he stood by patiently.

"Ken had enemies. Think anyone...you know..." It came out sudden enough to even surprise myself.

"Walt!" Ilsa squeeze my arm and gave me a death stare.

Karen turned to me, poised. "My late husband angered many people. But, they all respected his positions, whether they agreed with him or not."

"Let's go, Walt," said Ilsa. She didn't give me a choice. "Karen, call me when you want to come up."

"I will," said Karen.

"Take care, Karen," I said.

As I walked, and Ilsa stomped, to the car, I looked over at Ken's grave. It was a fresh reminder of how short our time is. How little control we have.

Ilsa hit fast and hit hard. A punch right to my shoulder. I almost lost control of the car.

"You are a cold son of a bitch!" she said. Unsatisfied with just one punch, she hit again to emphasize the point. I anticipated that one and grabbed her fist as it flew through the air.

"Calm down," I said. "I might have been a little quick with the questions, but she handled 'em fine."

"You just don't do that, Walter. She's grieving."

"I'm trying to help her."

A silent moment followed.

"Whatever is happening, if you get involved, then I do, too," she said. "I don't want any part of it."

"Fair enough," I said.

"So, will you stop? Please."

I didn't want to commit. But, I was starting to feel bad about how I'd put Karen on the spot at her husband's funeral. "Yes," I said.

"Please, you're a good man. But, I don't want anything to ever happen to you. Sometimes it is just better to look away, no?'

"Yes. Sometimes," I said.

"We've had too many days apart. I don't want to start our vacation by fighting." She leaned her head on my shoulder.

I turned up the music and reached over and ran my fingers through her soft, golden hair. No more words required. Les Baxter's 'Jewels of the Sea' swirled to life and filled the sonic space with its romantic exotica schmaltz. But, this was one of 'our' records. A Walt/Ilsa classic. Sure to soothe the mood.

A short while later we were driving southeast on the Florida turnpike. Ilsa had fallen asleep on my shoulder and I was alone with my thoughts.

Ilsa is *the one*. Hilarious, smart, and sincere. Brassy, yet kind. A personality to charm your pants off and a stranger to no one. And, she is stunning. Slim, fit, and busty. Sexy without trying.

We met fifteen years ago, working together on a project, me as writer her as a stylist. Friendly from the start. But, both married at the time. Then, she moved to Gainesville from Tampa and we went our separate ways. Through a chance meeting at a mutual friend's birthday party we re-connected and learned we had something new in common: We had both gotten divorced. Things clicked, hot and fast.

Perhaps like you, I've heard each person has three great loves in their life: Their first love when you start to get a hint of the magic and the pain it offers. Then, the first serious relationship, often a marriage that lasts for quite some time but is rife with inexperience that leads to heartache. And finally, true love. The love that doesn't have to try too hard but somehow works so well, a synergy is formed. You feel it when it happens. I felt it with Ilsa. That's how I knew she was the one. Despite that, we felt no compulsion to marry. Neither of us needed a piece of paper to say that what we share was legit.

Besides the sappy stuff...who could pass on a woman who digs Charles Bronson movies? I couldn't. She loved Bronson movies for the justice served. The bad guys were really bad, and Bronson made them pay. Hard. You don't see enough of that in the world.

Ilsa came to the States from the Netherlands as a teenager. The youngest of four sisters. She has that Dutch wherewithal to simply figure things out. And, she did that in spades, figuring out how to make a serious buck in the Gainesville bar business. Not a bad business to be in when college students invade your city nine months out of the year and you own four of the most happening bars in town. She was doing just fine.

She woke up as we arrived in Melbourne.

"Guten Tag, love," she said.

"Lady, I've worked up a killer thirst. And, it ain't for beer," I said with a sly glance her direction.

"Let's get to that hotel."

A couple of hours later we were flush faced and relaxing in the hotel lounge. A boulevardier for me, Bee's Knees for her.

"We could do that every day if you move to Clearwater," I said.

"Or, if you move to Gainesville, Herr Asher."

She knew I couldn't due to the terms of my divorce agreement, which prevented me from moving more than fifty miles away from my children. Fine by me. I wanted to be close to them in case of an emergency. And, I visited them every chance I got.

"Until that happens, you're worth the trip."

We clinked glasses.

"I'm sorry for getting on your case earlier," she said. "I know your intentions are noble, but your timing stinks."

I conceded the point with a nod. "But, you still don't want me looking into it."

"I don't think there is anything to look into. He was eaten by alligators."

"Hmm. I suppose so."

She set her drink down in dramatic fashion. "Oh, you! I see you are never going to drop this until your curiosity is satisfied, yes?"

"Probably."

"Fine." She grabbed her drink and sipped. She studied me a moment before swallowing. "I must admit you are an admirable man. Maybe a little stupid, too." She was a master of compliments that don't quite flatter.

"Thanks, I guess."

She continued, "There is only one way to solve this."

"How's that?" I sipped my drink and studied her over the glass. Finally...

"W.W.B.D?"

"Huh?"

She leaned forward, her face pushing into a beam of light, making her expressions very clear.

"What would Bronson do?"

She looked at me matter of fact. I knew the answer.

"He'd kick ass and get justice."

She nodded.

"Do you think you can do that?"

I had to think about it.

She spoke before I could answer. "Let me put it another way...do you think you can kick ass and get justice without getting hurt. And, without your loved ones getting hurt? Because that's what happens in Bronson movies. Many casualties."

She had a point.

"I really don't think it will come to that. I'm just poking around, asking a few questions. And, like you, I really don't think it's going to lead anywhere."

"Just be careful."

I nodded. And, that was when Ken's death began to scare me.

5

We spent the next morning relaxing at the beach and that afternoon roaming around Melbourne. It was a fine small town filled with rocket scientists and surfers. A great place to have no plans. And, we didn't. We just enjoyed each other's company in all the ways a loving couple can. Thoughts of Ken's murder cropped up every couple of hours, but I was able to keep them on simmer and not get too worked up. The crashing waves, blowing breeze, and warmth of the sun can make you forget plenty.

Infomercial writers don't get many requests for solving crimes. Not to mention, I'm not a cop or detective or a military veteran and don't have their crime fighting resources either. But, one thing my commercial work has taught me is how people think. What motivates them – greed, fear, social acceptance. I need to know what drives people in order to persuade them to buy a product they don't need or didn't know they needed. And, figuring out what happened to Ken was all about looking at motivations. Flat on my back in bed, with Ilsa deep asleep at my side, I started to do what I always do when I sit down to write...I asked questions to put myself in someone else's head.

Like, if Ken was murdered, why would anyone want him dead? Had he finally piss off the wrong person? What was he working on? What did the killer hope to accomplish? What could be so big and so important that the only option was to kill Ken? Or, was it the only option? Maybe these guys were just ruthless and that's how they handle problems big or small. That was a chilling thought. Was the killing timed to an event? Upcoming or past? Who did the killing and who was the killing for? Too many questions and too late at night. I rolled over and wrapped around Ilsa's warm, naked body. A perfect distraction. As I started to relax, I admitted to myself that I wouldn't be able to answer any questions without more information.

We returned to Gainesville the next day feeling rested and recharged. I dropped Ilsa off and headed back to the river. Work was waiting for me. While in Melbourne, a job came in for a two-minute spot about a super duper ever-ready, always sharp stainless steel kitchen knife. Familiar territory, which shouldn't take too long to write. As long as I didn't get distracted with other things.

But, a big distraction was waiting for me when I got to the house: Someone had been here while I was gone. It took me a few minutes to pick up on it. But, I noticed things were out of place – The door to the laundry room was open, I always kept it closed. The files on my desk were too neat. I'm never that tidy. Nothing appeared to be missing. But, someone had been digging around. Ilsa had the only other key, and she'd been with me.

Being in the house gave me the willies. The doors and windows showed no signs of being broken into. I had no alarm because life on the river doesn't require it. But, I knew someone had been here. That was troubling. Who snuck in and what did they want? More to the point...what could I do about it? The answer: nothing. I couldn't tell anyone. Ilsa would get spooked, and I had no smoking gun evidence to show the cops. I just had to live with it.

I re-checked all the locks, secured all the doors and windows. I even used my mom's old trick of balancing a metal cook pan on a chair behind the front doors. The idea was the pan would clang and bang if anyone snuck in and the noise would alert me. After that, I set a scaling knife under my pillow and slid my buck knife in my pocket. I tried to write, but the words didn't come. I too nervous to concentrate.

The next day, work became the distraction I needed to forget about the break in. I finished up the long-form script I had been working on prior to Melbourne. It was a good pitch and I felt the product would sell, which was all that mattered in this business.

But, just after sending the script off to my client, my mind drifted back to Ken. There was no way to avoid it. I was shocked by his premature death and it was going to take some time to recover. He seemed more alive, more actively functioning than anyone I had ever met. He just couldn't be dead.

Hunger pangs took my mind off the darker thoughts drifting into my mind. The ones that come knocking whenever we were faced with a blow close to mortality. I closed the laptop, locked up the A-frame, and headed for town.

I'm not an overly religious person. But, if there is one temple worthy of praise in Dunnellon, it's Reymo's. When I lived full time in Clearwater, I would get a craving for one of their down and dirty barbecue biscuits and make the two-hour trip without hesitation, reservation, or regret. Some things you just don't deprive yourself of. Dr. Pepper helped slide them down the throat. A healthy belch and the rest of your day is properly calibrated.

But before I could eat, I ran into Nadine Evers. She was one of Ken's regular activist colleagues. He introduced us when I was single. Hung out with her at a party, but the way she went on about saving the river, it sounded like she wanted to have sex with it more than with me. I took that as a barometer of things to come and pursued no further.

After sharing a few mutual "what a shames" she surprised me. "There's no way his death was natural, you know that, right?" she said.

"What do you mean?" I studied her face. Was she serious or just messing with me? She looked worried, bitter.

"He had really been up a number of people's asses. I mean really just dropping his dick right in their caviar." Forgot how classy she could be.

"I know he could be confrontational, but I wasn't familiar with his particular methods."

"He said he found some information that was really going to hurt someone or something. A company, I mean."

That felt right.

"Know who?" I said.

"No. He didn't say."

"If you had to guess?"

"He probably had fifty companies he wanted to turn the screws to."

"How'd he get the info?"

"I don't know. But, I could tell it was really big. Like devastating."

"Well, I'm not discounting your concerns. But, I'm the one who found him with the alligators," I said.

"For all his sustainability efforts, he hated alligators. Wouldn't get close to them. They couldn't have snuck up on him."

"My thoughts, too," I said.

"Glad I'm not the only one." She brightened with the hope I had given her.

"The circumstances were very odd," I said.

"He totally could have gotten away. Those things are fast. But, not that fast."

"Have you mentioned this to anyone? Besides me."

"Yes. I told a few people. No one's buying it." She looked off frustrated. "Look, I don't mean to hold you up. I'm just really upset about Ken. He was the best. He got things done. He made a difference for all of us. I just wish I could find a way to make a difference for him," she said.

"Well, I think if you carry on his work, that would make him happy," I said.

An awkward hug ended the conversation and I wandered back to my car. I didn't start the engine. My suspicions had just been validated, even if Nadine was her own kind of handful. Social proof. If other people say it so, then it must be so. I used that technique all the time in my writing. Why wouldn't it apply here? I started the car and headed home.

Back at the house, I ate, digested for a few then called the Sheriff.

"Please hold. I'll patch you through," said the receptionist. It turned into a ten-minute wait. The sheriff answered, "This is Sheriff Baker."

"Hi, Walt Asher. We met the other day."

"Alligators."

"Yes."

"Awful shame. Heard a lot of nice things about that man while we were following up on the case. How'd the wife take it?"

"As expected."

"That bad, huh?"

"Yes. So, I won't keep you long. I wanted to follow up on that vial I gave you. The glass one with the letter codes on the side."

"That liquid was pesticide. And, the lawn man had just been there the day before."

I was hit with a mix of emotions – relieved it wasn't looking like murder, bummed because it was dumb that Ken would die from gators.

"Did the lawn guy say he used that type of pesticide?"

"He did indeed."
That answered that.
"Okay, thanks for looking into it," I said.
"Sure thing. Take care," he said.
I hung up. Case closed.

6

I felt even more relieved the next morning. Mourning plus suspicion had been occupying too much of my mind. The difference was tangible when I sat down to work an hour later. The words flowed. Ideas came quick and I fell into a groove. I was Walt the writer again. Within two hours I had most of my pitch mapped out, short of a splash of showmanship to make it memorable. Leaning back in my chair, I knew what I wanted to say, but not quite how to--

A movement in the reflection of my computer screen.

Deep pain stung my neck. I grabbed at it in a panic. Arms yanked me back as a thin, sharp, metal wire – a garrote! – twisted tighter and tighter around my throat, choking the air out of it.

I twisted on my desk chair to create slack. Nothing doing. Two black-gloved fists cranked the wire tighter. No mercy. I sliced my fingertips trying to loosen the wire. I swung at the attacker. He dodged left and right, keeping tight control. The garrote cut into my neck. I felt my face turn heavy and hot with blood. Unable to yell, losing breath. My vision started to darken. I set a foot against a support brace under my desk and kicked. The thrust pushed my chair over and back, landing on the attacker. It knocked the wind out of him and the garrote loosened. I spilled over and away, grabbed my throat, and scrambled to my feet as he charged for me. I dodged him and shoved his back as he leapt past me. His head dented my metal filing cabinet. Papers flew through the air and wrapped around my leg as I kicked his ribs.

"What do you want?" I said, more scared than tough. I stepped back to create room between the attacker and me and took in his appearance - his face was covered in a cloth hood. Black, with just two eyeholes. Not like the Klan. Like a...medieval executioner. His arms were lean and ropey, yet all muscle and scars. He pulled a sinister, ornate hand scythe from his back pocket. I ran to the kitchen and grabbed two knives out of the block. Adrenaline crackled through my body. Footsteps – behind me. I turned and slashed.

"Get the fuck out of here!"

The attacker, shook off the blow and lowered into an attack stance. His crazy eyes narrowed behind the holes in his hood. He gripped the scythe handle and swung it through the air. He knew it was intimidating. He laughed.

I ran the opposite direction, through the kitchen and around the corner towards the front door. He chased after me. Hoping for this, I ducked around a nearby wall in the dark living room. As my attacker ran past, I jammed the cooking knife into the side of his gut. I turned queasy feeling the blade slice into his abdomen muscle and let go out of shock, stunned by my impulsive actions. No time to dwell on it.

He screamed and ripped the blade out. Blood drizzle flowed out of the wound. He raised his scythe and swung with rage. I ducked and ran as he sliced the air with the blade, swinging harder and faster. The last swing smashed the blade into the wall and sprayed drywall dust around the room like a powder firework. He grabbed at his eye with his free hand, turned, and ran after me.

I dashed out of the house. No car keys. A Ford Mustang I didn't recognize was parked just down the road, lights out, a silhouette behind the wheel. He must have seen me right as I saw him because the headlights flicked on and lit me up bright. Now, he could see me and I couldn't see him.

I raced across my neighbor Al's yard and down the dirt road, not sure of where I was headed. I looked back. The Mustang had pulled up to my house. The attacker jumped in. The hi-beams went on, illuminating the dust I had kicked up from the road...and me. The Mustang raced my way.

I hauled ass and cut through Tom and Tammy Pepper's yard. Their long, low ranch house was dark. They were part timers on the river. I cut around the corner of their home, ran down towards the river, and stopped. The Mustang grew louder. I stopped behind the blind side of a tall, thick pine tree and held still.

The Mustang pulled onto the lawn and stopped. The hi-beams were pointed straight at the tree I was leaning against. I looked for an escape route.

They revved the engine. I tensed. A pain grew in my chest as I tried to hold my breath. I didn't want to make a sound. *What the hell is going on?*

A thought: There were two of them. The attacker and a driver. If they got out of the car and walked this way I was in trouble. I couldn't fight both of them.

The car engine idled in the darkness. My eyes scanned the area ahead of me. The hi-beams had illuminated the entire backyard. The only direction I could run where they might not see me was straight ahead. But, they'd hear me splash into the water. I stayed put and listened for their next move.

My heartbeat pounded in my ears. Mosquitos buzzed. Both made it difficult to hear what was happening behind me, on the other side of the tree. A car door opened. I heard a few footsteps press down on the thick Bermuda grass. Someone cocked a gun. Then...nothing.

The lights continued to shine past me, the tree keeping me in the shadows. If it were winter they'd have seen the steam of my breath waft out. I stayed motionless, worried my broad shoulders were peeking out either side of the tree.

A voice. I couldn't make out what he was saying. A different language?

"We are your death, Asher."

Definitely accented.

And, damn. This was no random attack. They knew my name. The assured delivery of his words was terrifying. Like my death was inevitable.

I peeked out the corner of my eyes, both directions, hoping my peripheral vision would catch a glimpse of them coming around the tree. I worried they would swing a rope around the tree, tying me down before I could make a move.

I still had no plan. My heart thundered. It was so tense any kind of action, good or bad, would have been a relief.

More footsteps. Hold my breath. The car engine revved like a growing menace. *Dammit, come on!*

I decided my best chance was to run straight down the sloping yard, then cut behind another cluster of pine trees, run onto the dock and dive off the end of it. That would get me the farthest from them the quickest. The dock and water meant they couldn't follow me with their car. The river was black at night and would provide some cover if they tried shooting at me. And, if I were lucky enough to reach the far riverbank, I could hide amongst cypress knees and eventually make my way out the other side.

There was just one problem. Alligators. They stayed away during the day when crowds of people floated down river. But at night, the river was their domain. And I, didn't want to meet the same grisly fate as Ken.

More footsteps. Closer. The alligators were becoming better odds. I caught my breath and tensed up, ready to run. My palms were behind me, pressed against the bark of the tree for an extra push off. *No other way. I gotta run for it. Three...two...*

Words. Foreign. French? Impatient? Urgent. I couldn't make it out.

Quick footsteps...*the other way.* The car door slammed shut. The engine revved loud and wild. I stayed frozen. I heard the clutch shift and saw the headlights recede across the lawn.

As soon as the lights were off the tree, I ran – WAIT! STOP! Think first!

What if...what if they slammed the door shut and backed the car out just to make me think they left. But, what if...one stayed behind ready to attack when I pop up? I listened. I waited. No sound. The longer I stayed, the more time they had to sneak up on me.

Fuck it.

I ran and slid under scrub brush closer to the river. Better cover. I let out a big breath and allowed myself to relax a little. I continued to stare in the direction the car had been. I could still see the wash from its headlights illuminating trees down the road. Was anyone hiding in the shadows? There was no movement.

So now what? They knew my name and where I lived and they wanted to kill me. They knew I was in the area and couldn't get far without my car. Likely odds, they were staking out my house, if not the whole street. And, there may have been more of them. Best way out? The river.

7

Count to ten...Catch breath...Go!

I crawled out of the bushes. My eyes were adjusted to the moonlight, so I could better scan the property. It looked clear. I rose and ran, careful to stay in the tree shadows, weaving towards a storage shed near the back of the house.

The shed was open and, as I had hoped, there were paddleboards inside. I felt along the ground inside the shed to make sure nothing was in the way, then pulled out a board and laid it on the grass. I peeked over my shoulder. No attackers. I shut the shed door without making a sound then grabbed the board and ran to the edge of the river.

I didn't use the dock. Too high, and I'd be too visible for anyone who might be watching the area. Water rippled as I slid the board across the surface, steadied it, then belly crawled onto it. I grabbed a pylon and pushed out to the end of the dock.

The board was stealth, no sound to its movement. At the end of the dock, I grabbed the last worn, wooden support and stopped. As if pulling out into traffic, I inched forward and looked both ways. No sign of life in either direction. But, it was there...at least the amphibious kind.

I pushed off and drifted forward until the current took me. The good news: I wouldn't have to paddle so much. I was too close to shore and the sound would carry. As clear as I could hear the barred owls hooting and the gators croaking, I knew those hunters would be able to hear any sound I made. The bad news: the current was taking me back towards my house where my attackers could be waiting for me. If I made it past there undetected, I knew a safe place three-quarters of a mile down river, where it splits.

Hunters? Attackers...assassins?! What the hell is going on? I thought. But, then I knew. There was just one possibility. It had to do with Ken.

Despite this mortal terror creeping into my mind, I couldn't help but notice what a stunning night Florida provided – clear skies, a balmy breeze, and mild temperatures, which in Florida means anything lower than 90-degrees. I dunked my hands in the river and wiped cool water onto my face. That helped me to relax and adjust my patience to the river's pace. I felt happy I'd lived to float down it again.

The pleasure was short-lived. As I passed my house I saw two separate orange glowing embers floating in the darkness. Cigarette tips. Each in a different mouth and on opposite sides of the property.

They were waiting for me. I leaned to one side of the board and watched them as I floated past the house, ready to roll into the water if they spotted me. They didn't.

Once the current had taken me around two big bends I felt secure enough to paddle without revealing my location. So, I did, picking up the pace and steering my board into the long tree shadows and out of the bright, white moonlight. Intermittent splashes let me know when a fish broke the surface or an alligator slid off the muddy bank into the water. I knew the river was crawling with them. But, I couldn't think about that now. *Just keep paddling.*

It took twenty minutes to get to the fork in the river. By then, I was on my knees, hunched over, and paddling harder. The extra effort was necessary to cut across the current and over to the left fork in the river. A few moments of turbulence, then calm. It wouldn't take long to reach the safest place around.

The safe house was three-quarters of a mile down river and belonged to Donwald Jefferson Gary - abbreviated to Donnie Gary or Dongar or DG. And, that's the only thing abbreviated about this loud, proud, and obnoxious redneck biker. He was big and brawny with a sun-scorched, bulldog face—the automatic center of attention in any room he entered. He gave people who didn't know him the willies and the people who did know him a great time, every time—as long as you weren't looking for discretion, social grace, or manners. Since I wasn't looking for social niceties, I was glad to know him.

I entered Donnie Gary's good time, no bullshit orbit a few years back. He and his biker friends, best described as a wolf pack, had built some kind of floating human catapult contraption for kicks and were towing it down the river with a pontoon boat. As the boat floated, the catapult launched people into the air. They'd kick and flail, and most often look surprised at how high and far they'd been flung, all before splashing down into the water. Donnie Gary sat in the catapult as the pontoon chugged past my house.

"Do it! Launch this big ole hunk of love," he yelled to the boat driver.

However, Donnie Gary's girth shanked the launch and he shot at a side angle right into my small dock house, leveling it. His friends looked on from the boat, shocked yet drunken and amused.

"Holy goddamn shit!" one of the boat revelers said.

To everyone's surprise, DG had broken no bones and avoided impalement as his body tore through the wood and spilled onto my lawn. I was on my back porch writing at the time and witnessed the entire spectacle. As I walked down the lawn, scowling mad at the condition of my dock house, Donnie Gary climbed out of the rubble laughing. It took him a moment to get his balance and bearings. But, this was a high moment of hilarity he wouldn't soon forget. His friends went from cautious snickering to high voltage laughter once they saw he was okay.

"Nice flying. Hope you brought your wallet," I tacked on a smile to keep it civil.

Donnie Gary bent over and held his knees with more hysterical laughter, almost gasping for air through his beet-red face. He looked at me and pointed, still howling.

"Look at your stupid face!...haha...you're so mad...Oh, my god, that's the best!" Perfect. Now, I had the insult to go with the injury. Or at least my dock house's injury.

"Thought I was gonna hit the riverbank...but, my fat ass just kept flying," he said as he looked up to the sky, held his belly, and continued howling.

His laughter was contagious and it was easy to see the humor in it. Once he caught his breath, he walked over to me, threw his arm around my shoulders, and apologized. He brought me in tight, like we'd been friends all our lives, and pointed down the river.

"To get to my place, you take the fork left and look for the dock with the barbed wire," DG said. "Trust me. You'll know it when you see it."

"Okay," I said.

"Swing by later today and I'll have your money – in cash – and the best damn barbecue hog you'll ever eat."

"Will do," I said.

He was right. I stopped by DG's later that afternoon and had the time of my life. We've been buddies every since.

As my board finished its approach, I paddled over and took hold of Donnie Gary's dock. Unsure of what creatures might be lurking underneath it at this time of night, I did my best to leap onto the dock without touching the water. Once aboard, I pulled the paddle board out of the water and set it on the wood surface. I looked down river from where I came. There was no sign of human life behind me. A breeze made my dripping wet body shiver as I walked up the long dock towards Donnie Gary's cracker shanty house.

I had to watch my step. The moon only lit up so much and the towering trees blocked half the light. The mosquitos had quite the gauntlet set up for me, stinging my neck, arms, and legs along the way.

I heard a splash and a snap. I stopped, lost balance, and almost fell off the dock. Good thing I didn't. Waiting below was DG's alligator pen. Twelve of the nasty bastards looked up at me, ready to feast, as they sloshed around in the dark muck.

Knowing Donnie Gary, there was an assortment of possibilities as to why he had a pen full of alligators. Could be food, for skinning, maybe even rehabilitation. They creeped me out. Even more since Ken's accident. But, it could no longer be called that. Not after tonight. I stepped off the dock and scooted up the dirt trail.

As usual, something loud and feisty was happening at DG's. I heard it before I saw it. Laughter, music, and grill smoke wafted through the night air and made my stomach grumble. Just as I veered off the walking path, I saw strung-up fiesta lights dangling from the trees.

Something slithered fast under the leaves around my feet. A rope loop cinched around my ankles and yanked me flat onto the ground then hoisted me into the air where I dangled and swung.

DG's voice: "Trespassers get shot!"

A gunshot ripped right past me and splintered a nearby tree.

8

"Hey, it's me! Walt!"

"Who?"

"Walt! From down the river."

DG appeared around the grill, a rifle in his hand. He looked ready to kill.

The rope creaked as it swung me in a slow circle. My cheeks and jowls sagged down, my arms dangled, and my soggy shorts dripped cold water into my face. Everything was upside down.

DG raised his gun and took aim.

"No!"

Gunshot. The rope shredded and I dropped hard to the ground. This night was taking its toll.

As DG walked down the slope in my direction, I felt along the ground for my belongings and realized I didn't have any of them – no keys, no wallet, no cell phone. They were all back at the house. Which meant the attackers could have taken them. That was bad news.

The rifle barrel pressed against my nose. I stopped moving

"You know I don't like people sneaking up on my place, Walt."

"Hello, DG."

Up at the house, on the porch. DG brought me a plate of barbecued meat slathered in his legendary special sauce. He handed me a cold beer and sat down. After guzzling his beer, which was still attached to the six-pack, he belched then looked at me through eyes that were either watering from the grill smoke or copious amounts of weed. Or, both. I couldn't tell.

"Chew that up then let me know why I caught you sneaking up to my property," he said.

"I thought you said I was welcome anytime."

"Only through the front door. You know I don't cotton to sneaking around."

I did know that. Because all signs point to what DG does for a living as being a criminal enterprise. I was never sure what specific thing or things he dealt, bought, and sold. Probably a little of everything or a lot of everything.

His house was always guarded. The only employees were bikers, most hardened by prison. Draw your own conclusion. I did know that whatever illegal or dangerous enterprises DG dabbled in, it didn't prevent him from living with carefree ease. That's because his business was buttoned up. And, because he had all kinds of protection.

I'll tell you why. From a Governor to gutter dwellers, elite business enterprises to down and dirty dealings, the Gary family sprawled wide across Florida and deep into its history books. You've heard of the good ole boy network? For the most part, that was DG's family. He had more connections than a telephone exchange. In every industry, in every county, at every level. He did whatever he wanted to do and made enough money to spend most of his time playing. Despite his lowdown appearance, I couldn't begin to imagine how wealthy he was.

"Look, people were chasing me. I didn't have any other option. Besides, the back door is like the front door on the river. And, you come into mine with a belch instead of a knock every time," I said.

He belched. Point taken.

"Look, I wasn't sneaking up. I came here for help."

"What kind of help?"

"The kind that keeps me from getting killed."

"What? Which customer did you piss off?"

"Funny. Look, you know Ken Kerenz died the other day, right?"

"Yes."

"I discovered his body being eaten by gators, which seemed odd to me."

"Gators eat," he said.

"But, they don't attack unless you provoke. Ken was afraid of them. He was all about protecting nature. And, too fit not to be able to get away.

"Once they clamp on..."

"If they catch you. It just vibed strange. Especially because I found a strange vial of liquid on his lawn, not far from where Ken was being eaten. So, I told the Sheriff, talked to a few people. Next thing I know I was attacked in my house."

"When?"

"Tonight. Forty minutes ago. Two guys, one tried to slice my throat then filet me with a vicious looking blade. I got away and floated down the river to get here."

"And, you didn't get chomped. I'm impressed."

"Me, too."

He sat there looking perplexed. I presumed he was cycling through his mental Rolodex of thugs, degenerates, and hit men to see who fit my description. There was no eureka moment.

"So, how can I help?" he said.

I finished the food and set my plate down.

"That was good, thank you. I came here because I didn't know where else to go. This place is guarded. I figured they wouldn't get me here."

"And, you have no idea who *they* are."

"None. Could be one of Ken's enemies. Someone he used his activism against. But, I have no clue why they'd come after me."

"Bet your ass it's murder if they're showing up trying to kill you."

"But, I don't have any proof. It's been written off as a gator attack."

"Bullshit. Someone didn't like you poking around."

"But...who? It's not like I'm a reporter or, you know, a detective."

We looked at each other thinking the same thing.

"The Sheriff?" he said.

"What? No."

"Sheriff Baker's a dirty motherfucker. I can prove that."

"But, wait. Why Ken?"

"Maybe he was up to something. That's usually the case."

"He was an activist," I said. The circumstances were moving into areas I couldn't fathom.

"He had enemies you said."

"But, the gators."

DG leaned forward and looked me in the eyes. "Walt, you're not putting the pieces together. Whatever Ken had going on, it pissed someone off. And, if that someone has the right connections he could have Sheriff Baker take care of a few matters. That Sheriff can be bought. I've done it."

My mind reeled with questions and possibilities. "The vial?" I said.

"You gave it to the Sheriff?" said DG. I nodded.

"He said it was pesticide," I said.

"You may have handed over the only piece of evidence he overlooked."

I felt like an idiot.

DG's face pinched with uncertainty. "Only thing I don't know is why they'd kill you if they had all the evidence."

Pieces clicked together. "My house was broken into. While I was in Melbourne," I said. "They were looking for something."

"They think you still have evidence. Because you were poking around."

"They're not taking any chances, are they?"

He shook his head and looked grave. "You in some trouble, boy."

My body tingled with new fear. If Sheriff Baker was tied in with the attackers I couldn't go home. I couldn't even stay in the area. Plus, I had no proof to convince anyone this was real.

DG interrupted my accelerating thoughts. "I'd strongly suggest you let me hide you for a while. Underground. As long as necessary," he said.

"You can do that?"

"I have guys I've kept hidden for ten years."

"Do they ever go outside?"

"They live normal lives where their enemies won't find them."

"I think giving me a place for the night will do," I said.

"Done. Starlene will set you up," he said, referring to his newly acquired nineteen year-old wife with size humongous breasts. Don't judge, you'd notice, too.

"Thanks. I also need to get back to my house. They may still be there. But, I need to get my computer and phone, car, keys, and wallet."

"They probably took 'em. That's what we'd do." I gave him a curious look.

"Don't ask," he said.

"Okay, I won't."

"We can go over and check the place out for you first."

"That'd be great. I also was wondering if, um..."

"Yes, I'll reach out to my connections to see if we can find out who might be doing someone's dirty work. What the Sheriff might be up to."

I was somewhat relieved.

"Let's go get your stuff," he said and got up. I followed.

9

I rode to the house with DG in his redneck Rolls – a jacked up, mud-covered camouflage pickup truck complete with gun rack, fishing pole rack, dog cages, and coolers. He held me back as I started to climb out.

"Let them scout it first."

He was referring to his pack of bikers who had come along in case of any trouble. They parked their bikes on the lawn and entered the house. No key required - the front door had been left open. A few moments later they came out, coast clear.

I went in the house and couldn't believe the amount of damage. A huge hole was knocked in the drywall where we had fought. Glass was broken and scattered across the tile floor. Chairs were turned over. It took me a minute to realize not all of the damage was caused by the scuffle – they had torn the place apart looking for something. They still thought I had evidence proving Ken's death was murder. It gave me the willies.

"I don't want to stick around here. Give me five minutes," I said.

DG nodded to me, then signaled his boys. They scattered to other parts of the house while I walked into my writing office. Laptop gone. Phone gone. Wallet here, but turned out. My car keys were hanging on the wall. Two out of three ain't bad, but one out of four ain't good. I grabbed the keys and did a quick pass through the house, closing windows, locking doors, turning down the air.

DG and crew were waiting for me out on the lawn. I held up my keys to show I'd found them. When I made it over to them, DG held up something small, black, and wired.

"What's that?"

"A detonator. Your house was wired to explode," he said.

Chills.

"Should be safe in a few. They're dismantling some C4 now."

"Thanks."

"That's a lot of damage inside. If you can cover a basic hourly wage, I can have some guys start fixing the walls tonight. They can also keep their eyes open for anyone lurking around. Some protection. You good with that or are you going to still be a cheap bastard when you have ass-saving to worry about?"

"Yes, do it," I said. "But, I'm not staying here."

"Going to Gainesville or Clearwater? By the way, how is lovely Ilsa?"

"Gainesville. And, she's good."

"My boys said she treated them right fine at her bar the other week."

"If anyone can handle that rowdy bunch, it's her."

He flashed a smile, but grew serious again.

"Walt, these guys aren't messing around. I really think you should let me hide you. Least, 'til I can check my grapevine, see what's up," he said.

It was hard to refuse DG.

"I'm grateful, DG. Really. But, I'm not ready to hide yet."

He nodded and accepted it. "Keep me posted. I can have them killed, too." He was serious.

"Let's hope it doesn't come to that," I said.

I patted his back and walked over to my car. As I did, I saw a biker pull a tool belt and tools from his saddlebag. Two other bikers stood guard on the front porch. I realized that dangerous biker gangs are like lawyers. So much better to have them looking out for you than coming after you. Good to have friends like DG, too. Just in case.

Whoever turned over my house and riffled through my wallet would now know my Clearwater address. That made Gainesville the safe destination. I hit the road and headed that way, relieved to be leaving the river.

On the drive, I realized Gainesville might not be as safe as I thought. With my phone missing, that meant whoever was out to get me also had a list of all my contacts. They could check my text messages and see that Ilsa was the person I text the most, then find her number and address in the 'contacts' app. They could be waiting for me there. They could be going after Ilsa at that moment.

I drove faster.

10

I found Ilsa serving up drinks at Betty's Bomb Shelter, her fifties-themed joint named after her mom and built in one of those arch top sheet metal buildings. It had been an electrical supply business for forty-five years before Ilsa took over. I grabbed a stool at the end of the bar and waited for her to walk my way. She was surprised but pleased to see me.

"I didn't expect to see you," she said leaning in for a kiss. "Explain yourself."

"Can we talk in your office?" I said. The concern on my face appeared on hers. She nodded and we walked to the back of the bar.

We sat on the couch in her office. She looked at me, anxious for me to elaborate.

"What's going on?"

"Two things. One, when I got back to my place after Melbourne I found signs that someone had been there. I think they were looking for something," I said.

She sat up and demanded an answer. "Why didn't you tell me?"

"Because I wasn't sure and I didn't want you to worry. But, I'm sure now."

She looked very worried. "That's the first thing?"

I nodded. "The second is this..." I lifted my neck and showed her where the garrote had cut the skin on my neck.

She gasped and covered her mouth in shock.

"I was attacked. At home. Earlier tonight. I barely escaped. I had to float down river to DG's."

"Are you all right?"

"Yeah."

She leaned in to hug me; grateful I was in one piece. I hugged back. When we released a moment later, she looked me over like a mother caring for her child.

"I don't want you going back there," she said.

"Don't worry. I'm not. And, DG has a couple of his guys guarding the place."

Her expression grew stern. "You don't think this was because you were..."

"I think that's exactly why."

"Oh, Walt! This is why you should mind your own business!"

She wringed her hands. But, not in a helpless way. More like she wanted payback.

"Well, they've made it my business," I said. "So now, I have to figure out what's going on. Who's after me and why."

She grabbed my wrists. "No, you don't! We are going to Europe. We will stay with my parents until this goes away. I do not want you getting hurt."

"That's not a bad idea. But, the problem won't go away. DG's asking around, so we'll see what comes out of that. In the meantime, I'd like to stay up here with you." I smiled trying to make like it was all for the better.

"Of course, you can stay. But, I don't think you are up for such a fight."

Despite the previous evening's exhaustive events, I woke by nine, ready to tighten up my backstroke. I needed a new phone, new computer, and access to money. I called the bank first to cancel my old cards and have a new one sent to Ilsa's. In the meantime, I'd have to borrow some cash from her. She always kept an emergency stash around the house. I took half. Should last me for a while. I also borrowed her phone. I texted DG her number and let him know that was the best way to reach me.

I wasn't in the mood to cook so I stepped out to get breakfast at a nearby greasy spoon, The Sugarcreek, known for consistently good grits. While waiting for my food, I read a newspaper another diner had left behind. It made me wonder how Florida must appear to the out of state observer.

Only the most sensational Florida headlines captivate the nation (and parts beyond) with a new type of freakishness -Alligator humpers, triple-breasted wannabe starlets, and crazy preachers threatening to burn a Koran and bring about the only thing that Florida was missing, a jihad. But, the everyday, non-viral Florida newspaper stories read more like a catalog of crimes - government corruption, corporate malfeasance, white-collar embezzlement, drug mayhem, and murder. The recent turn of events made me feel like I was being sucked into that perilous world. I was determined not to end up as a morbid headline.

Like Nadine Evers, the woman I had run into after the funeral. She was convinced Ken had been killed. And now, her morbid headline was splashed across the pages of the Gainesville Sun. Found dead, late yesterday. Cardiac arrest. Only 42 years old. I wasn't buying that.

My order came up. I tossed the newspaper in a wastebasket as I walked out to the car. I stopped. Paranoia washed through me. I looked around. Nothing suspicious stood out. But, knowing they were after me — whoever they were - I couldn't lower my guard. And, I knew I couldn't stop this madness by running away. I was only going to stop it by fighting. The trick would be convincing Ilsa of that.

The stoplight turned red before I could turn onto Ilsa's street. I waited patiently for it to change green.

That's when I saw them -

Three out of place cars parked near her house. One was facing my direction closer to the intersection. One was a hundred yards past and facing away from Ilsa's place. The third car sat across the street from the first, but facing Ilsa's. Each car had a Union County license plate. Union is the smallest county in Florida. So, even though it's the next county over, you still rarely see Union plates in Gainesville. To see three at once was weird. A man sat in each car. The sun glare on the windshields obscured their details. They were watching.

11

The light turned green. Instead of driving into Ilsa's neighborhood, as planned, I flipped off my signal and drove through the light. I checked my mirrors to see if any of the cars followed mine. They didn't.

I hooked a left into the neighborhood beyond Ilsa's and parked about a hundred yards up. No movement from me. Birds called each other, from tree to tree. I sat and waited.

The coast remained clear for five solid minutes. So, I got out and walked up to a dull one-story home, which I estimated was right behind Ilsa's property. There was no car in the driveway. The house's dated design and wood exterior indicated an early eighties build. Not my favorite era.

I walked up to the front door and pulled my keys out of my pocket as if I were returning home. Like I was supposed to be there. I glanced over my shoulder again. No one was watching. I cut away from the front door and dashed around to the side of the house. The fence gate wasn't locked so I went right in.

Cutting across the backyard, I was happy to see no dog on patrol. That would have screwed things up. I walked over to the back of the yard and hopped the fence.

I landed on the soft dirt and stayed down. A small creek trickled below me. The water rolled towards a thicket of kudzu overgrowth, which helped to divide this neighborhood from Ilsa's. Her house was straight across the water. I could see her inside the house, puttering around. She didn't have a clue her house was being watched. Maybe that was good. If those were the same guys who busted up my place at least they weren't hurting her. Yet. Maybe I could sneak her out the backyard without them noticing.

My next move was risky. If someone were watching the house from the creek, I'd walk right into their view. They'd signal the others and thugs would pounce from all directions. No thanks. I studied the creek. No sign of other watchers on either side of me. Large tropical foliage swayed in the breeze. Do it, Asher.

I hopped the creek and landed with a thud on the far bank. From there, I made quick work of it; I scrambled up the bank, across Ilsa's backyard, and up to the rear sliding glass door. I looked back in the direction I had come. No thugs, no pounce. I turned back to the glass door, shaded my eyes, and looked in. It took a moment for my eyes to adjust from the bright sun to the dark interior.

Ilsa strolled through the living room looking occupied in thought. She had almost passed me by when she startled at seeing me out of the corner of her eye. She screamed. I gestured for her to keep quiet, then for her to hurry and open up. She let me in and started to speak. I put my hand over her mouth, then closed the door and pulled her down to the floor. I didn't want to be seen.

Whispering...."Three cars outside. All watching the house. I don't know who they are but I'd feel a lot safer with you outta here," I said.

She looked at me with a procession of expressions – annoyed, confused, worried. She finally looked like she understood and I confirmed with a nod.

"I'm parked in the next neighborhood over. What do you need to bring?"

"Just my purse, I think."

"Get it and let's go."

She nodded and started to stand. I pulled her back down. She got the message. She hunch-walked over to the front door and found her purse on a table in the foyer. She grabbed it by the strap and—

The doorbell rang. She looked back at me worried. I dove into the kitchen and peeked back around the corner towards the front door. A shadow outside. I waved for Ilsa to get down. She did as the shadow cupped its hand up to the frosted glass window framing the door and peered inside. I ducked out of site, and snuck out through the other kitchen entrance. My heart pounded.

Crawling through the living room I saw one of the men from the other night – gaunt, scruffy, hair with a homemade chop and a scar running from elbow to shoulder – walking along the side of the house towards the backyard. I hurried to the front of the house, until I could see Ilsa, holding still in the foyer.

"Psst."

She looked my way. I pointed to the door implying someone was right there. I waved her towards me. She moved slowly and against the wall, careful not to make noise or any noticeable movements.

I held her close and whispered.

"There's one in back."

She acknowledged then took the lead back towards the kitchen. We were almost there when we heard the slow whoosh of the rear slider door open. I peered around the corner.

There was the man I had seen out the window. He stood with his head tilted back. Like he was smelling the air. Tall and skinny, but he vibed menace. He moved his hand over the kitchen counter and set down a small micro-syringe tipped glass capsule with golden liquid inside and a label with code letters wrapped around the outside. Just like the capsule I'd found at Ken's. Connection. Proof. Worst suspicions confirmed. Anger bubbled up, but I couldn't let it distract me.

Something big was going on. And, they weren't here to ask us questions. They were here to kill. The intruder pulled what looked like a small, homemade gun out of his pocket. It had a handle and a trigger – but with an open track on top, like a crossbow but without the bow string. He set the glass capsule inside the track, pressed it into place, and held the syringe gun up, ready to fire.

I pulled back as he looked our way. Ilsa gripped my arm. Slow now...I looked into the kitchen and saw the heel of his scuffed work boot as he disappeared down the hallway leading to the foyer. Without looking back, I grabbed Ilsa's arm and pulled her to follow.

We crept through the kitchen. I listened for more of the intruder's footsteps, to gauge his location. I could only hear the blood in my ears. Outdoor heat poured in through the open glass door. Our escape route. It was close. All we needed to do was sneak out and run like hell. Yes, I know I said this wasn't a problem to solve by running away. But, knowing this operation went beyond these three yokels made it clear we had better to run and fight another day. Plus, I didn't want Ilsa getting hurt. And, as willing to fight as I may have felt at the moment, I was nervous about taking on one guy. I was real worried about taking on three.

A sound. A door unlocking. I peeked around the corner. The intruder opened the front door to let the other thugs into the house. We needed to run, now.

I grabbed Ilsa's wrist and pulled her. Quiet steps at first. But, then the front door opened. Another man walked in and saw us stepping out.

"Hey!"

The other thugs turned to follow his gaze. The scrawny man raised the syringe gun and fired. Glass shattered against the doorframe next to my head. Glass shards stung my skin. I pushed Ilsa out the door and we ran.

"To the creek!" I said.

We hauled ass. Ilsa knew where to go. Looking back, I saw one goon coming after us. The other two ran out the back door, then broke off and ran back to the front of the house. To their cars, I presumed.

Ilsa staggered down the riverbank, hopped over with no hesitation, and landed on the far bank. The force of the landing slowed her momentum, so I decided to run right through the ankle-deep creek. Big mistake.

My wet shoes slipped on the far bank and I slid back down, ankle deep in the creek. I scrambled to get up, but kept slipping, the soil turning to mud under my wet clothes. My heart thundered, fear crept in.

Over my shoulder I could hear the scrawny thug's approaching footsteps.

Ilsa was at the top wanting to come down and help but worried about the man approaching.

My hands found a knotty tree root jutting out of the soil. I grabbed it and pulled myself up. Still not enough. My feet kept slipping and I could only get so much leverage.

The scrawny man landed on my back and knocked the air out of my lungs. We rolled down the bank and splashed on our backs into the creek. I landed on top and flipped myself over. I delivered three rabbit punches to the gut then pushed off to create space. The blows didn't faze him. He got up and dove at me. I jumped out of his reach, but landed off-kilter on the riverbank and fell back into the water. It would look funny if someone wasn't trying to kill me.

The man grabbed a rock and slammed it down at my head. I rolled away in time, but not fast enough to dodge his follow up blow to the side of my neck. That hurt bad. I screamed rolled onto my back. He pounced. I kicked and connected with his gut. He lost his wind. His spittle laced my cheek. I shoved him off me and he tumbled into the creek.

I found a rock bigger than his and threw it, feeling the pain in my neck as I extended my arm. The rock hit the side of his head after hitting the creek first. It was only a mild blow, but enough to buy me a couple of seconds.

I grabbed a thick, wet log, raised it high, and slammed it down hard on him just as muddy water trickled into my eyes. I wiped them clear with my arm. As I blinked the last of the water away I saw his hand pulling a glass capsule from his pocket. No gun this time. He held the capsule stabbing style, ready for my next approach.

So, I didn't approach. I made another attempt to run up the riverbank. This time my shoes caught dry dirt and I got traction. Ilsa was straddling the privacy fence I had hopped earlier waving me up, It was a quick three step move from the top of the bank, to the fence, and over.

"That way!" I said and pointed to the gate across the yard.

Out the gate, around the house, and over to my car. She took the passenger side; I took the driver's. I hadn't locked the doors. We slid in. I reached in my pocket.

No keys.

I checked by the floor mats. Nothing. I opened my door and checked the pavement. No. I looked back towards the house and found them...twirling in the man's hands.

He sneered as he stalked towards the car, muddy and angry.

"What? What's--?" Ilsa saw him and gasped.

The man raised the syringe gun in his other hand and fired.

I ducked back into the car, forcing myself onto Ilsa's side. The gearshift in the center of the console dug into my gut. I was too adrenalized to feel the pain. The syringe flew in with a whoosh and pierced the rubber coated steering wheel horn. Too close. Then, another. Even closer.

The man staggered up to the car. I shot out like an NFL safety, shoulder aimed right at his belly. It knocked him flat on the pavement. I grabbed his hair with my left hand and cocked back my fist. He kneed my balls. I keeled over and felt the sun-soaked pavement hot against my face. He sprang up and landed astraddle of me.

He fired off series of one-two punches to my gut that made me nauseous. I punched the side of his throat and he froze, shock on his face.

I let go of the glass syringe and let it dangle from his throat. I had grabbed it on my way out of the car. It drained slowly but the poison acted fast.

He gazed down at me, a terrible look. Disbelief and sadness. I wondered if Ken had the same dumbstruck expression when they poisoned him. I pushed him off me and he was dead by the time his head smacked against the pavement.

No time to worry. I grabbed the keys off the street and ran to the car. Ilsa looked back at the body on the ground.

"Is he dead?" Ilsa said as I started the car.

"I hope so." I wheeled the car around and drove us out of there. I swerved to avoid running over his legs. But, I didn't swerve far enough. Thump, thump.

The car raced through the idyllic suburbs that lined 22nd Street leading up to University Avenue, where I cut west towards Interstate 75. Ilsa and I didn't say much the first few minutes of the drive; we were too busy checking the mirrors and catching our breath. And, we were in shock.

Ilsa spoke first. "Are you okay?"

"I'm okay with not being dead. Bruised to shit, otherwise."

"We need to call the police."

"I'm not so sure about that."

A hand on my shoulder. "Someone just tried to kill you. Again."

"They tried, I succeeded. The heat will be more on me."

She started to speak but came up short.

"Besides," I said. "I'm not so sure the cops are going to help us with this."

"Why?"

"I have a hunch these guys found me thanks to the Dunnellon Sheriff's department."

"But, this is Gainesville."

"Look, Ilsa. Something big is going on. Nadine Evers, another one of Ken's activist friends was killed last night. It's in today's paper. Whoever these guys are, they're working for someone powerful enough to use killers to solve their problems and have the cops assist as needed. Like pretending Ken's murder was a natural death."

I pulled on to I-75 and headed south towards Tampa.

"Why are they trying to kill you? You're not an activist!"

"I found the body and I made my doubts known from the beginning. I'm a loose end and they can't have that. And, now that I know they're trying to kill me they won't stop until I'm dead."

"So, I can presume they will probably kill me, too?"

"Not if I can help it."

"If the police are involved, what can you do?"

"Maybe the press. Once I have proof."

"Make the roaches scatter," she said sly grin, which melted away to a worried grimace.

She sighed and leaned back on the headrest. "I can't go home, can I?"

"No," I said, gripping the steering wheel and pulling myself up in the seat. "Clearwater house is out, too. They're probably watching it."

"And, probably all roads into Dunnellon."

"Think they'd be looking for us in your car?"

"It's possible."

"Then let's disappear until we know what to do next."

"Go west on Archer. I know a place."

I did as she commanded.

12

Two hours later we were in a dive motel off U.S. 19 near Crystal River. To our relief, they took cash. I didn't want our credit cards showing up on any tracking system. It sounded crazy. But, who knew what kind of reach the bad guys had? They had access to hired killers. They made a police department look the other way, or so it seemed. They might have had access to the different law enforcement agencies and therefore access to their toys—the kind of toys that find people in an instant.

The room was a depressing tomb fashioned with cinderblock walls painted a bland baby blue, chunky brown curtains that looked like they'd accelerate a fire, and thin, brown indoor/outdoor carpet with cigarette burns in it. The place smelled like a damp ashtray and bathroom sanitizer.

Ilsa tended to my wounds with ice and first aid items from the car trunk. To her credit, the kit also included whiskey, which we imbibed well beyond any doctor's orders. With the edge off and the pain numbed, my mind cleared enough to start working out next steps.

I needed to know two things: what did DG find out through his network, and what did Tom find out about the glass capsule? I'd seen the capsule's lethal ingredients in action. Ingredients that surely killed Ken. There was no doubt about that now. It would be good to know what those ingredients were. Maybe they could be tracked down and that could provide a clue. I placed a call to DG. No answer.

It wasn't very late when Ilsa showed up with food - fried chicken and southern fixings from a nearby gas station.

"Walt, I did some thinking. We need to leave." Ilsa said.

"Agreed. Crystal River's a drag," I said.

"Listen to me. We need to leave the country. Things are only getting worse."

"But, I can't fix anything if I'm thousands of miles away."

"You can't fix things if you're dead!" This wasn't "worried" Ilsa anymore. This was Ilsa getting fired up and ready for battle. She wasn't going to back down.

"Ilsa..."

"No, you listen. We can stay with my parents in Holland. We have some money to last for a while. We have friends there. You can even write from there. To not go there while this blows over is insane."

"What if it doesn't blow over?"

"We make a very nice life there. The key word is 'life'. I'd be fine moving back."

"I can't leave my kids."

"You won't see them if you're dead. Fly them over."

"Carol won't let them go."

"Take them."

"That's kidnapping," I said. "Look, what if they're willing to wait however long it takes to kill me? Running may not solve this."

She slumped onto the far corner of the bed. "I love you and I'm scared and I don't want anything to happen to you...or me. Why is that not enough? Why can't we just protect ourselves first and then deal with it?"

Her logic was sound. But, I couldn't stomach the idea of sitting back and hoping for the best. Even though I had very little idea what to do next. I just stared back at her.

She opened the greasy bag and tossed over my food.

"We're going to Holland."

I caught the food but didn't respond. We ate in silence. The food wasn't fancy, wasn't hot, and wasn't delicious. But, it worked. Once fed, the exhaustion overtook us and we conked out hard.

13

I woke up thirteen hours later. The shower rejuvenated my wherewithal, but I felt like I was wrapped in one giant, swollen bruise. It hurt to move my body. I dried off with the kind of crispy crunchy, paper-thin bath towels these types of motels were famous for as I checked out the massive bruise spreading across my neck and chest. It matched the bruises on my arms.

Ilsa didn't stir when I sat down on the bed next to her. Now dressed, I dialed DG and got him on the line.

"DG, it's Walt."

"How's it going?"

"More of the same."

"And, you're not dead? I'm impressed. These are some bad dudes you're messing with."

"What'd you learn?"

"I learned you're wanted for murder."

I went cold.

I looked over at Ilsa, perhaps wondering if she'd heard the news. "It's in the papers. Police are after you," said DG.

"Donnie, that guy tried to kill me. It was self defense."

"Don't worry. I know you're not the killing type."

This was bad. Now, I couldn't go to the cops or the press. Flying to Europe was the better option. But, they'd grab us before we got on the plane.

"What'd it say?" I said into the phone.

DG described the paper's breakdown. Neighbors had seen a suspect, believed to be me, wandering through Gainesville's Raintree neighborhood yesterday afternoon and had witnessed me murdering a man named Barry Wilson.

"DG, there's no way that guy's name was Barry Wilson. He spoke French and was definitely European."

"Just reading like it's printed. Every P.D. in the state's waiting for you to show up."

I couldn't go home. Not to Dunnellon. Not to Clearwater or Gainesville.

"Did it say anything else?"

"They're looking for Ilsa, too."

My heart sank.

"What do I do?" I felt lost. I'd read about things like this happening in crime novels.

"You need to get proof, that they killed Ken and came after you. Once you get that, I can tap my connections to make sure the information gets to the right people," he said.

It helped to know I wasn't in this alone. But, any hope he gave me was squashed by the impossible notion of getting the proof I needed. In the end, it was all I had.

He continued, "But first, you need to disappear for a bit. I can hide you like I said before."

"My first concern is keeping Ilsa safe. She's with me now."

"She can stay here while you take care of business."

"Thank you. I also need to get into Ken's house. To check his files. That's the only lead I have."

"You mentioned that the other night. I had a couple of my guys save you the trouble. All of his house files are on my desk."

That was a relief.

"Where are you?" he said.

"Crystal River. The Manatee Motel, right on 19."

"We'll be there to pick you up in an hour. Be ready. I'll bring someone to drive your car. You don't want to be seen in it."

"Okay. Thanks."

"Who was that?" said Ilsa behind me.

I turned around to see her blinking the sleep from her eyes.

"DG. How much did you hear?" I said.

"Enough."

Three days ago my life was in perfect order. A good job. A great love life. Happy kids. Everything in balance. Now, depending on who found me first, I was about to get fired from jobs, get arrested for murder, or flat out killed. Perhaps my girlfriend, too. Three rotten choices, none of my making. And that meant only one thing: I now had to do the best sales job of my life and convince everyone I didn't do it. And, there's only one surefire way to change people's minds and convince them to buy it: proof.

But, that would have to wait. Because when I got up to glance out the window I saw a police car parked directly behind our car, blocking it. Two cops were speaking to the manager of the hotel, who pointed to our room. The cops walked over and knocked on our door. Not good.

"Ilsa! The cops," I said.

"Huh?"

I ran into the bathroom and learned the only window in the room was along the front wall above the air unit. The only way out was through the front door.

"What are we going to do?" she said as I walked from the bathroom. I shrugged and gestured towards the door, like I have to open it. She got out of bed and hurried to slip on her clothes. Once they were on, she nodded, straightened out some wrinkles, and I opened the door.

"Hello, Officer."

He was big and packed tight into his formfitting uniform, bulked up around the torso by a bulletproof vest. A buzz cut, clean-shaven, with a pair of spires from a neck tattoo peeking above his shirt color. His right hand rested on his gun, holster open. A pair of cops stood flanked behind him, hands on their guns, too.

The motel manager scampered back to the motel lobby, shaking his head like he'd be glad to be rid of us. And, we were quiet tenants. Jerk.

"Walter Asher?"

"Yes."

"Is that Ilsa Jorissen?" he looked past me to the bed.

"It is."

"Anyone else in there?"

"No."

"I need you two to step outside, please."

I nodded and turned to Ilsa. This looked bad. Real bad.

"We gotta go outside."

She looked at the cop and nodded. We walked out into the scorching sunlight. It was already hot and humid at that early hour. I could smell the salt in the air wafting off the nearby Gulf of Mexico. Wind blew nearby palm fronds as cars zipped by on the highway.

With no other options, I figured I'd better turn the charm up to eleven.

"How can I help you, sir?" I said.

"I have a warrant for your arrest. And, for Ms. Jorissen."

And, there was said warrant right in his hand.

Dammit. Charm to 12.

"I can tell you're looking at me like this must be some kind of mix up. That it is. But, you have orders to follow. Even though I probably don't look anything like someone who would have a warrant out on them." I said as I noticed the sleazy motel, which set the scene. "Except for the fact that I'm staying in this grimy motel, which you've probably had to pay numerous visits to, right?"

Persuasion tip: Get them agreeing with you.

"By the way, you guys need a drink? I know how hard you guys work. I have some water and sodas in the ice bucket?" Persuasion tip: Acknowledge and appreciate.

His expression read impatience.

"No sir, I need you and Ms. Jorissen to get in the squad car peacefully."

"What are the charges?"

"Murder."

"We need to call our lawyer," said Ilsa stepping out the door behind me.

"Ma'am you can do that at the station. I need you both to enter the police vehicle now."

She looked to me for answers. I looked to the officer.

We got in the car. The officer radioed into the station. No sale.

Our squad car raced down Highway 19, through Crystal River, a quaint, low-key downtown area filled with outdoor recreation enthusiasts and manatee seekers. The town looked like it had changed very little over the past fifty years. But, like most small towns in America, chain stores and retail glut were spreading at the city limits. For reasons I never understood, Crystal River also had a disproportionate amount of New York transplants.

I watched as banks of mangroves blurred past. They were growing out towards the Gulf of Mexico. The water would have been warm and calm. The way things were going, I couldn't help wondering when I'd see the Gulf again.

I looked at Ilsa. She wasn't sad and she wasn't mad. Just frustrated and I could tell her Dutch ingenuity was working overtime for a solution. She looked at me and forced a smile. I forced one in return and mouthed the words "I'm sorry." She shook her head letting me know it wasn't my fault. But, she couldn't look me in the eye.

Things were getting serious. The dark powers that be had already pulled enough strings have me arrested. But, the thought gnawing at my guy was a suspicion that we'd never make it to court. They didn't want us talking. They wanted us dead and quiet. I didn't want to tell Ilsa.

As I sat there rolling the situation over in my mind a huge, camouflage painted four by four truck with an enclosed metal box on back raced past our police car. That was bold.

But, not as ballsy as what happened next:

The 4x4 hit its brakes and turned, tires squealing, to a stop across the middle of the road. That cut the lead police car off from our car. And, it was making our car slow down. Forget reaching court. We weren't even going to make it to the police station.

14

"What's happening?" said Ilsa. The police offer driving the car didn't respond. Instead he called the other car through his shoulder radio. Our car slowed then stopped.

"What's going on?" I asked the officer.

He started to get out of the car but stopped. He reached back across the dashboard and hit a switch. It took until he was out and walking towards the truck for me to realize what he'd done.

"He turned off the dash cam," I said.

"They're not supposed to," said Ilsa.

"I have the feeling none of this is supposed to happen."

A gaunt man climbed out of the truck. Jeans, t-shirt, a hardened, familiar look – he was one of the men watching Ilsa's house.

The cop pointed at the car, at us. The police officer from the lead car walked around the camouflage truck and joined them. They walked our way.

"Ilsa, that's one of the men from your house," I said.

"But, how?"

"Maybe they followed us."

"I think they would have come after us at the motel."

"Then, they heard about it on the police radio."

The police each took one side of the car. Guns out, they opened our doors.

"Out of the car. Now!" said the officer who'd been driving us.

We got out. The zip cuffs were hurting my wrists.

The Gaunt Man sneered at me. Evil in his eyes. European features on his face. Just like "Barry Wilson".

I had just gotten on my feet when the cop hit my back and pushed me stumbling forward. I regained my balance just as the officer grabbed my arm and lead me towards the gaunt man's truck. Ilsa received the same treatment not far behind me.

The Gaunt Man moved ahead of us, jiggling keys off his belt, and opened the back of the truck. Nothing inside except hot, hard steel.

I stopped at the bumper and turned to ask the cop something. Before I got a word out, the Gaunt Man grabbed my arm and the back of my pants. He and the cop hoisted me into the truck. I landed hard, hitting my chin against the metal floor. I rolled onto my back just as Ilsa was tossed in.

"Hey, wait!" she said.

The doors slammed shut. It was dark, hot, and stuffy.

"Walter, what the fuck?" said Ilsa.

"Stay calm."

The truck rumbled to life.

"We've been patient so far. When they open this door we fight," I said.

"How? Our hands. My ties won't budge." If she was holding her hands up for me to see, I couldn't. It was pitch black. Sweat had beaded all over my skin.

"Use your head. People never expect head butting. It hurts and does serious damage. Aim for their nose," I said.

The truck continued to rumble but didn't move.

"That weird guy's the one that tried to stab me at my house. I've fought him once and gotten away. No reason it can't happen again."

"But, the police. They're helping them. They handed us right over!"

That was more than troubling. It was one thing to think these killers would intercept us before we could squawk. It was a bigger problem to be handed over to them. The Gaunt Man and the other attackers didn't look like types who could call shots that big. They had to be working for someone. But, who could have the power to make a police department surrender us and look the other way?

I realized the truck still hadn't moved just as I heard the sound of another vehicle pulling up, equally loud.

"Another vehicle."

"I don't want them to separate us, Walt."

"We won't let them."

The truck's loud rumble made it impossible to hear what was happening outside. The heat was stifling. And, being in here too long would weaken us. We'd be no good for fighting.

Ilsa said, "What's going on?"

"I can't hear."

A loud clang from something striking the metal walls. We jumped. I scrambled onto my knees, turned, and placed my head next to the door. Nothing.

"Can you get to your feet?"

"Yes," she said.

"Good. Do it. When they open the door we can charge them. Remember, top of your head. Aim for his nose. Try to land on him or your shoulder. Then, run. "

"Okay."

She stood up from the sound of it.

"Walt," she said.

"Yes?" I said.

"Find me and kiss me. Just in case."

We shuffled through the dark, finally bumping shoulder to shoulder. I found her head with mine, smelled her hair, and used my nose to follow the curve of her cheek down to her lips. It was a long, tender kiss that re-ignited my spirit.

Then we waited. The truck continued to rumble. My hearing continued to prove insufficient for picking out details.

After a moment, she said, "Do you think—"

Keys rattled, the handle cranked, the doors opened. Light blasted in as we blasted out. "Go!"

We leaped out of the truck. I tensed, prepared to ram against flesh and bone. But, I fell shoulder first against the dusty, rocky ground. It hurt like a mother.

"Take it easy, boy," a voice sad. "No need to get uppity." A boot stepped on my chest, pinning me to the ground. The sun was so bright I couldn't see anything. Might as well have been blindfolded.

I blinked and squinted until I could make out a scruffy, denim-clad man standing over me. His shadow blocked the sun, which allowed me to see. He was a biker. Stitched to his denim vest was a patch. DG's colors. I looked around for Ilsa. She had a dirty face and a bloody nose. And, several more bikers were standing around her. All wearing DG's colors.

"What's going on?" I said looking up at the biker hovering over me.

He pulled me to my feet and dusted me off. The other bikers did the same for Ilsa. I was about to ask my question again when I saw the Gaunt Man chained up against the side of the camouflage truck and held in place by two of the biggest, meanest looking bikers I've ever seen.

"We got here just as the fuzz took off. I'm Bannon. We have a mutual friend."

"DG," I said.

He nodded and moved his toothpick to the other side of his mouth.

"How did you know?" I said.

"He had us scanning the police radio after your name appeared in the paper. The call came in and we caught up to you."

I looked to Ilsa. "You okay?"

"Yes, I'll be fine." She sniffed blood.

"What about him," I said, gesturing to the Gaunt Man.

Bannon smiled like a devil. "You're gonna ride back with the pack. Me and Sonny and Waffle are gonna stick around and ask our friend with the funny accent a few questions. We'll let you know what we find out."

It's an awful feeling knowing someone is about to experience brutal pain on your behalf. That's why I didn't look back after hopping on one of the choppers. As its engine revved, I heard the metal slink of a long chain sliding across the ground, plus a few nefarious laughs. I didn't want to see what was coming next. But, after being attacked, stalked, almost killed, forced to kill, and kidnapped – by the police, no less – I wanted some goddamn answers. And, I didn't care how they got them.

15

Returning to DG's house put me at ease. Well, as much as could be expected given the circumstances. Having been arrested for breakfast, the first thing we did was eat. After that, Ilsa found a spare bedroom to lie down in. The day had already exhausted her.

I needed a hit of normalcy, so I put in a call to my kids. It was fantastic to hear their voices. Just small talk – how was your day, what have you been up to...that kind of thing. I didn't tell them about my day. For a few moments, they calmed me down and made me forget the last thirty-six hours. But, when they asked if they were still going to see me this weekend, I could only say that I hoped so. It reminded me just how much was at stake. They need their father. That meant I needed to get to work.

DG pointed to a quiet room at the end of a dimly lit hallway, past stacks of boxes of assorted items, everything from pungent leather biker vests to jars of moonshine. Whatever was selling that week, I assumed.

The room's tongue and groove wood paneling made it cozy. I sat down at a wobbly desk and took in the mountain of files and papers from Ken's house. Where to begin?

I started shuffling through the files, first organizing by category – personal, business, then activism. I had trouble distinguishing between files related to investments in corporations and files related to activism against corporations. But, once I reminded myself that Ken would never invest in any company with activities he would protest against things became easier to identify and sort.

My gut – and Nadine Evers' – told me activism is what got Ken killed. So, I started looking through those folders first. They didn't paint a pretty picture. Corporate greed, illegal dumping, politicians bought, paid for, and performing heinous acts against their constituents. Greedy men and women running amuck like rotten kids in a theme park bounce house.

It was not a new story. All you have to do is read the Florida daily papers to see the bad guys in action. So, the real question was...what information had been so damning that Ken needed to be killed before he could expose it? And, was that the same bombshell information Ken had teased to Nadine. I kept digging.

I'm not anti-corporation. If you are brilliant enough to create a breakthrough product or service that the population at large needs, good for you. You deserve success. But, I am anti-corruption. You don't get to re-make or break the rules to get what you want. And, in Florida that seemed to be the path most travelled:

Phosphate runoff. Natural preserve destruction. Everglades siphoning. Bribes, buyouts, bamboozlement. The public misled. The public outraged. The public ignored. Fat cats getting rich. Fat cats getting richer. Politicians in close alliance with questionable corporate partners. Heavy-handed development. Developers lunching with State Senators. Private meetings between CEOs and the Governor. Secret retreats between politicians and big money, including the Attorney General. All nasty, but all common knowledge. I made a list of the biggest offenders, guys Ken clearly had in his sites.

He had been busy. Peaceful protests, scathing editorials that named names, boycotts, shaming guilty parties on TV talk shows and news reports. He did everything he could to get the word out and direct Florida's powerful sunlight on state corruption. He was fearless. He was effective. He was inspirational. He was no more. And, that made me mad.

Several hours passed. My eyes started to blur and my butt was numb. I got up to stretch and go grab a drink. But, the corner of a folder caught my eye. It had been placed with the Business/Investment folders. The label read "Capital Punishment." A quick glance inside and it became obvious Ken was not a fan of the practice. I tossed it on top of the activism files.

Ilsa walked in rubbing sleep dust from her eyes.

"Good snooze?" I said.

She nodded. "I needed it. But, I needed you to snuggle with even more."

"I would have been restless."

"Find anything?" She pointed to the stack of files.

I shook my head. "Ken was a very busy guy and it appears he did everything he could to muck things up for a bunch of people. I just don't see what he would have done to get himself killed. Not to take away from his efforts, but I'm really not sure how much he succeeded."

"He built a following. He mobilized people around the state and made it harder, no?" She leaned against the desk waiting for an answer.

"Yeah. I'm sure eventually it would have reached critical mass and gotten real results. But, I don't think he was there yet. Not from what I can tell."

Ilsa took my arm and nuzzled against me. Her soft warmth thawed my bones. I leaned my head against hers.

She sighed and said, "We're in a lot of trouble, lover." It wasn't panic or a plea. Just matter-of-fact. And, she was right.

"Well, the good news is we're not idiots. So, we might be able to figure this out."

She looked about to argue that point, but didn't. "How 'bout some food?" she said.

I nodded.

She led me out of the room.

16

DG seemed to always have some kind of gathering in progress – a party, biker meeting, tribal council, redneck rodeo, what have you. Today it was a party for a friend just released from prison. Biker mamas were cooking in the kitchen. The boys were outside barbecuing and boozing. A spectacular array of food had been laid out in the parolee's honor. He had arrived while I was in back reading Ken's files.

We picked our way along the food spread across the dining room table. It all looked delicious and my plate filled up fast. DG stumbled into the dining room with his arm around 'Oater,' of the newly emancipated Oaters. I wondered if his handle was a nod to western movies. Both he and DG were elated, laughing and smiling with red, cherubic cheeks.

DG pawed my shoulder and turned me their direction. "Walt, this is my main man most, Oater Dicks, formerly of Raiford State Prison. Oater, this is my good buddy and neighbor, Walt, and his hot as hell girlfriend, Ilsa."

Oater smiled at me then devoured Ilsa with his eyes.

"Hey man, keep your appetite on the food not the females," DG said with a fist thump against Oater's chest.

Oater laughed, held out his hands and said, "Can you blame me? I ain't seen a slice like that in three years. I thought about breaking out, but hell, have you seen the women in Union County? Bunch a homely nags!"

They howled and DG grabbed a chicken wing off the table and shoved it in Oater's mouth.

Ilsa smirked and said, "Thank you for the very nice compliment, Mr. Oater." I smiled politely, but DG was already dragging Oater out of the room. The fun was just getting started.

I grabbed the rest of my food, a napkin, a fork, and poured a soda. With no hands free I bit the lip of the cup and carried the soda in my mouth. Ilsa was amused. I almost spilled the drink smiling back at her.

We sat on DG's back deck, which looks out towards the river. What I'd do for a swim right now.

"You should get in," she said.

Ilsa seemed to be reading my mind.

"I could use it. Just not so sure I should be showing my face around here."

"You think they're watching for you?"

"If I was a cop or one of the killers, I would."

I looked around at the dense woods surrounding us and started to feel uneasy. Anyone could be watching right now. If they could get close enough. Which was possible if they knew the woods. And, if they know how to avoid DG's traps. Maybe I shouldn't even have been out on the deck. But, I needed the fresh air. Especially after that moldy motel room. And, DG's place was pretty remote. I figured it would be okay, at least for a little while.

"I guess I shouldn't go either," she said.

"I'm sure DG's ladies have some fresh rags around here. You could change your appearance and swim looking like a biker mama. No one would suspect." I smiled.

"You know I swim naked."

I did indeed.

The first time I witnessed her sleek, busty body dripping with fresh spring water still ranks as one of the greatest sights of my life. She just stood there, water up to her knees. Droplets glistening in the sun as they slid down her hips and hung from her nipples. My eyes were still thanking me for it. I'd been with plenty of women. But, then and there I knew I'd never be with a better one.

A pair of motorcycles rumbled onto the property. Their loud, choking engines slaughtered the serene vibe of the wooded area. It was DG's boys, Bannon and the other guy, back from Citrus County. Their chains hung from the handlebars.

And, they were bloody.

They parked the bikes and walked into the house. A moment later DG led Bannon onto the deck and over to me.

"We beat the piss outta that boy and he took it," said Bannon. "Chain whipped him hard."

He meant the Gaunt Man.

"Takes a special kind to suffer that sort of beating without yapping. Only words he said were some I didn't even understand."

"Where is he now?" I said.

"We left him. Chain choked him purple and he fell right over. Couldn't tell if he was dead or just passed out. But, couldn't stick around. Traffic was starting to pick up."

DG spoke. "You get a wallet or anything?"

"Just this," he held out a small, torn out piece of newspaper. "We scoured his truck, couldn't find nothin'. Nice truck, too. We'd a stole it if we coulda gotten our bikes loaded in the back. So, we just crashed it into the swamp along the side of the road. Should slow the boy up a while if he's still breathing."

The torn out piece of newspaper featured a brief write up about how the police were looking for me next to my driver's license photo. It was chilling to see my face next to those words.

Me. A wanted man.

I started to wonder what my clients would think, if they'd ever call to hire me again. And, if not would I have to go back to the dreaded nine-to-five life. Fuck it, I'd just tend bar. I didn't need that corporate pressure. I could get by with less.

"All right, thanks brother," DG said to Bannon as they shook hands. "Go eat."

"Gladly. Inflicting chain pain always builds a mean hunger." Bannon laughed and walked back inside the house.

DG looked to me. "Sorry we couldn't do more."

"You saved our lives. That's plenty," I said.

"I'll keep my ear to the vine, see if anything turns up. Meanwhile, stay here long as you like."

He moseyed back into the house.

Ilsa took the newspaper out of my hand and studied it.

"This is surreal," she said.

"Beyond belief."

"It says we're wanted for questioning. That sounds better than wanted for murder."

"We saw what kind of questions they were ready to ask us. That article was published to flush us out so we'd be easier to find."

She let out a long, agitated breath and leaned against the wood backing of the bench. She flipped over the newspaper to read the back side.

"Dante's For Men is having a sale in Lake Butler."

I looked at her like huh? She handed me the newspaper.

"Two-for-one men's suits, this weekend only. Are there even occasions formal enough to dress up for in Lake Butler?"

"Church and funerals," she said.

I nodded, conceding the point.

"And executions at the state prison," she added.

I nodded, but stopped and caught my breath. Thoughts connected in my brain.

"Wait a minute—"

DG's house exploded.

17

My skin tingled and my hands shook.

Smoke filled my nostrils.

My ears rang.

Muffled voices were inarticulate.

I sensed panic and anger.

I blinked my eyes open to tiny shafts of sunlight beaming through gaps in the darkness. At first, I couldn't move. I tried again, with extra effort, and it was enough to force a pile of wooden planks to slide off me, unveiling the world. A crooked house nail sticking out of a plank caught against my head and scratched it deep until I could shake it off.

DG's house was gone. What remained was a disaster zone, landscaped with smoking, burning rubble. Chunks of wood and concrete were scattered in every direction. Trees five deep and surrounding the house had been whacked in half by the blast. The air smelled burnt and gas tinged.

I used my hands to pull my legs out from under more wood. It was part of the deck I had been sitting on moments before...

Now, I remembered.

I was talking to Ilsa when everything exploded to hell.

Ilsa!

I looked behind me, under me, all over for her.

"Ilsa!" I yelled.

No sound.

I stood up and had to pause as pain rippled through my body from the inside out. I felt bruised from head to toe as I scanned the ground for Ilsa.

"Ilsa!" My voice echoed across the river.

A classic mid-afternoon Florida rain started to fall making every surface slick. I reached down and hoisted away deck planks. I was careful putting them down because I didn't want to accidentally throw them on top of Ilsa or anyone else who might be buried in the debris. I avoided nails jutting out at odd angles, metal braces with twisted sharp corners, and roof tacks scattered across the ground.

I pulled up a sheet of plywood that had been torn in half. Underneath, I found a dead biker with half his head missing. The metal top of the barbecue grill that had smashed his skull lay next to him. His lower teeth were sticking out of his mouth at odd directions towards the sky. I pushed the plywood to the side and moved on.

I recognized Ilsa's shoe first. Her leg was sticking out through a window frame. Fear chilled me as I wondered what terrible condition I might find her in.

Bannon walked past me, still stunned from the explosion. He had splinters sticking out the back of his neck.

"Help me get this off her," I said.

He looked at me, perhaps still incoherent, but started helping anyway. He wedged up some wood while I pulled the window frame off her leg. Ilsa was flat on the ground and she looked bad. Real bad.

I knelt down and touched her. Please don't be dead.

"Ilsa. It's Walt. Are you okay?"

I stroked hair away from her face and kissed her cheek. I wiped globs of soggy pink insulation fibers off her neck and chest as I sat down on the dirty ground and carefully pulled her into my arms.

Her eyes fluttered.

"What...hap...?" She winced with pain.

"It's okay. Hang in there. You're alive and I'm going to get you taken care of," I said.

I picked her up and carried her over to a tree stump. It had been a tall, majestic pine tree a few minutes ago. I leaned her against the stump. She was coming to. She looked around, bewildered.

"Oh, my god, Walt. The house is gone."

"Yes."

I gave her a moment to pull it together. She straightened one leg then looked to me with worried eyes.

"I can't move my leg," she said.

I looked down at her left leg. No gashes or punctures. But, it was bruised from calf to upper thigh. It appeared bad enough to make me think her bones were cracked underneath. She wasn't going anywhere.

And, that was a problem. No clue yet as to why the house exploded. But, anything coincidental wasn't believable. People were out to kill me and I think they just took a shot. That meant a couple of things - If the guys gunning for me just bombed DG's they might presume we were dead. That could be good cover. Or, they could be in the woods right now, waiting to see who climbs out of the rubble, ready to finish the job.

Fear jolted me and I squatted down and glanced around for any sign of snipers. Nothing.

DG's crowd — those who had survived — were staggering around, many of them bloody. I was relieved to see DG himself marching through the mess like a defiant general surveying his losses. Blood trickled from his temple down his neck. His swagger was still intact, as he helped people out of the rubble.

I turned to Ilsa. "Bit of a problem. We need to get you medical attention fast. But, I don't know that we can go to any hospital without getting arrested."

"And, we don't have much time, do we?" She paired it with an expression I was familiar with. The one where she puts guilt on herself.

"True. Stay here until I can see what our options are."

"Obviously. I'm not going anywhere with this mangled leg," she said.

Her sarcasm was more than encouraging. She still had fighting spirit. I kissed the top of her head and hustled over to DG, keeping low and keeping an eye on the property's perimeter.

DG had command of the situation, pointing bikers in various directions.

"You all right?" I said.

He looked at me with a furious scowl, like he was ready to kill Satan himself. "I'm fine and I'm pissed," he said. "How 'bout you?"

"Sore but good. Ilsa's propped against what used to be a tree. Her leg is shot. I need to get her to a doctor, but..."

"I getcha." He pointed to a van on the far side of the rubble, facing away towards the entrance. A biker and a mama were helping another injured biker up into it. "These boys never go to doctors or hospitals. That van is loading up to go to our...private practitioner."

"Like a real doctor?"

His facial expression and matter of fact delivery made it clear he didn't want to debate it. "There are plenty of doctors who owe us favors. First class medical service. They do whatever we tell them."

"Got it," I said. "Let's get her in that van."

She was in the van in less than ten minutes. DG reassured her she would be safe and underground. He said he'd let me know where she ended up.

"Don't leave me, Walt," said Ilsa.

The move from the stump to the van had been painful, and the shock was wearing off. The pain in her leg was intense and made her eyes water. She was scared.

"I have to do something about this," I said.

"No. Please. Just stay with me." She winced and clutched her leg. The van started up.

"No more running, Ilsa. You'll be safe. And, so will I."

I leaned in to kiss her. She'd couldn't move her head away so she settled for closing her eyes, tolerating the kiss, not happy with me. I shut the van doors and gazed at her for a long moment through the back window.

A minute later the van drove off and I had the terrible feeling this could be the last time I would ever see her. I sure hoped not. It'd be a rotten farewell.

18

I turned to find DG giving me a skeptical look.

"What?" I said.

He started to say something else but settled on, "Now, what to do with you?"

"What do you think caused the explosion?" I took in the surrounding debris as I said it. "Think this is my fault?"

"Sure would be a strange coincidence if it wasn't," he said. "But, don't get too cocky. You're not the only one with enemies around here. The Devil's Destroyers have been trying to get at us for years."

"Could they get close enough to plant a bomb?"

"Wasn't no bomb."

He walked over to a part of the concrete foundation, still in place. A jagged piece of scorched white metal sat on it. "We found this." He held up the metal and pointed to a hole near the middle of it.

A bullet hole.

It gave me the willies, thinking that whoever fired that shot was still watching me from the woods, their rifle sight set on my head.

"This was part of the big propane tank that ran under the deck."

"I was right there."

DG smirked briefly, then looked worried.

I got the message. I scanned the woods again, more alert than ever.

Fire engine sirens cried in the distance.

"If I'm not hiding you, you better split," DG said.

"How?"

DG used his big, meaty hand to stop Bannon from rushing past.

"Flamers and pigs are closin' in. We gotta hide this shit," Bannon said gesturing to the battered, but not broken, wooden box in his hand.

"Take the four-wheeler, and you and Walt boogie out Black Path. Now."

Bannon nodded and looked to me, "Come on!"

We ran around the rubble to a small shack that was still standing near the river. Bannon opened the wooden door and inside sat a high-end, all terrain four-wheeler, keys in the ignition. He threw the box on the back of it and strapped it down.

"Hop on," he said.

We both did. He started it up. Three revs of the engine later we were out of there, and riding over house debris. We almost jostled off, but he put some body English over the handlebars and we kept rolling towards a part of the woods where no driving trail appeared to exist.

As we reached the trees, we slammed through wide palm fronds and found ourselves on Black Path, its name clearly coming from the dark, rich color of the soil and the density of the trees. There was little sunlight to guide the way. That didn't slow Bannon down.

I had no clue where we were headed. But, I trusted DG and, therefore, Bannon. They hadn't steered me wrong so far.

I watched the woods whip by, and grew anxious wondering if we'd pass the man who shot the propane tank. Was he fast enough to shoot us off the ATV? It had to be driving close to forty miles per hour. That doesn't sound like much, but when you have less than a foot of space on each side of your vehicle and the road keeps twisting and turning, it feels like too much speed.

A few moments later, I stood corrected. We hadn't been on Black Path. We were just now entering it. The ATV rumbled down a rough log ramp that went into the earth and led towards a tunnel. So much foliage covered the opening. You'd have to fall into it before you'd know it was there.

The opening led into a dark underground pathway made from natural caves caused by the sinkholes. The same type of sinkholes you hear about on the news when they swallow a house hole. That happened a couple of years ago in the City of Mango, on the outskirts of Tampa. The sinkhole took the house and the owner down into the earth forever.

Bannon flipped on the ATV's headlights, illuminating the way.

Thick wood beams had been installed to fortify the chasm. It was wet, dirty, and the ATV's engine echoed loud inside. Too loud to ask Bannon where we were going.

So, I did my best to think through the latest events. Cops arrest us and turn us over to the French speaking – yes, it had to be French - man along the side of the road. Thanks to DG's police scanning, we get saved at the last minute. Bannon tries to chain whip information out of the Frenchman and gets nothing. That means Frenchy and his gang were some fearless motherfuckers. One of them was already dead back in Gainesville. Bannon might have killed Frenchy. I didn't feel bad for hoping so.

Then, I remembered the one small possible clue Bannon found - the newspaper clipping announcing my fugitive status. But, that wasn't the important part. What mattered was the flip side of the newspaper. The side with the advertisement for a men's fashion store located in Lake Butler, Florida.

Lake Butler was the county seat of Union County. Frenchy and the boys all sat in cars outside Ilsa's place with Union County plates. It's one thing to steal a car from Union County as a way to throw people off your trail. Presuming word would get out about a murder at Ilsa's. But, it seemed hard to believe these guys would clip a newspaper from the smallest county in the state and not actually be from around there. If I was right, I now had a fix on where they came from. It wasn't much, but it was something.

But, that wasn't even the most significant detail.

Ilsa's flip comment about executions had reminded me that Union County was home to Florida's Death Row. Ken had a Capital Punishment folder. I thought it was out of place and meant nothing important. But, maybe it did.

Had Ken been campaigning against Capital Punishment? Had he pissed off one of its supporters? Would anyone want capital punishment to exist so much they'd kill for it? Maybe. The prison industry was huge and growing. Prison privatization brought in mega money. It could all be connected. There was no way to get the file now. It was either destroyed or soaking in the rubble that had been DG's house. And by now, that rubble was surrounded by cops and firemen.

I needed to get to a computer and research the names I'd written down from Ken's files. Find out who they were, what they did, and figure out why they might have killed Ken. See if any of them connected to Union County, the prison system, or capitol punishment.

I also needed to talk to Tom and learn the contents of the glass vial. That could give me another lead.

Bannon raced the ATV through the swerves and curves of Black Path. We passed several tunnels that forked off in other, undisclosed directions. My guess: the Black Path was like the Underground Railroad of illicit activities.

Daylight appeared up ahead. Bannon raced towards it. Moments later we exited the tunnel and roared into another wooded area.

A few turns later and Bannon had us driving down a hilly pass into a small, unremarkable town just to the south of Dunnellon. He pulled up and parked the ATV behind a barn just off the main drag. My ears were ringing after the engine shut off.

"Where are we?"

"Citrus Springs. East side," said Bannon. "But, not for long. I gotta stash this shit and boogie over to DG's other place, get it up and running."

"What about me?"

"What about you," he said as he unlatched the barn door.

"I need a computer. I need to get to Clearwater."

He carried the banged up wooden box full of mysterious contents into the barn and set it down next to a car. Before exiting the barn, he pulled a ring of keys off a wall hook and tossed it to me.

"I need the buggy. You can take these wheels."

I looked at the car. If the meanest, nastiest group of bikers you had ever seen decided to trade in their bikes for a car, this was what it would look like - Flat, deep charcoal grey paint job, polished chrome grill, and a blower erupting out of the hood. Silver detailing. Spikes on the tires. Attitude to spare.

"Thanks. A little flashy for someone trying to stay under the radar. But, I'll take it," I said.

"Well, if you attract too much attention, it'll get you out of a jam quick. Just bring it back in one piece," said Bannon.

We shook hands and I hopped in the car.

I ignited the engine, and it roared to life. It rumbled with such force I worried it would shake the old barn apart. I drove the mean machine out of the barn, waved to Bannon, and hit the road. Next stop, Clearwater.

19

My route was I-75 through Tampa then the Courtney Campbell Causeway across Old Tampa Bay into Clearwater. I grew up there. It's right on the Gulf of Mexico, most noted for it's white, powder sugar beaches and Scientologists. It was a screwy combination to say the least, but somehow it all worked. It wasn't backwoods like the northern part of Florida, it didn't have the cocaine and Cuban flair of Miami, and it's not the family fun wonderland of Orlando. Clearwater also doesn't have the sleazy vibe of its better-known, lesser-dressed city across the bay, Tampa. But, both are part of the Tampa Bay area along with St. Petersburg.

I made two stops on the way to Tom's lab. First, I swung by to check my "winter" house. It was a modest suburban home built in the late 60's. My ex-and I bought it from a home flipper who bought it from a one-legged drug dealer who hosted thugs, crooks, and prostitutes, all while dealing in a bathrobe out under the large jacaranda tree. Unlike most dwellings in Florida, ours had some charming history.

I liked it enough to hang onto it after I bought the A-frame up at the river. Now, it was where I crashed when I returned to town for business. After all, this area was one of the capitals of infomercials ever since Home Shopping Club started here back in the late 70's, first as a radio station, then as a local cable channel (where the TV hosts would personally deliver the products to your doorstep after they got off they air), then as a national cable cash cow that moos to this day.

There would be no stopping by the house. A recent model white pickup truck sat parked two houses down. It was facing away, but its side mirror was aimed at my driveway. I could see the shaded outline of a man inside, slumped down. The truck was too clean to be the killers'. I guessed cop. Best to not stick around. I turned down a side road then looped out of the neighborhood.

I left DG's car in the parking lot of a Peruvian restaurant two blocks from Tom's office. He and I ate there often. It was cheap and good.

As I walked to Tom's, I realized just how beat to hell my body felt. My wrists were sore from the handcuffs that morning. My whole body ached from the explosion. My ass hurt and still buzzed from the vibrations of the ATV. And, my nerves were shot. But, I had no choice. I needed to keep going.

Tom's office had front and rear entrances. I opted for the back door, presuming that the killers or police were staking out the place,

Tom answered my knock and startled at my appearance. "Walt."

"Can I come in?"

"Is it true? I saw the news."

"Invite me in, offer me a drink, make me feel like a lady first. Then, I'll give you the full scoop."

He looked past me to see if anyone was watching, then let me in. He closed and locked the door fast.

"Man, what's been going on?" he said, worry in his voice.

I brought him up to speed on current events the best I could.

"So, did you really kill that guy?"

I shrugged and felt a pang of guilt. He looked disappointed.

"It was self defense. I had no choice," I said.

He blew out a big, slow breath under wide eyes as he grasped the weight of the situation.

"So, that glass vial you brought me is related to all of this."

"Yes. Find out what was in it?"

He nodded, looking grave and puzzled. "It's dangerous stuff, Walt. Really dangerous."

"Like?" I said.

"Like I could get arrested for having it here dangerous," he said. "Pure, liquid nicotine, VX, and Batrachotoxin." Saying it made him look like he had just tasted something awful.

"Sounds like a chemical weapon," I said.

"Essentially, yes," said Tom.

Jesus. My heart sunk with this revelation. If these guys could get those chemicals, they could get anything they wanted. Anything they needed to stop me.

I looked down at my hand, worried I may have gotten splashed with toxins when I jabbed the glass vial into "Barry Wilson's" neck. I wiped it on my pant leg.

"No wonder it works so fast," I said.

"If Ken was hit with a dose of this, he didn't have a chance. It's a brutal cocktail."

I wandered around the room, thinking.

"Any idea if these elements could be traced in the body?"

"What are you a detective now?"

"Survivalist, it seems."

"Don't know for certain, but I would presume they could."

"So, they weren't worried about hiding the murder." I thought for a moment. "Because they don't expect to get caught."

"Why would they believe that?" said Tom.

"Because they're connected and protected. By someone who can manipulate cops, who can plant bogus murder stories about me in the papers," I said.

"So, they're just the hired help."

I nodded. "I need to figure out who hired them. And, approach them."

He held up the glass vial. "I'm pretty sure the guys using this stuff are going to stay in your way. Unless you can get to their boss first."

I paused and wondered how the hell I would pull that off. It was a fresh reminder of my complete inexperience in this realm, how unprepared I truly was. "Where would they get those chemicals?" I said.

Tom shrugged and said, "Don't know. Pure liquid nicotine can be had with some ease. The other two not so much. I did some research...Batrachotoxin is a super potent non-peptide—the most potent, in fact. Comes from frog excretions and is used for poison darts. VX was developed for pesticides in the nineteen fifties, but..."

"What?" I said, drawn in.

He gave me a blank look. "It's so dangerous the world's stockpiles were supposed to have been destroyed."

Tom continued, "The last place said to have it was a stockpile in Anniston, Alabama."

I had no response and looked out the window, at the trees swaying in the breeze across the pond. I no longer had the time to appreciate the small, simple things.

"There was also a European company that had it, Velmont," said Tom, surprising me with more information.

"Had?" I said.

"Went out of business eight years ago. They had a sales office in Rennes, France with manufacturing in Vitré, a village not too far away," he said.

I hopped off my stool, excited. "These guys were French! They had French accents. They could have gotten it there." I started pacing around the room.

Tom nodded, conceding agreement. "Makes sense. So, what can you do with that information?"

"I have no fucking idea." My excitement fizzled.

"I could find out who worked there, maybe. Match that with travel logs, passport records," I said.

"And you have access to all that sort of information?" Tom looked at me skeptical.

"No."

"And, you're in good enough standing to work with the authorities to make those types of queries?"

"Definitely not. Shit. I could look for French people in Union County. How many could there be? It's Hickville."

"Probably not many, if you're ready to find and confront them."

"I'm ready to get them off my back."

Anger flared in my voice and Tom looked surprised to hear it.

"Didn't mean to aim that frustration at you, friend," I said.

"You get cranky when you're hungry. When was the last time you ate?"

"Too long."

He reached for his keys and a jacket. "I'll walk over and get us some chow. You sit tight." Tom walked over to the front door.

"Mind if use your computer?"

"Go for it. Password is ProfessorPowertron, one word. "

"God, I knew you were a nerd."

He smiled and out he went.

I fired up Tom's laptop, punched in the password and checked my email. My inbox was bursting and the majority of emails appeared to be from clients losing their patience. They wanted to know what was up with their particular script.

The majority of my clients were based outside of Florida, so only one inquired about me being a wanted man...and was that going to prevent me from delivering work on time? Classic client behavior. Always thinking about themselves. I told them not to worry. Something as trivial as murder wasn't going to jeopardize my ability to make deadline. Sure, it was probably a lie. But, why scare paying clients off?

I reminded myself that emails and business weren't the reason I'd hopped on the computer. I needed answers, so I pulled out the scribble-scratch list of names I'd taken from Ken's files and started to Google them.

I spent a good thirty minutes punching in names, all corporate titans with a penchant for thumbing their noses at Florida and its citizens. It was amazing to see how those guys, who always complained about the poor and taxes and so on, were the biggest welfare queens around; always wanting exceptions from the state, a break from the rules, money from the government till.

An article popped up about Phoscore Industries, one of the state's largest sand dredging companies. They've pock marked the state for years, buying up land, digging up sand, and selling to the highest bidder. The article quoted Ken and his informed opinion about Phoscore's detrimental business practices. It also quoted Phoscore's CEO, Jert Maynard and his position on Ken Kerenz. He wasn't a fan. And, he went so far as to say, "if Ken Kerenz is going to continue trying to undermine Phoscore's business, we have no choice but to go after his business."

That sounded like a threat. But, would they go so far as to kill Ken? Would they kill him after letting a quote like that get in the paper for all to read? The article was just a few months old. If I were a detective, I'd be very interested in speaking to Mr. Maynard in light of Ken's death. In truth, I was a detective now.

20

I picked up the office phone as I tried to recall Kathy Kerenz's cell phone number. I took a guess and stabbed the phone buttons. As it rang I started feeling overwhelmed by it all. I thought about Ilsa, missing her, wanting to be with her. If we both wanted to be together, why weren't we? I didn't even know where she was. I should have listened and gone with her.

Kathy answered.

"Kathy, it's Walt. Asher," I said.

"Oh, Walt. What's going on? I saw your name in the papers. And, Nadine Evers. Ken knew her!"

She'd started to cry. "It's all just too much."

"It's all right, Kathy. I'm fine. You have enough to worry about without worrying about me."

"But, what happened?" she said.

"Look..." I took a beat to think of the best way to phrase what I had to say to a woman grieving the extra fresh death of her husband. "I'm pretty certain Ken didn't die of natural causes. I started looking into it—"

"You think he was killed?" she said. A heavy silence followed.

"It's looking that way. And, I've had a few close calls myself. From the same people."

"And, Nadine? The paper said she had a heart attack."

"I don't buy it," I said.

"But...why would someone do that to Ken? He was such a good man."

"Kathy, I only have a moment. I don't have the answers you need, but I will try to get them for you. And, I can do that if you'll help me."

All I heard on the other end of the line was a sniff then a long sigh. When she came back on, her voice was pinched, throat constrained, trying to hold back an avalanche of emotions.

"Kathy, I had a chance to go through Ken's files, to look for any information that would tip me off about who might have been after him. I didn't find much. I also ran into Nadine after the funeral. She said Ken had discovered something massive. Something that would make heads roll. Did he tell you what that was?"

"He said he had something that could expose a lot of people. Government people. And, corporate people," she said.   "Did he say who?"

"No. Just that he could kill about twelve birds with one stone. And, there'd be, um, what he called aftershocks."

"Sounds big. Nothing in his files pointed towards that. These were files out of the river house. Did he keep files anywhere else? In another room? A safe deposit box, maybe?"

"Not that I know of," she said.

"If I can find out what he knew I'm certain it will help us track his killers down," I said.

A moment passed with no response. Then...

"Talk to Duncan," she said.

"Who's that?"

"Ken's friend. They were talking a lot before Ken..." she couldn't finish the sentence.

"How can I get in touch with him?"

"Let me get his number off the phone." I could hear the phone pull away from her ear. A moment later she came back on. "You there?"

"I'm here," I said.

She gave me the number. I repeated it to be sure. Then said, "Tampa. Not far."

"He's the only other person I think might know. He and Ken were supposed to get together the day he died. But, that never happened." She sounded tired, of talking, of grieving.

"Kathy, you've been a great help. I will call as soon as I learn more. Be strong, for yourself and the kids," I said.

"Sure thing, Walt. Thank you."

I hung up and dialed Duncan. He answered two rings in.

"Hello?" He sounded cautious. I had to earn his trust fast.

"Duncan, this is Walt Asher. Ken Kerenz was a good friend of mine and I think someone did him wrong. Real wrong."

I paused to let him respond.

Nothing.

"I just got off the phone with Kathy, his wife. She gave me your number and said I should talk to you about some explosive information Ken received right before his death. If you want proof, call Kathy now at her number. She'll vouch for me." I gave him her number as further validation. He hung up without saying a word.

I waited by the phone, hoping he'd call Kathy then call me right back. Time dragged. I was starving and wondered what the hell was taking Tom so long with the food.

The phone rang. I picked it up.

"Yes," I said, not giving away anything.

"This is Duncan," he said.

"You call Kathy?"

"Yes. She vouched for you."

"Good. So, you obviously know about Ken. I could tell by your voice when you answered."

A long pause.

"I'm worried, yes," he said.

"Has anyone approached you?" I said.

"No. Not yet. I mean I hope never. But, Ken...and Nadine."

"I think you're wise to keep under the radar. I've had several brushes with the guys who killed Ken. They're bad news."

Another long pause. I continued, "Problem is, I don't know who they are. I'm trying to figure that out to take the heat off me, and of course, you and anyone else who might be in their sites," I said.

Still no response.

"So, I need info. What did Ken find out that was so damning someone would kill him?" I said.

"We should meet," he said. "I don't want to use the phone," Duncan said.

"Good idea. Let's keep discreet. Where?"

"You know the Sulphur Springs Water Tower?" he said.

"Yes. I can be there in thirty minutes."

"Okay. I'll be there," he said.

"Before you go, I gotta ask...am I onto something?" I said.

A long pause.

"Yes. More than you could possibly imagine." He hung up.

The phone started to slip in my hand. My palms were sweating. I had that feeling where you push and push and push to get something, then immediately regret it. But, I couldn't dwell on it.

Someone rattled the doorknob, trying to get in.

No keys were jingling. It wasn't Tom. I froze, scanned the room then dashed out the back door, not waiting to see who was coming in.

Good thing I didn't. As I walked back towards the car I saw Tom leaning against a police cruiser, our food going cold in a bag on the hood. Two detectives were grilling him—I'm sure looking for me. But, if he and the cops were talking on the street...who the hell was at his door? I hurried back to the car and got the hell out of there. The rumbling engine was much less subtle than I would have liked. Thirty minutes later I was across the Bay and weaving through traffic North of downtown Tampa.

21

The Sulphur Springs Water Tower was a Tampa landmark leftover from a 1920's. It had been a luxury arcade that was damaged beyond saving by floods that occurred when the Tampa Electric Company dam collapsed. Two hundred and fourteen feet tall, you can't miss it driving down I-275 right through the heart of the city.

I parked a couple blocks away on Florida Avenue near a tiny Cuban bodega that had been converted out of an old drive-thru only restaurant. I was tempted to get a Café Con Leche and Cuban toast since I still hadn't eaten, but there was no time. I hustled over to the tower.

The tower's surrounding area was all but deserted. Cars roared along the nearby interstate. The Tampa Greyhound track stood tall just beyond. The sun disappeared behind a thick patch of clouds. I made a point to hang out near a cluster of bushes, keeping out of sight. I was still a wanted man. And, a scared man. A dose of clairvoyance flashed through my mind – what the hell was I doing here?

Duncan showed up late at 3:40 p.m. He was obvious to spot. His stereotypical liberal attire – sweater, cap, khaki pants, and hiking boots along with a salt and pepper beard and a rubber wrist band dedicated to some cause – seemed like the right look for Ken's tribe. Paranoia had him checking every direction to see if anyone was watching. He spotted me and waved me into a small opening in the tower. I hurried over and ducked in.

It stunk in there. Birds, bats, and god knew what other creatures had turned it into a toxic shit pit. Critters came in through the ground entrance; birds and bats flew in via the openings at the top of the tower within its signature circular parapet wall. I had to put my shirt over my nose and mouth to breath. Duncan seemed unfazed.

"Walt Asher," I said. It came out muffled through my shirt. I held out a hand for shaking. He just nodded and backed away from the light spilling in through the entrance.

I stepped closer. "Who are you worried about, Duncan?"

He looked at me, almost surprised I had caught him being a nervous nelly.

I held my hands up, palms out, hoping to reassure him. "It's okay. I'm keeping a low profile, too, and made sure no one followed me here. Now, I need to know what you know. All you have to do is tell me and we can get out of here. It's that easy." I sounded like an infomercial Call-To-Action. For a very good reason. I wanted to close the deal ASAP.

He relaxed a little. "What I'm about to tell you has gotten people killed. It's dangerous information."

He had a flair for drama. But, I believed every word of it.

"Tell me," I said.

"There's a cancer in the state. And, it's metastasizing, growing out of control."

I knew what "metastasizing" meant and wanted to tell him to hurry the fuck up. I was nervous now. But, I let him tell it his own way.

He continued. "Everyone knows the corporations and the government are in bed together."

"Ken had files full of news clippings as proof," I said.

He looked irritated, like he wanted me to shut up. So, I did.

"Everyone knows the government changes the laws to suit the corporations instead of designing the laws to protect constituents," he said.

I nodded, showing I was listening.

"Everyone knows the corporations bribe them to do this. Everyone knows. They hardly try to hide it anymore. You know why?" He stared at me. I could tell what he was about to say next qualified as a leap of faith for him.

I shook my head, not knowing why.

"Because when the average person sees there's a protest going on, when activists raise hell, they think something is being done to stop these creeps. And, when that happens the public at large doesn't press the issue. They leave us to do the work. So, it's no longer a bother. And, that's what the creeps want. They couldn't handle the masses being fired up. They want them sedated and placated. That way, they only have to deal with a few squeaky wheels."

"Like you and Ken and the other activists," I said.

"Yes. You're getting it. And, usually we can only do so much. But, Ken was different. He had money, power, and passion. He could hurt them."

I nodded, agreeing. "And, he did. And, they weren't happy about it. His most recent coup was finding a capital hill staffer willing to testify to some of the collusion he had witnessed between the corporations and the State government. It had been going on for years. And, went all the way up to the Governor."

"And, they wanted to stop him from talking," I said.

"Presumably. But, that's not why they killed Ken."

I gave him a curious look. I felt like I'd missed an important detail.

"I made contact with the staffer first. Then, I introduced him to Ken, who was able to seal the deal that he would spill what he knew. But, the staffer was nervous. When we asked why he said it was because he'd heard a rumor."

He took a big breath. His pause gave me pause. He looked grave. Like all of his dreams and hopes had been shattered. Like the world had reached a point of no return.

I sensed he was about to spill the dirty secret and stayed silent.

"We've already established how politicians are for sale. But, so is everything else belonging to the State. Our parks can be rented for private functions. Our colleges can be used for private industry testing. Our police are hired to direct traffic outside of churches on Sundays. It's all for sale to keep the money flowing in. Everything."

He looked me deep in the eyes, knowing what he was about to say would shock me.

"The rumor the staffer heard was that a certain arm of the government was starting to be farmed out. But, not as public service. As a private service. Something bandied about in backroom dealing. Something that makes problems go away. For good."

He looked at me, reading my face to make sure I understood. "Now, ask your self which part of the government does nothing but make problems go away?"

"I don't know. What kind of problems? " I said.

"The worst problems," he said.

"You mean killing?"

He nodded slowly.

I racked my brain. And, then I got it. He saw I'd gotten it, too. A small, hesitant smile cracked onto his face between his thin, tight lips. Like he was happy to have served a public good.

I remembered Ken's folder.

"Capital punishment," I said.

He nodded. "Saved for the worst of the worst," he said.

My heart was pounding. It wasn't a big conspiracy. It was a huge one. And, I was right in the middle of it.

"Are...are you saying that the State of Florida executes people for hire?" I said, stepping up to him.

"It seems someone is selling those services." he said.

This was just the kind of information no one would ever want made public. And knowing Ken, he'd have done just that. That's why he was dead. That's why Duncan was on full alert. And, that's why they were after me. Loose ends, all needing to be clipped. And, who better to do the clipping than the official Death Row executioners of the State of Florida?

Just like me, they'd gotten a new gig. No more waiting months or years between jobs. Now, they were freelancing full-time.

22

The humidity grew oppressive. There was no breeze inside the tower, just swampy air that made the clothes stick to my body. Duncan's revelation had made me forget about the stench.

"The staffer gave Ken a signed affidavit detailing a full list of names. Buyers and sellers," Duncan said.

"I didn't see any lists in Ken's files. Just information on different corporations. Do you know where he put the list?"

He shook his head. "Some of those corporations might tie in," he said.

"The files were destroyed. I can't check. I have a list of some names, but..."

"You won't find any proof. They've kept it beyond secret."

"Who's doing the killing? Is this like government sanctioned assassination stuff," I said, hoping to have half my work done for me.

He shrugged. "I don't think it's official state business. But, someone has access to those resources. And, I'm guessing they don't want the state or anyone to find out."

"Who's the staffer? Maybe I can get to him."

"He's dead."

The air blew out of my lungs in a sigh of frustration.

"Did he tell anyone else?" I said.

"It's time for me to go," Duncan said, adjusting his hat and looking with caution towards the door. "I can no longer be a part of this."

"Where will I be able to reach you," I said.

"You won't," he said. He checked both directions then darted out of the tower. I gave him a moment, to make our rendezvous less obvious. Also, to let him flush out any killers should they be waiting for us.

And, they were.

I felt the whip of a blade as it slammed into the old, white concrete. Pulverized particles stung my face as I leapt back into the tower. Glancing out I saw one of the men I had seen at Ilsa's house. The same one DG's bikers had savaged. He had purple bruising laced around his arms, neck, and face. He had been worked over something awful. Yet, here he was ready to attack. Tough motherfucker.

Duncan was dead at his feet, throat red and ripped. The man ran at me. I looked around. The only place to go was up the stone, spiral staircase leading to the top of the tower.

Three steps up, my foot slipped on bat dung and I crashed against the stairs. Shaking, my hands covered in scum, I scrambled up the stairs two at a time. I held my hand against the curving walls for balance. When I heard the metal "ching" of the man – this executioner - lifting his blade off the concrete outside the tower, I double-timed it.

They caught a glimpse of me just as I disappeared up the curvature of the stairs. Two of them now, both climbing the stairs after me. I reached a plateau, a small semi-circle deck, which would have afforded me a glance below. But, I didn't trust its rotting wood to keep me from plunging through it.

I felt a breeze blow in through a window cut into the tower wall. I looked out and saw the Hillsborough River below. It was a survivable jump—if I could have slipped through the iron cross bars, but I couldn't. The killers appeared in my peripheral vision. I bolted up the steps.

Next level up, another plateau. This time with the wood deck already fallen away. Another window, more cross bars. I grabbed them and pushed. They budged. But, not enough. I pushed again, then pulled, watching over my shoulder, working them loose.

The bars broke free!

I looked back at the stairs, could hear the men approaching. I turned back to the window and started to climb out.

Stop.

It wasn't the river below. Just a hard concrete parking lot. No chance of survival.

I crawled back into the tower and turned just as one of the men stepped onto the plateau. A vicious dagger gleamed in his hand. He swung it. The blade ripped my shirt, but missed my skin. I fell back and kicked him. He tumbled off the plateau and rolled down and almost off the steps. I stood up and kept running.

Each step became more of a challenge. Excrement was everywhere, making each step slippery, like in a sloppy bar bathroom that hadn't been cleaned in...ever. The slippage slowed me down and the extra effort to stay balanced exhausted my legs. They were throbbing and sore. I was losing momentum. When I looked back, I saw the other man had surpassed his fallen comrade and was fast approaching. His hand clutched an ornate machete. I pressed on.

He gabbed my leg as I reached the fourth floor. I kicked him off, more panicked than precise, and raced higher into the tower.

Birds fluttered and flapped away as I stormed up the steps. Some flew out windows others flew down the deep interior. By the time I reached the fifth plateau, I could run no more. My legs felt weighed down. The other guy didn't seem to have that problem. He sprung up to the landing before I could figure out what to do next.

This was bad. The wooden deck looked sturdy and less rotten. But, if I stepped onto it all he had to do was push me off. If I circled around with my back to the steps, he'd only have to swing the machete at me to make me fall back. I had to go up or fight.

He swung first. I pressed against the wall near the window. Bars, parking lot view. Nothing doing.

He slashed again and I ducked. The blade cut a line into the cement, its powder raining down on my neck. I rammed my shoulder into his gut and slammed his back against the steps leading up to the next level. I heard the wind squeeze out of him and saw him gasp as I pulled back.

The machete was loose in his hand. I made a grab but he clenched his fist first then pushed off the steps and lunged at me, machete pointed like a sword. I screamed as it went under my arm and next to my torso. Way too close.

The machete and his arm went out the window. He grabbed my neck with his free hand. I pounded his face hard, harder...hard enough that he went limp for a moment. It was enough release to wiggle myself loose. I stepped back and kicked as he pulled the machete in from the window. But, he hadn't brought it in far enough. His wrist caught on the cement window frame and my kick snapped his elbow. He dropped the machete out the window and clutched his arm. His scream echoed throughout the tower. I ran past him and down the steps.

I stopped at the fourth level. The other man was stalking up the stairs. He was older and looked more menacing, with scarring across his cheeks and wrinkles around his eyes. But, he was fit. His arms were cut and massive.

About twenty steps down from the landing, he slowed his approach. He started creeping up the stairs, his eyes fixed on me. Now, I was stuck between the two of them. And, the longer he took the more time his colleague above had to recover and come down.

He said something to me. In French. There was anger in his voice. He pointed with his dagger to the landing above me where he presumed his friend was.

I didn't respond. I looked around. Half a wooden deck and a window. I tried the window. The iron crossbar moved. I tugged on it hard, back and forth. The ends of the metal dug through the decades old concrete.

He saw what I was doing and quickened his step.

I set my foot against the wall and tugged as hard as I could. Almost there, then it stopped. I was furious and desperate enough that I stomped the crossbar. To my surprise it flew out the window, creating a clear path for me.

The man was ten steps away. I ran over to the window and looked out. It was a long drop to the river below. Two choices: Fight or fly.

The man's dagger scraped against the tower wall; his head was level with the landing. He would be tougher fight than the other guy. And, I was low on fight fuel.

I looked up the stairs. The other man stomped down, holding his broken arm, but still looking ready to fight. There was no way I'd beat both of them in this small area. One choice: Fly.

I kicked a leg over the ledge and pushed myself out. The men picked up on my intention and started running towards me. No more thinking.

I kicked my other leg out and pushed off the wall.

I screamed to keep my stomach from floating into my throat.

I covered my face and closed my legs together.

The water came fast.

Splash!

Crashing into the water sent a jolt up my spine. But overall, I was fine, even with hitting the bottom of the river thirty feet deep. I swam fast to reach the surface before I ran out of oxygen. My lungs were tight and my wet clothes were slowing me down.

When I broke the surface, I inhaled deep. I wanted all the oxygen. It felt cold and good in my lungs as I bobbed in the water catching my breath.

I looked at the tower and counted four windows up. It was empty, which meant those guys were on the move. And, they'd want to make sure I was dead.

I swam to the far side of the river as a pontoon boat cruised up the channel. An old fisherman wearing a yellow cotton fishing cap with hooks attached drove while his just-as-old wife sat in a waffle weave lawn chair watching the scenery pass by. As the boat passed, I saw the two men rush out of the tower. They ran towards the river but I didn't think they had seen me. I grabbed the front edge of the nearest pontoon tank and let the boat take me, unseen, down the river.

23

Back on Florida Avenue, I made good on that café con leche and Cuban toast. Although I had to pay with soggy dollar bills. I hurried the food into the car and got the hell out of there. Once I felt safe and far enough away from the tower, I devoured the food. It tasted beyond amazing. Too bad I couldn't sell it over TV. I'd make an infomercial fortune.

Even though I finally had food, I didn't have any answers. Those assassins...the executioners...must have followed Duncan to the tower. Ten minutes later and I wouldn't have learned the truth.

But the awful truth just created more questions: Who sold the execution services? Who paid for them and why? Most importantly, who else have they been hired to kill? How long has this been going on? Talk about a trick of shit.

I still had the wad of cash from Ilsa's in my pocket, so I spent the night on the outskirts of Tampa, at an old style motel off Highway 301 heading towards Zephyrhills. The towels weren't quite as crunchy as the ones back in Crystal River, so I was able to shower without abrasions. But, sleep was fleeting. Between my mind racing and the prostitution ring being run out of the next room over, I was too distracted to get the rest I needed.

I did reach one conclusion before I fell asleep. And, it rang true the next morning after breakfast: there had to be a middleman—someone with the political juice and corporate connections to peddle the killings. Call me crazy, but anyone who served as a state executioner didn't strike me as also being an enterprising salesman. There had to be someone else marketing the executioners' services.

Okay big shot, you figured it out. What's your next move? You can go after the buyers, the sellers, or the executioners. All equal players in this black market butcher fest.

Duncan said Ken had been going after some of the corporations on the staffer's list of execution customers. I'm sure that brought him particular joy. Or rather, affirmation.

I pulled out the list of names I had written down from his files, each belonging to a corporate titan. No name jumped out. And, each would be hard to reach. What if I did get in front of them, even accused them? They'd never admit to anything. I had no leverage to make them confess. And, that's if they were involved. Someone in their organization might have contracted the killers on behalf of the organization. Compartmentalization and plausible deniability. Asses covered.

Okay, scratch the buyer for now. What about the middleman? I had no clue who that could be. Someone who had access to multiple corporations and wealthy leaders of industry. And, who also knew the executioners. How, the hell did that happen?

But, Duncan said the *state* was peddling the execution services. Just the thought of that was revolting. Did that mean someone who worked in the government was the middleman? That would make sense. Most logical would be someone in the prison system. The warden.

The Warden at Raiford would know who the executioners were. He'd also have ties to State agencies, perhaps even a direct line to the Governor. He was in the perfect position to sell killings for hire. And, how much money could a prison warden really earn? Raiford was big leagues prison. But, still the job couldn't pay all that well, could it? He'd still be susceptible to greed. That gave him the access, the means, and the motive to run that type of illicit operation.

Well, well, Walt Asher. You may have made a fine detective after all. If you live. And, that was only going to happen if I put my theories into practice That meant driving up to Union County, enemy territory. Although, if they were out looking for me, they'd have no clue I'd be sneaking right into their back yard.

At last…some momentum.

24

I took the back roads - Highway 301 up to Zephyrhills, east to Highway 471. Then, a straight shot north through the Withlacootchee State Forest and into small half-towns like Sumterville and Coleman. It took a while. But, traffic was minimal and to the average observer I couldn't have looked much like a wanted murderer. Just a white boy weekend warrior out cruising in some rebellious looking wheels. Fine by me.

I made a point to avoid Gainesville where I figured they'd have a stakeout waiting for me. But, seeing Gainesville in the distance reminded me of Ilsa. And, I desperately wanted to know how she was. So, I stopped at a convenient store in a little town called Shenks and gave DG a call to find out where she was. No answer.

Just north of Shenks was Waldo, the city. The same Waldo that made national news a while back when it was revealed the city's police force had a monthly speeding ticket quota they were required to meet. Turns out, that's illegal in Florida. I assumed the quota was now gone. But, this town had been so proud of their reputation for ticketing speeders they even sold commemorative shirts. Odds were, I was driving through a town filled with cops still itching to pull people over. I couldn't afford that.

I kept the speedometer right on thirty and didn't let it budge. Waldo wasn't a big town. But, when you're a wanted man and you're going that slow, time crawls and the town seems huge. I got through without incident. A few minutes later I was in Starke, home of Florida State Prison, home of "Sparky" the electric chair.

A green highway sign pointed towards the prison. As I approached I saw a sign for the prison itself. It read "Department of Corrections, Florida State Prison."

The prison was comprised of several flat buildings spread across a sprawling campus, all surrounded by razor wire. Even in the bright sunlight, one look at the place was enough to make you never want to never set foot inside of it. Also makes you wonder what it does to a man working there day after day.

The late afternoon sun shone bright, which made it difficult to see as I walked up to the entrance of the Starke public library. Inside, I hopped on the first free computer I could find where the previous user hadn't logged out. Time to work.

It didn't take long to find information about the warden. Warden James L. Durfee to be exact. He got the job back in nineteen eighty-six. There didn't appear to be any controversies or black marks on his record. I guessed that was why he still had the job. A quick skim through the online white pages coughed up his home address and even a phone number.

Now, the gamble - If he was booking gigs for the execution team, he'd know about me. What then?

To my surprise there was a working payphone in the library lobby. I slugged in fifty cents and dialed.

"Hello," said an older female voice.

"Hi, ma'am. This is Robert Martin from the Tampa Bay Times. Is it possible to speak with Warden Durfee?"

I couldn't let him know my real identity. Just in case. I checked my watch. Almost half past five, maybe too late.

A brusque, Southern male voice came on.

"Warden Durfee."

Wow, that was easy.

"Hello, Mr. Durfee. Warden. Bob Martin from the Tampa Bay Times. I was hoping to interview you for an article we're doing on the current state of Florida's Prison System."

"All right..."

I should have thought my story through better before calling. I riffed.

"Is that a 'yes'?"

"It is."

"Okay, great."

"Why don't you come by my office tomorrow? We can speak then."

"Okay, sir," I said.

Wait. No. Bad.

Even though the last place authorities would look for a fugitive is in the state prison, there was no way I was going in. Because if they found out who I was, I wouldn't get out. If the execution team saw me or if Warden Durfee placed my face, they could hold me there until authorities arrived. Or, until they took care of the problem themselves.

"Fine then, how about ten thirty?" the Warden said.

"Actually, sir. I'm in town and looking to get back to Tampa early tomorrow to write the story. If there is any way we could meet tonight, perhaps at your house, it would be very helpful."

"Hmmm," he said.

I waited. If he said 'no', I could figure out another approach. And stay free at least another day. I was not going into that prison.

"I don't really care to talk business at my home."

"I promise I'll make it fast," I said.

"How are you going to do in-depth reporting by asking fast questions?"

He was sharp. No wonder he wardens.

"I know what I want to ask. I won't waste any time. I'd even be happy to bring dinner for you and the missis."

"I guess that'll do."

"Terrific. That's a huge help."

"Forget the food. Just get over here so we can get it over with. Here's the address."

He gave the address and minimal directions. I thanked him and hung up. Time to face the suspected enemy. At least at his house, I'd have a chance to get away. Presuming he didn't also invite the executioners over.

As I exited the library, I caught a glimpse of myself in a pane of glass. I looked worse for the wear. So, I made a quick stop at Wal-Mart on my way, purchasing new slacks, a button down shirt, deodorant, even a notepad and pen. It wasn't much of a look, but it was a huge improvement.

Judging by the Warden's house, running prisons appeared to be a much more lucrative profession than I thought. All the more reason to suspect he was making money outside his nine-to-five job. Although, I wasn't really sure what the Warden's hours were.

The house itself was simple enough - A one-story, flat and wide ranch house with a quaint wooden porch that seemed to wrap all the way around the building. Wooden rocking chairs were set out with a view of the pastureland that sprawled in all surrounding directions. Had to be at least ten acres.

Behind the house I could see a large barn, a separate horse stable, and a tractor parked nearby. A crop of what I guessed to be cabbage grew in the distance. Two vehicles, an older, dusty pickup truck and a new-looking Chevrolet SUV were parked in the drive.

I pulled through a gated fence that spanned the property's façade and had a wood carved sign that read "Sun Beam Ranch". I checked myself in the mirror. *You're looking rough, Asher.* But, well, whatever. I got out, climbed the wooden steps, and rang the doorbell. A folk art cross hung above the door.

Mrs. Warden answered.

"Why, hello! Welcome to our home!" She seemed to smile the words more than say them with her thick Southern accent. I estimated she was mid-sixties and a former prom queen of a small rural town high school.

"I'm Loretta. Come in." She opened the door.

"Thank you, I'm Bob." I stepped over the threshold and eyed the interior, which was just what you'd expect – country quaint.

I turned to Loretta to compliment the digs, but didn't get the chance.

"Reporter, huh? I hope I have something interesting to say."

I turned and saw the Warden step through a doorway from a dining room area.

"Hi, Bob Martin. Thank you so much for making the time." I held out my hand. He shook it then gestured towards a sitting room.

"Let's."

I led the way.

The sitting room gave the vibe that it was his domain with Loretta only welcome part time. Numerous framed commendations and whatnot covered part of the walls. There was an orderly, old-fashioned roll top desk with just a few bills on it. A few small mementos were placed here and there. And, there was a shelf full of books, which all appeared to be prison related, save for a few Louis L'Amour paperbacks.

"This is nice," I said.

"It's peaceful, which is better than nice. A man can think here," he said.

We sat down.

"Has there been much to think about lately or are things running smooth at the prison," I said, getting right into it.

"Things always run smooth at the prison. At least, all that I can control."

"What can't you control?"

"Well, you know. The bureaucracy. Changes, regulations...changes to regulations, and so on. Boring stuff." He waved it off.

"I know how that goes," I said with a smile and a nod, method acting off memories of my torturous time in the corporate world.

"So, whatchu want to know?"

"Well, I'm kind of just checking the temperature on Florida's prison system. Lots of things going on. I know there's still a lot of debate about the death penalty, and so on. Really wanted to hear things from a Warden's perspective since you see first hand what happens after things are settled in the courts."

He frowned like it was a curious question then took a moment to formulate his answer. "Well, I would say the temperature is a healthy 98.6 degrees. Normal. There's always some good and bad. But, hell...it's prison. Everything is confined and any issues we deal with stay inside the prison walls. It doesn't affect the general public. That's why you guys never have too much to report."

"I guess that's why my editor sent me up here. To see what the heck was going on inside." I smiled. "We haven't heard from you. You never call home anymore."

A little humor to grease the wheels.

The Warden laughed at that knee slapper and said, "I'll try to be more regular about it, ma."

I laughed. My charm dial was set to ten. So far, he wasn't vibing murderous creep. Then again, he probably didn't have to do the actual killing.

"What about the death penalty?"

"What about it," he said.

"Is it working?"

"I ain't seen a man get up from it yet," he said and grinned.

"But, do you think it's deterring crime?"

He leaned in. "Know what deters crime?"

I shrugged.

He continued, "A fighting chance. A fighting chance to make money, earn decent wages, live the American dream. But, some people don't get that chance. It's gone before they slip outta their mama's womb. If every man, woman, and child was born with a fighting chance, they'd consider options other than crime. Of course, that don't count mental illness. Some of my, uh, clients, are simply crazy. Their rod's been bent and it can never be straightened out again."

His follow up look was pleasant, but serious.

"So, your prison is basically a way to get rid of the ones that can't be fixed? And, capital punishment is for the ones you think are doing more harm than good?"

"I don't think nothing. The court does the thinking. It's the brains that sends the message through the judicial nervous system to the penal system, to me, the fist. And, if it says strike 'em down, that's what I do."

"So, you stay objective when it comes to the actual killing."

"No, I don't stay objective. I'm human. I have a heart and a mind that responds to what's before me. Every time we put another boy down, whether it was with Old Sparky or lethal injection, or what have you, I do right to remember that this man, this criminal, this violator of social laws and morality, this beast...is still someone's baby. And no matter what they did, no matter how horrible their crime, they will always be someone's little baby. So, no. I do not like capital punishment. But, it serves its purpose. And, society has yet to conceive of a more persuasive way to punish and deter. So, until that happens, we do it. And, we do it to the best of our ability. Quick, clean, and as pain free as possible."

I relaxed a bit with the thought that in no way was he showing any signs of being the middleman in a murder for hire scheme. Although, if he wasn't involved, that left me back at square one.

"This is not the line of questioning I was expecting," he said.

"Who performs the executions?"

Any trace pleasantry washed out of his face.

"I can't tell you that," he said.

"Why not?"

"Executioners in the state of Florida are anonymous."

"You don't even know who's doing it?" This surprised me. And, it was another obstacle.

"That's for their sake. It isn't a glamorous position." He leaned forward. "Of course, I know who is running my executions. I lucked out in that department."

"Oh? How so?"

"Well, most prisons tend to use any guard who will volunteer for the job. A little extra pay. It isn't much," he said. "I made the acquaintance of a team of men who have specialized in these types of services over the years, and they're great. Nobody does it better."

I gave him a bit of a creeped out look because I was indeed creeped out.

He continued, "You know what I mean. I don't mean to belittle the act. They're just very proficient at, um, executing. They apparently did this kind of thing before. Over in France."

There we go. A connection.

He kept talking, "But, I guess you could say they were out of a job when the country banned capital punishment. Typical French. Although a beautiful country. Loretta and I visited about ten years ago. Anyway, these fellas always come prepared. They're like the Navy Seals of executions. Our simple little lethal injection's kind of beneath their skill level. But, everyone needs a paycheck. And, they know just what they're doing. The executed go out without a hitch. Like I said, it works every time."

He tacked on a make-nice kind of smile. So, did I.

I was relieved to get out of there twenty minutes later. It had been nauseating to be talking about killing with such trivial flair. And, disappointing to have to walk away without any names of the people involved. But, at least I knew where they came from. I was on the right path.

25

The town of Starke didn't offer much, but for the second time today it looked like it would provide a pay phone. However, when I walked up to the booth, the phone itself was gone. It had been removed.

I looked for the place least likely to have people who would recognize me from the news. That was a scum bum bar called Rope's, a block down and across the street from the Huddle House. That sounded appetizing. But, through the windows, I could see a television set to a cable news channel. They'd know about me. No dice.

Campaign posters for Archie Gagnon were pasted on the wall outside. He had a dumb face making a dumb expression under the slogan "March with Arch!" Sounds fascist. No thanks.

Inside, the bar was dark and stunk like stale beer, sweat, and depression. I don't imagine there's much to do in a town whose primary industry is incarceration and execution. This place had to be the dirt below in a town filled with barrel bottoms.

I got funny looks walking in. Tough guys perched on stools. Lots of camouflage and confederate flag apparel, hats with fishhooks, and back pockets filled with chaw. Fair enough. I was on their turf.

I nodded to them and asked the bartender if they had a phone I could use. I put a five-dollar bill on the bar. She pointed to the far end and walked in that same direction. When she reached the end, she set a cordless phone on the bar.

"Dial anything to get out?" I said.

"Huh?" she said flummoxed.

"I'll take an Intuition." My favorite beer. Out of Jacksonville.

I dialed DG again. This time, I got him.

"Yeah?"

"DG, it's Walt."

"You're alive!"

"Yeah, can you believe it?"

"Not really," he said.

That was depressing.

"Where are you?"

I hesitated. "Not sure if I should say. Could your lines could be tapped?

"Ain't no one tapping this line, brother. We're pirating off other users."

"Oh, okay. I'm in Starke."

"Starke? The hell for?"   "I've found a few things out and they lead here. To Union County."

I glanced down the bar. Some of the patrons were taking an interest in me.

"Hey, how's Ilsa?" I said.

"She's safe. But, messed up bad. Gonna take her a long time to recover. Doc says a few weeks before she can walk. But, she don't gotta go nowhere. They're taking real good care of her."

I sighed, worried about Ilsa. Felt guilty, too.

"I need to see her. When can I? And where?"

The boys down the bar were no longer down the bar. They were walking my way.

"Get up to Defuniak Springs and call me. I'll have some of my boys meet you and take you to her," DG said.

"Defuniak? Wow, that's like three, four hours...Okay, I'll try to get up there as soon as I can. Hey, I gotta go."

DG said something I couldn't make out as I hung up and turned to the lads, who were now gathered around me. I didn't bother greeting them.

One guy appeared full-time flummoxed. Another kept blinking. He looked skittish and had a pair of big farmer's ears. The third fella had a hard, angular face that seemed cut out of rock with Silly Putty for jowls.

"Do we know you?" said Farmer Ears.

"No," I said.

"Pretty sure we do," said Putty Face. The difficulty he had articulating that simple sentence made me think he'd had too many dumb-dumb pills.

That didn't stop me from getting nervous.

"Well, you may know me, but I've never met you."

"You were in the papers."

Shit.

"You read?"

Nerves shot that one out of my mouth before I could stop it.

"Yeah, we read it in the paper," said Farmer's Ears. He'd been popping dumb-dumbs, too.

"Oh?" I said. "Stranger things have happened."

I smiled quick and stepped through them. Flummox Face grabbed my shoulder and spun me back towards them. Putty Face stepped up. I coiled, ready to punch.

"You're that Gator's coach," he said.

Big exhale.

"Oh yeah. Should be a good season this year. Team looks strong."

"No, the one what got caught molesting the boys on the team." said Farmer's Ears.

Awkward.

"Oh, no. You definitely have me mixed up with someone else."

"You just said you was the coach."

Putty Face chimed in. "If you's a molester, we gon' beat you ass."

I held my hands up.

"I'm sorry. I thought you meant Florida State. That's my school. In Tallahassee. Not Gainesville."

"We hate the Seminoles."

"Me, too," I said and got the hell out of there.

26

It was nearly seven o'clock when I got out of there. I drove back into town, but when I reached the big intersection at Highway 301, I realized I had nowhere to go. And, being this close to the killers' home gave me the willies. Plus, I wanted to see Ilsa. I had to see Ilsa. So, I drove towards Defuniak Springs four hours away.

Besides seeing Ilsa, Defuniak would give me space — away from my home addresses, known associates, and other places most liable to attract the attention of the authorities and the executioners. I needed space to think and let my guard down. Plus, I could hit Tallahassee on the way. It was the state capitol and there was a chance I could uncover some valuable information there.

The sun was setting just as I reached I-10 West. This bland stretch of highway in the Florida panhandle had little scenic diversity. Moss draped oaks hung silhouetted and black against the deep blue, darkening sky. They added a gothic presence to the drive. But, I couldn't find anything on the radio to fit the setting. I drove in silence.

So here I was, three days into having my life turned upside down. I'd had near death experiences, been exposed to a murderous conspiracy, and covered a large portion of the state either fleeing for my life or looking for clues. Well, I wasn't bored.

But, I would have loved to get things settled as soon as possible. And by that, I meant save my ass. I missed my house. I missed floating in the river. I missed Ilsa. Sometimes normal was just fine.

I also missed my kids. Thinking about their sweet faces and winning smiles sent a chill down my spine. My ex had to know I was in trouble by now. If she hadn't read it for herself in the paper, one of her nosey friends had, and they would deliver the scandalous information without delay. If I knew my ex as well as I thought, she'd be shocked at first, like anyone would. But, then she would feel malicious triumph knowing that all of her worst instincts about me and my character had just been proven true. I knew he was a jerk! She'd ride that triumph over to the phone, dial her lawyer, and push for full-time custody of the kids. As if I needed more motivation to wrap this thing up and clear my name. Goddammit.

Thinking about the ex made my stomach sink and my blood boil. So, I distracted myself with details of the Warden's interview. I may not have gotten specific names, but I did get a few clues.

First, the executioners work for Warden Durfee. As in, present tense, still happening. So, they were still local or nearby. Unless they commuted for executions. And, he confirmed they were French and they had executed people in France. Would there be any record of that? Where would I find it? Would I find it if France kept their executioners anonymous like Florida? Didn't seem like the type of profession that inspired passing out business cards.

I came up with a list of people who would know who the executioners were. Prison guards and journalists attend the executions and would have seen who did the killing. However, they wouldn't have their names unless they tracked them. Was there anyone involved in the business of the executions, like the mayor or the funeral director? The medical examiner likely had a hand in things.

What about that guy, Gagnon? The State Representative, Mr. "March with Arch". Maybe. If one person didn't know I could ask the name of someone who might know. That networking approach worked great while growing my business. I bet it could still work.

But, that would bring me a lot of attention. Starke was a small community. Word might have gotten around—would get around. To the wrong people. And, they could find me before I found them.

After all, I was a wanted man with a face plastered all over the news, hourly on the local cable news broadcasts. I suspected they had spun it well – Madman on the loose. Killer on the prowl. This was serious business.

And so were those headlights in my rearview mirror. Right on my ass, two of them...but drifting together and apart from each other.

Motorcycles.

I tapped my brakes and got a momentary glimpse of the drivers in the red light. Bikers. Maybe DG's guys. Good chance they'd know this car.

Before I could consider any options in depth, the cycles split and rode up on opposite sides of my car. Looked like some tough characters behind the handlebars. They vibed long time on the scene.

The biker to my left signaled me to pull over. I rolled down the window to see if they were with DG, but the cycle roar was too loud. He pointed to the side of the road again. I nodded, and as soon as the guy to my right pulled up ahead of me, I veered onto the road shoulder and parked. I got the sense this could be important if DG's guys had to track me down in the middle of I-10.

I stepped out of the car. The guy who pointed parked his bike behind me. A semi roared past in the lane closest to us and with enough light to illuminate the back of the Pointer's jacket. The colors said "Panhandle Rippers."

Not DG's crew.

The Pointer walked my way, no expression.

"Panhandle Rippers? You guys affiliates with DG's—"

Pointer held up a fat wrench and smashed out my taillight. He followed that up with a whack against the back window. White shatter veins cracked through the glass, but it held strong.

"Shit, what the--?" I said.

A doubled-up metal chain swung in from behind me and wrapped tight around my neck. I gagged and felt like I was choking on my tongue. The biker twisted it tight and shoved me to the ground. I landed hard, chest to dirt, with gravel and glass pressing into my skin and that chain cutting off my oxygen.

Pointer got down in my face and pressed my jaw with his big, brutal wrench.

"No one flies their colors on Ripper roads, dickhead", said Pointer.

"What are you talking about?" I said with a strained croak.

Chains pressed his knee into my back to shut me up and said, "Your car man! DG's colors. We hate DG!"

"You crazy thinking you can drive DG colors through here after the other day?" said pointer. "That's fuckin' suicidal!"

"What happened the other day?" I said.

Another knee in the back created a wave of pain up my spine that rippled into my arms.

Pointer bent my nose with the business end of the wrench. "We didn't blow up your goddamn compound," said Pointer.

"We told DG that, but he still hammered us," said Chains.

"Wait, what?"

"Don't act dumb, scab."

They were kicking up road dust and it was drying my throat out. I attempted to roll on to my side to get more air in my lungs, but they shoved me down.

"I don't know what you're talking about. I'm not in DG's gang. And, he said the place blew up because..." I hesitated, "of someone else. He didn't even think it was a biker gang. I swear!"

They yanked me up and slammed me against the car, unworried that a highway patrol officer could drive by and react to seeing a man accosted. I wanted to avoid that anyway. I was thrilled just to suck in a little bit of fresh oxygen.

"How do you know what he was thinking if you're not in DG's gang?" said Pointer, leaning in hard with the wrench against my throat.

I could feel blood trickling down my forehead.

"And, you're driving a car with his colors. Why you lyin' to me?"

"Look, I know DG because he's a neighbor of mine. We live by the same river. I was there when the house blew up. I'm not in his gang. What he did to you guys had nothing to do with me," I said.

"Stop lyin' to me. You got his car and you're flyin' his colors," Pointer said.

Chains pulled me tight against the car, over the hood. My feet started to lift off the ground. No air in the lungs. I started to choke. Cars passed and no one stopped to help.

Pointer gave a hard shove against my throat and it felt like my neck was ready to snap. But, then he withdrew and Chains slackened up. I slumped down to the ground, gasping for air. When the chain was loose enough, I put a hand in the dirt to hold myself up and I rubbed my throat.

Some jerk honked as he drove by.

Pointer grabbed me by the back of the shirt and pulled me up. But, he spoke to Chains.

"Call the boys, Fang. Tell 'em to come pick up my bike. I'm gonna drive this sucker back to camp."

A moment later he slammed the trunk shut with me inside. The car revved to life and off we went.

27

Their camp was a makeshift trailer park in the middle of a wide sinkhole amidst a scrub filled, un-farmed field. At its center burned a large bonfire with filthy, rundown mobile homes parked around it, like an old west wagon circle. Several of the mobile homes had junk wood patios built off of them. Choppers were parked next to each trailer.

At one end of the wagon circle was what looked to be a motorcycle junkyard replete with bike skeletons, tire stacks, and scattered spare parts. A three-legged dog hobbled through the mess. At the opposite end of the circle was the dirt road. I presumed it was the path we drove in on.

But, I didn't find any of that out until after Pointer popped open the trunk, a beer already popped and spilling suds over his fingers. A few of his friends were gathered around for the big unveiling.

"Shee-it, Panther! You got a car and a soldier!" said a biker who looked like a desperate weasel.

Panther, no longer "Pointer" said, "Pull him out."

And, they did. They let me fall onto the dirt. Sand spurs stung my knee. I swiped it away as they yanked me up and prodded me towards the campfire.

At the campfire, they sat me down on the ground while Weasel Face scampered over to the most prestigious looking trailer in the compound. He knocked on the door. A biker mama answered, listened for a moment, and then went back inside. Weasel Face headed back towards the fire, around which more of the village goofballs were now sitting. They stared at me with dumb, amused faces, like eight year olds fascinated by an ant they were burning alive with the sun and a magnifying glass.

The door to the prestigious mobile home swung open and out stepped a very short, very stocky man, done up with all sorts of biker regalia. He looked pompous for a biker, the way he strutted towards the fire – chin up, right arm bent and holding the lapel of his denim biker vest, like an old-time plantation colonel.

His lips were pursed as he surveyed the crowd. It wasn't until he stood fully in the soft orange glow of the bonfire that I saw his lengthy hair was rolled up in curlers. My heart sank. This was the last thing I needed - a Fancy Biker Napoleon. It looked like my evening was just getting started.

"You're not listening to me," I said.

"I don't have to listen to you, nave! I am in control here," said Fancy Biker Napoleon a.k.a. 'Artimus'.

"Look, Artimus—"

"It's Emperor Artimus for the last time. Panther!"

Panther kicked his heavy biker boot into my kidneys. I toppled into the dirt. The pain was excruciating.

"You shall address me as such whenever I am in your presence and in the midst of my kingdom," said Artimus. He sneered down his nose at me.

Emperor Artimus had his act in full swing. As if they didn't get very many guests around here. It was obvious he wasn't going to squander this opportunity. He wanted respect and adulation, but it vibed desperate and small potatoes. These were the Grade-Z wannabe bikers, especially compared to DG's A-list crew.

"Hail Artimus!" said the rest of the gang.

The short emperor continued, "You have trespassed while donning enemy colors. You have resisted arrest And, you have besmirched the general atmosphere of our Kingdom."

"And, I'm sorry for everyone of those things. But, I'm not your enemy. I'm just heading up the road to see my girlfriend," I said, losing patience.

"Well now I know you speak false," he said with a wave of his hand.

All this clown needed was a powdered wig and a beauty mark above his lip.

"No woman would lie with such a brute!"

I glanced at the rest of the gang. They looked like a rag tag pack of adopted loners. No wonder they fell for this guy's garbage.

"Look, man—"

"Silence!" he said. "The court rests its case. The verdict is in. The punishment?" he balled is hand into a fist. "The Skull Crusher!"

The gang roared. Two guys grabbed my arms and dragged me across the lot towards a wooden wall made of thick, cut loblolly logs, like old power line poles with straps attached. The goons lit two torches atop the wall then buckled me in, wrists and ankles strapped down and spread apart.

I couldn't move and I couldn't believe this kind of medieval behavior was still thriving in the Florida panhandle. But, then again, it was Florida. If this made the front page tomorrow, no one outside the state would be the least bit surprised.

Would I even see tomorrow? These guys weren't mean. They were crazy. And, crazy scared the hell out of me.

A crusty gang flunky hustled a small, hard shell brief case over to Artimus. The Emperor held out his right hand. The flunky opened the briefcase while a topless biker mama took hold of The Emperor's hand and slid it inside the briefcase. A beat later he pulled his hand out. It was enveloped by an oversized black leather glove with curved iron fingers and sharp metal studs on the knuckles.

The gang started chanting "Skull Crusher!" as Artimus sashayed over to me. He held the menacing metal fist up to my face.

"You are condemned to die. Have you any last words, heathen?" said Artimus.

The Skull Crusher looked like it could more than adequately live up to its name. More painful was the thought of dying here in a lousy dirt lot surrounded by a bunch of drooling rejects.

Stop judging and start escaping, Asher! You don't want a taste of that pain.

I tried to pull my arms loose but the restraints wouldn't budge.

Bloodlust was in the air. Artimus' arm cocked back.

"Au revoir." His arm tightened, his torso recoiled, and his fist started to move towards my face.

"Wait! I can make you the number one biker gang!" I yelled.

My eyes flinched closed. The Skull Crusher smashed the thick log next to my face. Wood splintered into my cheeks.

I opened my eyes and saw Artimus draw back his weaponized fist. The force of the punch had shaken a few of his rollers loose. He looked surprised.

"How dare you say the Panhandle Rippers are inferior," he said.

I caught my breath and surveyed the scene. All the bikers were creeping closer, as if I had just blurted out the answer to some ancient riddle they'd been trying to solve for centuries and wanted to hear it again, for clarification. They were mystified.

Artimus looked at to the curious crowd.

"Do not listen to him! He speaks no truth. He is crazy. We are sane. We are number one. The Rippers are Number One!"

He was exposed. I took a deep breath and decided to gamble.

"Uh, no...you're not doofus." I said.

The crowd hushed and murmured.

Artimus turned to me, the look of a madman on his face.

I pushed my luck further.

"Fucking save it, Artimus. You guys are living in a ring of shit box mobile homes in the middle of forgotten Florida. You're not a biker gang. You're a pack of hobos."

"You will taste the fury of my iron fist," he said, holding up his fancy glove.

I couldn't think about that. I had to stay focused on my pitch.

"I've seen DG's house. One of his many houses. Filled with women, money, food. DG...*he* lives like a king!" I said.

Gasps from the crowd.

Brewing rage on Artimus' face. My ploy had worked...or I was about to have my brains smashed in the next two seconds. Time to hedge my bets. All or nothing.

"And, you can, too! With my 5-Step Success Plan. No matter who you are, no matter what you do, especially if you run a motorcycle gang in the middle of Bumfuck, Florida. You, too, can start to live the good life you deserve! Imagine never worrying about money, getting all the women you want, and all the respect you deserve! You can and you will! Just like DG, leader of Florida's current number one gang"

Artimus shot me a curious glare. I couldn't tell if he thought I was insane or if I had something of value to say.

I continued, "DG was a broke as a joke biker pulling small time heists and losing men left and right to arrest and death. But, once he started following *my* 5-Step Success Plan, he turned his business, his gang, and his life around! Kings and queens would kill to have an existence so royal. Now, I don't work for DG...I work *with* DG, consulting and advising to ensure his success in perpetuity. You like fancy words, Artimus. That means, FOREVER!"

The tiny emperor appeared speechless.

His gang looked enchanted.

"Artimus, if you act now, you too can live a life of luxury and riches, of bitches and bikes – as many as you like! No more sleeping in mobile homes. No more sucking sand. No more having all the other superior biker gangs laugh at you and laugh at you and laugh at you and laugh right in your face!"

"All right!" Artimus cut me off. Veins throbbed at his temples, his eyes looked ready to burst. He started strutting before the gang:

"We are the most vicious, violent, and bloodthirsty gang on the highways. We are the Panhandle Rippers. We show no mercy!"

He looked up at me through a shrewd glare.

"But tonight, I believe we have been visited by a messenger. A messenger brought forth to fulfill our divine right of greatness and power," he said as he thumbed back at me. "This is such a messenger. A messenger...which I have been expecting!"

I didn't think the crowd bought it. But, they were pretty dumb.

"I knew before I even saw his face shimmering next to the fire. I merely had to test his sincerity, his courage. He faced the Skull Crusher with bravado. And, he passed the test," he said.

He stared into their eyes to prove conviction.

The skepticism drained from their faces.

"Now, we must confer. Cut him down," he said with a wave of the Skull Crusher.

I let out a huge sigh of relief and smiled.

"Shall we talk in your office?" I said.

"Come," he said and we marched towards the prestigious mobile home.

28

What a dump.

Just what you'd expect from a beer swilling, woman raping, biker pig. Only King Artimus had a throne, all right. It was a beauty salon chair with a fancified helmet heater attached to the back. His biker mama stood next to it, ready to serve. She was a sad looking woman with leathery skin and topless tits that appeared to have been deflated.

Artimus lead me into the cluttered living room, stopping to set the Skull Crusher on a TV tray that also held a leftover tin with congealing Salisbury steak sauce and a few rogue peas in it. It has been converted into an ashtray.

"Come in," he said.

"Lovely place," I said. It wasn't.

He sat in the dryer chair and crossed his legs lady style.

I sat on an old copper velour sofa with vintage cowboy pattern on it. It sunk too deep. That made leaping up and escaping more difficult. But, the Skull Crusher was within reach.

His biker mama walked over and tightened his sagging rollers.

He maintained eye contact with me through bitter, battle worn eyes.

"DG has foiled the Panhandle Rippers for years. I take it as a personal affront. So tell me, messenger. What are the five steps of your success program?" he said.

"Well..." I said, glancing at the Skull Crusher, getting ready to wing it. "Number one, you gotta believe in yourself. Totally eliminate doubt from the equation."

"I already do that. Tell me something new. And, get specific."

"Funny you should mention specifics, because that's point number two"

I looked casually around the room, as if collecting my thoughts. But, I was really mapping the quickest escape route possible.

I continued, "Instead of speaking in generalities and vague ambitions, you have to get specific with your men and most importantly your goals as a leader."

I could move first and grab the Skull Crusher on my way out the front door, right into the middle of the gang's "kingdom" as he had put it. No good.

"Break it down to its finest level – start at what you want to accomplish for the year, then figure out what you need to do each month, then each week, each day, each hour. Specifics sell. They also give you focus and a real plan for success," I said recalling some copy I had written years ago for a get rich quick program. I neglected to tell Artimus that the purveyor of said program was now residing in one of the state prisons for defrauding the public.

"That makes sense," he said nodding. "But, it speaks to the little man. I lead these outcasts because I have a very specific vision already in place. I need to know the secret that makes it possible for a baboon like DG to rule. What is the source of his power? And, tell me quick. You are trying my patience. Had I purchased this advice off the television I would be ready to send it back."

His highness looked most displeased.

Biker mama finished tightening his rollers and pushed the heating helmet down over his hair. She turned it on and the steady sound of cycling air began to hum.

I looked past her towards the hallway leading to the bedroom. I could grab the Skull Crusher, smash him with it, shove her out of the way, and punch through a bathroom window, then get the hell out of there. Maybe.

"Look, this plan has already helped millions of people around the world tap into their secret power source. But, there's a methodology to it. Incidentally, what am I getting for this?" I said.

Biker mama pulled up a stool and sat right in the middle of the hallway escape path. She lit a cigarette and it looked like smoke exhaled from her every facial orifice.

"Your life. I could have smashed you to oblivion as I have so many others," said Artimus.

"Okay, well good point. Look, I have a whole book I've written about the five step plan."

Kitchen window? Maybe too close to them. But, a possibility for escape. I needed to get this just right.

"If you'd just let me get back to my home, I can send it to you. Not only that, you'll also receive my latest insider information for building automatic wealth that literally pours into your bank account while you sleep. That's a free bonus, my gift to you." I said, stretching, stalling.

"Tell me now, before my hair is set. Or it's back to the rack for you." he said gripping the arm rests on the chair.

"That bonus information is normally reserved only for my select gold level clientele and they each have to pay ten-thousand dollars for it. Per year. I'm offering it to you absolutely free!"

Any of the routes could work as long as I could get past these two. The real trick awaited outside. Even if I got out, I didn't have the keys to the car. And, I've never driven a motorcycle before.

"I want the secret. Now!" Artimus pounded his fist on the armrest. His face flushed red.

Biker Mama kept smoking with her head cocked and a look that was sizing me up.

I scanned the room again. There...keys on the bar counter. Next to a jar of hard candies...and denture cream?

I looked to Artimus. "Okay, you got it. Here's the real secret for success. The same secret that DG and just about every other successful person you ever met knows. A secret that could mean the difference between—"

"Artimus, what the fuck are you doing?" said Biker Mama. She shook her thumb at me. "This guy's wanted by the cops. I saw it in the paper. Just turn his ass in and collect the reward money. It's probably like a million dollars."

Shit.

29

She looked at him like it was the easiest decision ever.

Artimus looked at me, surprised. Then, serious. Then, devilish. It was obvious he liked that plan.

Nobody moved.

The hair drier dinged.

"Get him!" Artimus yelled and pointed.

Biker Mama leaped at me like a cat, right off the stool and claws out. I grabbed the Skull Crusher and clobbered her in the head. She landed on me limp and unconscious. I pushed her off and pulled myself out of the deep soft couch.

Artimus moved to get up. The heater helmet locked him down. I got my balance as I slipped on the Skull Crusher. It was heavy and menacing. Artimus reached to push up the hair dryer. Two steps forward and I smashed the Skull Crusher down on the heater. The metal studs shredded the plastic casing, the dull iron smashed the unit apart causing it to impact against Artimus' head. Sparks fried his hair and his head flamed up. Artimus let out a shrill cry as his arms and legs jerked straight out and his body flailed violently in the chair.

A knock at the door. "Artimus, you okay?"

"Uh, yes...feeling...divine!" I said over my shoulder.

Panther kicked the door in: "What the shit?"

He whipped his chain at me, smashing the candy jar and knocking over a lamp on the pull back. I ran down the hallway.

A glance into the bathroom – the window was too small to crawl through. I ran back to the bedroom. A musty smelling pigsty. No window.

Dead end.

I turned towards the hallway. Panther appeared and slowed up at seeing me. More bikers fell in behind him.

"He killed Artimus!" someone yelled.

"Dude's fryin' and shit," said another.

Panther closed in.

I stepped up and shut the bedroom door. Panther pounded against it as I pushed over a dresser to keep it closed. Artimus' extensive hair supply collection spilled onto the floor.

Panther's fist smashed through the door.

"Tough luck, jerk. First we're gonna kill ya, then we're gonna rape ya."

I jumped back and scanned the room for options...then paused, realizing just how gross Panther's threat was. I ran to the closet. A rifle. No bullets.

An arm reached through the hole in the door. It bent and felt around for the doorknob. I hit it with the rifle butt. Panther screamed.

"Let me at it," said another biker who peeked through the hole in the door. I smashed his face with the rifle butt and he fell back wailing.

A voice from down the hall said, "Lookout! I got a gun!"

I moved back behind the bed, watching the bikers clear a path in the hallway. My back bumped into the far bedroom wall. The Skull Crusher knocked against the wood paneling. I dropped onto my knees behind the bed.

The rifle cocked.

"Gonna blow that sumbitch's head off," said the shooter-to-be.

Would this bed stop a bullet? I looked around for a better option.

Moonlight shined through a small crack in the wall. Right where the Skull Crusher had knocked against it. These mobile homes were made cheaper than I thought.

A gun shot. The far side of the bed blew up; cotton and metal coils flew around the room.

"Aim better, Rape-O!" said Panther with a critical, impatient tone.

The gun cocked.

I looked at the Skull Crusher then at the wall. What the hell...

I punched a hole in the wall. My whole fist went through.

Another gunshot. The headboard shattered.

I pulled back my iron fist and smashed the wall again. This time, rather than a straight punch, I swung across the cheap wood and took out a large section about a foot high and three feet wide. I didn't wait for the next shot.

I dove through the wall and fell onto the dirt outside.

Another shot. Part of the wall exploded above my head. Pieces of wood paneling blasted out into the field beyond. The bikers cheered inside.

I got up and ran around the wagon train of mobile homes. The bonfire blazed in the gaps between. It was bright enough that I could see the bikers gathered outside Artimus' trailer. But, that would only last up to when they got in the bedroom and figured out I'd slipped through the wall. I had to hurry.

I stopped behind the trailer closest to my car. It sat unguarded twenty-five feet away. A few of the bikers appeared around far side of Artimus' trailer. They were looking at the hole I'd slipped through.

"Find him!" Panther shouted.

The bikers scrambled in all directions, including a pair of big dudes running my way.

I had to act fast.

If I ran to the car now I could get in and get out of there quick enough to make space between me and their bikes. That could give me enough time to lose them, presuming I could find the path back to the interstate. If I ran to the car and it was locked or had no keys, I was screwed. I need to stall them in case I couldn't take the car.

The two big bikers stopped at the bonfire. I checked around for a rock, something to fight with. I found gas cans. The bikers were lighting torches in the bonfire, to aid their search. I opened a lid and smelled. Yes, gas. I picked up the open gas can. It was heavy, but light enough for what I needed.

The bikers moved towards me, their torches leading the way.

I did three practice swings then threw the gas can as hard, as far, and as high as I could. It flew across the night sky tumbling over and over, spurting out droplets of gas. It landed with a crash on the near edge of the bonfire and exploded. The metal canister blasted through the air and over a nearby mobile home.

The sound and bright flash of the explosion stopped the big bikers. They turned around to see what had happened.

I opened another gas canister. Two more practice swings and I launched it. This time it was a line drive aimed straight for the bikers. They turned from the fire without enough time to react. The gas can hit one biker in the chest and knocked him back while its gas splashed over both of them. They ignited in a flash of fire and were wrapped in flames as they fell to the ground. They screamed. A crowd of bikers ran over to help while the big boys flopped around in the sand trying to extinguish the flames.

I grabbed the third gas can and pulled off the lid. No practice swings. I threw it right in the middle of the crowd trying to put out the burning bikers. Gas exploded and at least five more bikers caught fire. Wild screaming and panicked running commenced. Incinerated anarchy. I had my distraction.

I ran over to the car. The door was open, the keys in the ignition. You didn't have to lock your doors out here in the middle of nowhere. I got in, fired it up, and floored it in reverse without turning the headlights on.

Ahead of me, the silhouetted and flaming bikers danced and hollered amongst the trailers like they were taking part in an ancient white trash ritual.

I ripped the car into drive with the Skull Crusher still on my hand. The heavy glove snapped off the top half of the gearshift. I hauled ass down a dirt trail I hoped would get me away from the flaming freaks.

Ten minutes later, the car raced onto a small, paved country highway with signs pointing towards I-75. It wasn't until I merged on to the interstate that I took off the Skull Crusher. I checked my rearview mirror every few seconds for the next hour and a half. No one had followed me. I escaped clean.

It was the middle of the night by the time I crossed over the Tallahassee city limit. I was too tired to go any further. I parked in a Piggly Wiggly parking lot, crawled in the backseat and went to sleep, naïve the surprises I'd encounter the next day.

30

I woke up at eleven thirty the next morning. Pain blasted my body. It took two tries to sit up and another ten minutes to get out of the car and stretch. My bones creaked.

There was a hat in the trunk and a pair of sunglasses in the glove box. I put those on to disguise myself then went inside the grocery store for some breakfast. Welcome to Tallahassee, the state capital of Florida.

A choice: Drive two more hours to Defuniak Springs to see Ilsa, which I desperately needed. Or, stay in Tallahassee and see what I could find out about the staffer Ken met with and/or the middleman who may have been selling the executions. I decided to stick to night driving in the hopes of keeping a lower profile. That meant I had to get busy around town.

Tallahassee was like no other city in Florida. It's quite hilly in a state that's flat and features a weird mix of government, college students, and rednecks. I had never known what to make of this town, so I didn't visit often. And, I didn't really know my way around.

First stop, the library.

The LeRoy Collins Leon County Public Library sat on the west side of downtown Tallahassee. It was sandwiched between a slew of government buildings and Florida State University, alma mater of the greatest actor who ever lived, Burt Reynolds. Don't argue with me.

I parked several blocks away near a small shopping plaza that reeked of hipster. My unconventional car would blend in well there.

It was still warm in Florida this time of year. But, it was a nice change to get out and walk. I guess I could have worried more about someone on the street identifying me as a wanted man. But, I figured it best to hide in plain site. Plus, I only had so much time. I needed information and fast.

The library was ice cold. I headed for the periodicals section and rounded up a week's worth of issues of the big city newspaper, the Tallahassee Democrat. Five papers in I found what I sought.

Eight pages deep into the A section of the paper was a small write up on Ross Chambers, twenty-seven, unmarried, an assistant to Representative Trip Wingart, Democrat representing parts of Florida's Fourth District. He had been found dead. The official prognosis: heart attack. The funeral occurred yesterday in his hometown of New Smyrna, Florida, over on the east coast.

Senator Trip Wingart. I didn't know anything about him. I looked up the Fourth District. That's Nassau County, Jacksonville. The northeast tip of the state. Quite a ways away from Dunnellon and Ken.

I took a minute to think it through. Ross Chambers worked as an assistant to Representative Wingart. It's probable Chambers learned Wingart was dealing with the middleman. Why? Because he had a problem that needed to be solved. What kind of problem could the Senator have that required the services of the middleman and his team of executioners?

He didn't have a problem. But, one of his constituents might. Not constituents. Supporters. No. Donors.

Big money donors.

And, there was a ninety-nine percent chance those donors were corporations. Which would make the specific purchaser nearly impossible to find.

So, which corporations were big money donors to Senator Wingart? I checked the search engine. OpenSecrets.org popped on screen with links guiding me to the names of donors and their bought politicians on both a national and state level. I punched in Wingart's name.

My adrenaline kicked in. I had clues giving me direction again and that was exciting. I typed as fast as I could. It was like a road map of cronyism revealing itself to me. And, I just wanted to discover more.

Within a few moments I had a full run down of all of Wingart's big money donors. A slew of corporations and independent businessmen. I could only guess which one – or ones – had hired the executioners.

How would that conversation have gone down? *Hey, Larry, I know you've been having that problem. I know a guy who knows some killers who take care of problems like this all the time.* Could it be that easy? Could it be that attractive an option? Would his donor recognize the moral implications of such an act? Or would they be so focused on business, on the bottom line, they'd go with the fastest, bestest solution? I couldn't help but presume they'd choose the later.

Another scary notion: Wingart was a duly elected member of the *U.S.* House of Representatives. Not the State House. That means the execution services may not have been getting pedaled strictly within the state. They could be working outside of Florida, too. An armed Congress? Dear god.

I remembered the list in my pocket. The list of companies from Ken's files. I retrieved it and held it up next to the list of Wingart's donors on the computer. I cross-referenced.

No.

No.

No.

No.

No.

Yes!

A match.

INNOVATIVE TOMORROW GROUP

What the hell did they do? More digging. The search engine belched up ITG's corporate website along with a few miscellaneous mentions linking to business journals, real estate transactions, a community giveback program. And, a Florida Times-Union story on their newly appointed CEO, Doug Tanjeris.

A quick glimpse of Tanjeris' picture showed him to be a fresh-faced thirty-something straight out of the new breed of corporate prodigies – young, smart, and elite enough to be cocky. Cocky enough to take big gambles and demand fast results, no matter the risks. I presumed he was a real dick to work for.

I clicked back to ITG's corporate website. The vague, yet aspirational, copy tried to be charming: We innovate, develop, and perfect this and that for a better tomorrow. A corporate jerkoff page. Digging deeper though, I found a small mention about their "portfolio of assets," which included significant land holdings and mining.

I tried to think what Ken's files had said about ITG. But, by now with so much insanity, the details had melded together. However, this much was clear - ITG did meddle with the environment. And, that would have gotten Ken's attention. I was creeping closer to the truth.

If Ken's actions had caused enough problems for ITG, it was conceivable – from a very cynical viewpoint – CEO Tanjeris could have accepted Representative Wingart's offer to 'get rid of the problem'. The problem being Ken. The dots would have been impossible to connect to Representative Wingart. But, Ross Chambers found out about it. And, he spilled the beans to Duncan and then Ken. Ross, you were already a hero.

So, what next? Assuming compartmentalization was in play, I figured Tanjeris would not know the names of the middleman or the executioners. Only Wingart would. At least, in this particular deal. Wingart seemed to be the most accessible. And, he had to have an office in town.

I found his office address online and punched it into Mapquest. It was located a few blocks away on West College Avenue.

As I walked there, I thought about how to play things. Wingart wasn't going to volunteer the information. His trusted assistant was dead and rotting just for finding out about the executioners deal. That told me one thing: No playing nice.

I went back to the car to grab the Skull Crusher. That thing was coming in handy.

31

I found Wingart's office building fifteen minutes later. It was an uninspired four-story chunk of beige concrete in the heart of downtown, a block north of the Capital Building. The sign in the lobby listed the Senator's office on the third floor. I took the elevator up.

I noted my appearance in the reflection of the brushed metal paneling. It wasn't my best look. The duds I'd purchased to meet with the Warden were close to filthy and stained with sweat. Battling bikers had me too fried to care.

With a ding, the elevator doors opened up to the glass door entrance of the Senator's office. Thick, plush carpet. Air conditioning humming out the vents. The only other place to go was through a door leading to a stairwell.

The iron fist in my pocket clanged loud against the elevator's metal frame with and knocked me off balance. I recovered and walked in to U.S. Representative Trip Wingart's official the reception area.

The girl behind the reception desk had to be an intern and had to be a sorority sister from nearby Florida State University. You could just tell from her fake bake tan and bleach blonde hair. She smiled, but her eyes showed skepticism and boredom.

"Hi, may I help you?" she said as she gave me a repulsed once over.

"Yes, I'd like to speak with Representative Wingart."

"He's out of the office. Did you have an appointment?"

"No, I'm...one of his constituents and I just had a few questions."

"Well, I'm sorry. He's in session most of the day and will be in meetings well into the evening," she said, a sorry/not-sorry expression on her face.

"Oh, I see."

I looked over at an oil painting of Representative Wingart. He was either made of leather in real life or the artist had squeezed too much "golf course tan" brown on his paint palette.

I turned back to the receptionist. The plaque on her desk featured her name: Kyleene. Oh boy.

"I can let Mr. Wingart know you stopped by. What is your name?"

"Oh, I'm, uh, Doug Tanjeris."

She didn't seem to buy it.

"Junior," I said.

She still wasn't buying it.

"My dad looks young for his age," I added a smile to seal the deal.

That appeared to make sense to her. If still waters run deep a whole pre-school was splashing around in her mental kiddie pool.

"Okay, I will let him know," she said as she finished writing the name down.

I left the office disappointed by the delay and rode the elevator downstairs.

The door dinged open in the lobby and who should be strolling in but Representative Wingart himself. Two guys flanked him until he broke off towards the restroom.

I followed him in.

He was taking a leak at the far stand up urinal. No one else was around.

I slipped on the Skull Crusher, walked up behind him, and placed the cold heavy iron on the back of his neck.

"You move and this iron fist will break your goddamn neck, got it?"

"Huh, uh, yeah, sure. How can I help you sport?" he said.

"We need to talk about Ross Chambers," I said.

I could hear he had finished peeing. He zipped up and turned to face me.

I shoved his neck with the iron fist.

"I said don't move."

"We can't have a friendly face to face conversation? Yeah, I know Ross. Great kid. What about him?" he said.

I was about to ask a question but then my face smashed against the cold ceramic tiles. Before I could turn to see what had happened, fat hands grabbed my shirt, stood me up, and punched me in the gut. Had I eaten within the past hour I'd have puked on their shoes. I had not, so it was just a painful dry heave that made my eyes water.

My assailants were Wingart's flankers from the lobby.

"You need to get the hell out of here while you can still walk," said the ugly one with the pock marked face. He slapped me hard.

Wingart walked over to the sink and washed his hands, barely paying attention. Like he was done with me.

"Hey, Wingart! I know all about your secret service," I said. My lips felt like they were swelling up.

He ignored me.

The thugs yanked me off the wall. Each grabbed an arm, and they pretty much carried me out the door. I missed trying to spit on Wingart as I passed by. My bloody saliva splotched on the mirror.

Back in the lobby, they moved me towards the exit. When the bruiser with the feathered hair reached out to push the door open, I shot my metal fist back and cracked him right between the eyebrows. He dropped like a sack. That gave me room to swing at the other guy. I missed, smashing a brass column.

Wingart walked out of the restroom towards the elevator. He pressed the button and the elevator doors parted. He stepped in.

"I know all about your executioners, Wingart!"

Ugly smashed me against the wall and drew his hand back to punch.

"No!"

Wingart's voice echoed throughout the marble lobby.

I looked over. His hand held open the elevator door. A worried look on his face.

"Bring him to my office," he said.

32

Back upstairs. Wingart lead me into the office. His goon stayed downstairs to tend to the other goon who hadn't moved since he dropped to the floor.

The sorority girl at the reception desk smiled at Wingart then looked very surprised to see me.

"I found him," I said and smiled, revealing bloody smear on my teeth.

She cringed.

Wingart lead me down a hallway towards his office in the back. I passed a room that still had Ross Chambers' nameplate on the door. I glanced in, but it had been cleaned out. No clues.

Wingart shut the door behind me and offered a seat in front of his desk. He walked over to a liquor cart and started fixing a drink.

"Whatever you're having," I said. "Also some ice."

He looked over his shoulder, bothered.

He dropped ice into two glasses then brought me the ice bucket.

I held ice cubes up to my swelling face. It wasn't neat, but it helped to numb the pain.

Wingart finished the drinks and handed me mine, but in my ice wet hand the glass slipped out and spilled onto the floor.

Wingart looked irritated, thinking he'd have to fix another.

"I'm good for now," I said.

He nodded, sipped his drink, and sat behind his desk. Then he just stared at me. Sizing me up? Deciding how to play me? Wondering how dangerous I am?

"Who are you with?" he said.

"No one," I said.

"Well, then I simply don't know what you're talking about."

I sighed and set the ice bucket down.

I looked around the room.

"Power...access...money...you have a lot to lose, Trip."

"So, do you," he said.

"Oh?"

"Oh yeah." He didn't smile when he said it.

"Why's that?"

"Because just knowing what you know is going to get you killed," he said.

"By who?"

"You know who."

"How do you know?" I said.

"I know." He slumped back in his dark leather chair, a hangdog expression on his face.

"If I'm not careful it's going to get me killed, too," he said.

Not what I was expecting. I sat up.

"What do you mean?"

He didn't look at me. "You find out through Ross?"

"Not directly. No."

"So, he told people. That means it's out. And, that means they're going to start wiping away their tracks. I'm one of those tracks."

"Tell me how it works. It's the executioners for the state, isn't it?" I leaned against his desk as if closer proximity would will the answers out of him.

He said nothing, did nothing.

Then, a slow nod.

Confirmation.

My pain faded behind my desire for answers.

"Who are they?" I said.

"Who are you?" he said.

"I'm a guy who accidentally got mixed up in all of this and I'm trying to save my ass."

"I don't know who they are," he said. "The ones that actually do it."

"So, there is a middle man. You dealt with someone who does know. Did you hire them for ITG?" I couldn't get the question out fast enough.

"I won't admit to anything. I will only acknowledge that it exists."

"It helps to have some confirmation. Of what I suspected."

Nothing from him. He just watched me carefully.

"Who is the middle man?"

He shook his head. "Not gonna tell you that."

I slammed the desk with the iron fist. It left a huge dent. "Tell me!"

"I can't do that."

"Why?"

"Because. I need a way to cover my ass."

"They're either gonna kill me first or I'm going to get them. If I get them, they won't know you told. If they kill me they won't know either."

"There's no guarantee they won't find out. And, say this whole thing gets exposed. What happens to me? I get arrested. I go to jail. They work for the prison system. There'd be nothing stopping them from getting to me."

"Unless they were stopped first," I said.

"I just want to be clear that I didn't actually do any killing. You know that," he said. "The service did. I merely passed a name along. There was no conspiring, no nothing. You understand that, right?"

"Politics as usual," I said.

Now, I was mad. I leaned into his desk and pointed.

"Your passing along a name was directly responsible for getting my friend killed! A good man. With a family!"

"But, I didn't do the killing, I—"

"No, you accommodated it. You made the deal. A deadly one."

He sat up, a pleading expression on his face.

"You gotta understand, once you're privy to this kind of information, these services—"

"There are other services?" I said with genuine surprise and air quotation marks, which looked odd because I couldn't make quotes with the Skull Crusher.

"Of course, there are. Why else would a man spend seventy-five million dollars of his own money to become governor? Or Senator? It gets him access. To unimaginable privileges. That's what this is all about. Access, power, and prestige. Maximum Freedom." He waved around the room, meaning government/politics.

It was sickening.

"But, you don't learn about these things until it's too late. When you already have blood on your hands," he said.

"What do you mean?" I said.

"I'm not going to get into details. But, I got into some trouble last year. This connection offered to help out. I was desperate so I took his help. It wasn't killing. But, enough to give him something to hold over me and use as needed."

"Get to the point. My face is swelling up. And, I want to barf," I said.

"The point is, they made me pass the name along to my client. My donor."

I had to think for a moment. He said a lot that was vague. But, then I got it.

"So you figured it would be best for everyone if you played along. You save your ass, you help your donor, and you make these creeps some money, right?" I said.

He nodded. "And, that's exactly what happened."

"Who cares if someone has to die."

"It wasn't like that," he said.

"Only your faithful assistant Ross caught wind of it."

"He wasn't supposed to know."

"And so, now that the fuck up came from your office, it's your ass in the sling."

"Yes." A grave expression appeared on his face.

"So, we've talked ourselves right back to my original request. Tell me who the middleman is. Stop trying to cover your ass, because it sounds like you're already dead," I said standing up. I'd had enough.

He shook his head and smirked.

"No. That's not gonna happen."

"Why the hell not? I'm the only chance you got!"

He looked me over.

"That's not much of a chance," he said.

I sighed.

"You're being a real dumb dick," I said.

"Perhaps. I'd love for you to get the bastards. But, my money is still on them."

He tapped a newspaper sitting on his desk. There was an article about authorities stepping up their search for me.

"And, I'd increase my odds if I just turned you in right now."

I held up the iron fist.

"I'll smash your face before that phone reaches your ear," I said.

Hate brewed inside me. This guy was jerking me around. And, he was working against his own best interest.

"Then we've come to an impasse," he said as he stood up.

I was starting to worry but didn't want to show it. He could call the cops – or maybe even the executioners – and they could be here before I walked out of the lobby. Then, it would be all over. I'd disappear and they'd get away with everything.

I looked down at the phone on his desk. Then up to him. He stared back. I looked back at the phone and smashed it to pieces with the iron fist.

He jumped back worried I was attacking him.

Someone from outside the office spoke loud, "What was that?"

He composed himself. "There are other phones in this office."

"You piece of shit. I tried to help you."

"You can't help me," he said, straightening into a defiant posture. "But, I can help you."

"That's what I've been asking for all along."

"I'll help by giving you a ten minute head start. Then, I will call Capital Security. Then, I will call my connection. I want everything to appear as if I tried to stop you," he said.

"That is no fucking help," I said ready to pound his face.

"I will also tell you your instincts appear to have been spot on. You were shrewd enough to find me here. You're obviously moving in the right direction."

His flattery felt like an insult.

He continued, "You know who the killers are, you just don't know their names. I don't either. But, I'm sure you can find that out." He added, "If you're willing to get close to them."

"Every time I get close to them they try to kill me," I said.

"You'll need to be careful then," he said.

That did it.

I leapt over his desk and grabbed him by the tie. My momentum pushed us back onto the table that ran along the wall behind his desk.

"Tell me who the middleman is, asshole!"

I grabbed his throat and punched him in the stomach with the iron fist.

He gasped, his face beet read.

One of his staffers walked in. "Mr. Wingart, is everything—" They screamed. "Call the police!"

I hopped off Wingart and ran out of the office.

An office flunky tried to block me. I plowed through him and ran towards the front door.

Up front, the sorority sister shrieked and hid under her desk when I came around the corner. I must have looked like a charging bull. I shoved the front glass door open. When my arm swung back and the Skull Crusher smashed the glass shattering it onto the floor in a thousand jagged pieces. I hustled down the stairs and out of the building.

33

I was barely off the block when police cars converged from every direction. They surrounded the Senator's building. I ducked into a doorway and watched as half the cops secured the area and the other half stormed inside the building. Then, I looked for a clear path and got the hell out of there.

After twenty minutes of cutting through alleys and working a roundabout route I made it back to the car. I had to presume Wingart – that prick – had already told the cops I had been in his office. So, I'd be billed as armed, dangerous, and in the vicinity. I had to get out of town fast.

Easier said than done. Roads leading to I-10 west were closed down and checkpoints were being set up. The only way I was going to get to Defuniak – to Ilsa – was by going way out of my way, taking small roads and cutting through small towns. But, just getting out of the downtown area proved challenging. Traffic was already backing up.

A police siren squelched. I startled as a cop car raced past on the road shoulder. The car pulled up to the intersection ahead and stopped. The officer, wearing a bright yellow vest, started setting up a new checkpoint. I couldn't U-turn. I couldn't back up. And, I couldn't pull out of line. It would look suspicious.

Two more police cars and a police van arrived at the intersection. Two cops pulled wooden barricades out of the van and began placing them on the street to funnel traffic into a single file line. The other cops directed traffic and checked cars.

The car behind me honked. I hit the steering wheel, frustrated and un-nerved. My foot lifted of the gas and my car crawled forward as I looked around for an alternate route. Slim pickings.

The cops waved traffic forward. Time was running out.

Mine was three cars back from the checkpoint. I could see the cops up ahead – the ones checking passengers in cars – they referred to some papers. It had to be a picture of me. They'd identify me the moment I pulled up. *You're screwed, Asher!*

The ding of a service bell drew my attention. Right side of the car. A large, jacked up pickup truck had just pulled out of the service bay at the tire repair shop and was looking to pull into traffic. This could work.

A police officer whistled and waved. The cars ahead of me pulled forward. I didn't. I waved the truck ahead of me. He thanked me with a nod and pulled onto the street, creating a shield to prevent the police from seeing me drive into the tire shop parking lot.

But, I didn't stop in the parking lot. I pulled into the empty service bay the truck had just exited. Service technicians watched my car pull in and gave me a signal to stop. No thanks. I pulled straight through the bay and out to the other side of the building. I swerved around an assortment of cars waiting to be repaired and cut onto a service alley for deliveries. It was the break I needed. I drove for five alley blocks then turned off and took an intersection that hadn't been cordoned off.

Three streets later, I was on Highway 319 driving south. It wasn't my preferred route. It would take almost twice as long to reach Defuniak Springs. I'd have to cut down to the Gulf coast, around the Apalachicola National Forest then up through Panama City. But, at least there were no cops. Yet.

34

The hour and a half trip from Tallahassee to Defuniak Springs took more than seven hours. Defuniak Springs is just north of Interstate 10. And, there was a ton of heat looking for me. Police cars were parked near every major Interstate on and off ramp. I had to double back and cut through small towns like Ebro and Vernon, even going so far as to cross over into Alabama before looping around and driving straight south into Defuniak Springs. I was relieved to arrive.

I found a payphone at the far end of a poorly lit convenience store. This was the bad part of town and plenty of the locals watched as I dialed DG's number under the glowing cone of a bright streetlight. A woman with a hard Southern drawl answered my call.

"DG's," she said, pleasant enough.

"Hi, this is Walt. Calling for DG," I said.

"I'm gonna connect you now, sugar," she said.

Of course, DG had an answering service for his underground network.

I said, "Okay, thanks."

A trio of teenagers walked over and sized up my car. From here, they seemed impressed.

A different voice came on the line. I didn't recognize it.

"Hello, Walt?" Female, pleasant. I guessed early twenties.

"Yes," I said.

"Don't write this down. I'm gonna say it twice, so listen."

"I'm ready."

Twice she gave me the address and directions to where I would find Ilsa. I thanked her, hung up, and walked back to the car, repeating the address in my head.

The teenage trio breezed away from my car as I walked up. One smiled, "Sweet wheels."

"Thanks."

I got in and drove off.

The woman's directions lead me to a dead end. A chain-link fence cut off the road. I killed my lights and waited. Nothing happened for fifteen minutes. I turned the car on and backed down the road to check the street sign. I glanced at the rearview mirror.

Stop!

A pair of men stood in the road behind my car. They looked mean. One walked up to my window and swirled his finger, telling me to roll it down. I did.

"Who are you?" he said, a menacing look on his face. His hand on the handle of a pistol tucked in his front waistband.

"Walt. DG's friend. I'm here to see my girlfriend, Ilsa. She's the one laid up," I said.

He looked over the roof of the car and nodded approval to his friend.

They hopped in the car. "Beams off. Turn here, cut around the house, and follow the road," he said.

I turned into what looked like the front yard of a small two-bedroom home. But, as I pulled around to the back yard, I could see the house had been built right in the middle of an intersection, disguising it and obscuring the side street we were on now which, a moment later, lowered and banked until it ran parallel along a creek of respectable size.

I had to follow the road using the moonlight that beamed through the trees and reflected off the creek. Good thing it wasn't overcast. It was slow going, and despite the ridiculous rumble of the engine, things seemed more peaceful without the headlights.

I saw a family of deer on the far side of the creek. They were partially silhouetted by the moonlight. Their heads perked up at hearing the car. They watched me and I watched them between glances at the road. It reminded me that life was still happening as normal for people and beasts outside of my predicament. I hoped to get my life back to normal soon.

We arrived at a small alcove with a gravel path that led to barn-sized doors set against the base of a hill. My passengers – who remained silent for the ride – hopped out and pulled open the doors. They waved me forward and I drove the car into what looked like a small cave. I parked, turned off the car, and got out. I could smell the minerals in the soil.

"This way," my guide said, waving me out of the cave. They closed and locked the barn doors behind me.

We walked along the river for about the distance of a typical big city block. Then, we cut down a worn grass path that meandered towards the river.

"Careful," my guide said.

He led me across a small bridge of stepping-stones, hardly visible above the surface of the water. No one would see them from the road or even from higher up in the nearby hills.

I made it across the water despite almost slipping off twice. Once on fresh land, we picked up the pace, jogging through a densely wooded area until we arrived at a wooden gate. My guide opened the gate and we went in.

The set up was familiar in that it was similar to how DG had his property arranged down by the Rainbow River: A winding path led back to a flat, spacious house set in the middle of a parking lot's worth of vehicles. All the vehicles pointed away from the house for the fastest possible getaway, and they were parked under thatched roofs to avoid aerial detection.

My guides took me into the house and led me up to a buxom woman whose scoop neck top let it be known that her cleavage ran long and deep.

"You must be Walt," she said. "I'm Stella."

"Hi," I said.

"You hungry? Thirsty?" She turned to my guide. "Smash, get him a brew. Make it two."

He nodded and went to find libations.

"I want to see Ilsa. I can eat after," I said.

She smiled and led me down a dim, wood-paneled hallway.

Ilsa was sitting up in bed, brushing her hair. She sensed my presence at the door "I wanted to spruce up once I heard you were coming," she said with a smile.

"You look extraordinary," I said and moved into the room.

I took her face in my hands and gave her what had to be the best kiss in all the many years of our relationship. I couldn't kiss her enough.

I moved my hands off her face, down the sides of her neck, across her shoulders and behind her back then squeezed to hug. It was a strong enough embrace to nearly lift her off the bed.

"Oww!" she said.

I relaxed my grip and she settled back against a small mountain of pillows. She squirmed around for an angle that would put the least pressure on her body. She smiled, but the kiss and hug seemed to have exhausted her.

"I'm sorry," I said.

"Don't be. I've needed that kiss," she said.

I sat on the bed next to her.

"Well, here I am. The woman of your dreams," she said.

"You are indeed. How you feeling?" I rubbed her left leg.

She smiled. She hesitated, but forced her concerned expression away. She was trying to keep up a strong front.

"Before you answer that," I leaned forward and gave her another kiss. I couldn't get enough. I held it and held it and held it until she started to laugh.

"Sorry, I just had to," I said.

"Take all you like," she said, a genuine smile on her face this time. "Your kisses numb the pain."

"Is it bad?" I said.

"It's getting better. Just takes time to heal."

"What does the doctor say?"

"That I might be able to walk on my own in six months. But, I will limp for the rest of my life. And my long, lean, lovely leg will not be worthy of showing off at the beach." She forced a smile.

My hand caressed her injured leg. I looked down at the L-shape it formed under the blankets. I wanted nothing more than for my hand to emit a healing heat that would restore her leg back to full health, and forever ease her heart and mind.

I looked into her eyes.

"You will always be the most beautiful. Always," I said.

She waved me off like I was getting too serious and needed to chill out. But, when she leaned back to rest her head on the pillows and looked out the window I could see the beginnings of tears glisten in her eyes.

She started to say something then stopped and caught her breath. She closed her eyes then blinked the tears away. One escaped down her cheek. She wiped it away, looked at me, and smiled. Then, more tears surfaced.

We hugged, with less force this time.

"Okay, enough of that silly stuff," She said. "I will be fine. There are more troublesome things to worry about, and I think you know what I mean."

She gave me a stern look, as if I was the misbehaving student and she the disapproving teacher. She's given me that same look on friskier occasions.

"How goes the work of the hunter?" she said.

I gave her the full report. Everything from what I learned about the execution team to my meeting with Wingart, and even an aside about the Panhandle Rippers.

"You have done well, love," she said. "But now, it is time to get serious."

"What do you mean?"

"I have spoken to DG. He can get us out of the U.S. and into Holland. It would be expensive, but I have money hidden at my house. It would cover his fees and give us plenty to live on for a while. At least a year," she said.

"Didn't I just say I was making progress?" I said.

"And, I heard you. It sounds like you've taken very dangerous risks and I am grateful you survived. But, now you have enough information to give to other people so they can handle this. Someone better equipped for this. And, I don't want to risk losing you again. I won't," she said.

I didn't say anything. I needed a moment to consider her proposal. She watched me and waited for my answer. But, she wasn't going to like it.

"I'm not going to Europe. I've seen these guys, what they do. I'm not walking away now."

"You are foolish."

"Running is foolish," I said as I got up from the bed. "They won't stop chasing us. Are we really having this conversation again?"

"Yes, we are. And, we're lucky to be having it!" Her face flushed red with anger.

"Lucky? Or, maybe I'm better at this sort of stuff than either of us knew."

"Don't flatter yourself. How soon until your luck runs out?"

"They're *from* Europe. How soon until they find us there? I have no choice!"

She didn't respond and I didn't follow up. Things had become too tense.

"I'm the one who has no choice," she said.

She turned away and several minutes of silence followed.

I hated fights like this. We both wanted the same thing – to stop the bad guys, stay safe, and get back to our normal lives. But, we saw varied degrees of risk. It was a drastic difference.

"I think you're making a terrible, careless, unkind decision," she said.

"Maybe. But, it's the right one."

She looked away frustrated.

Another long silence.

Her body relaxed and she sunk deeper into the pillows. Tension in her face revealed a war of thoughts going on inside her head. Her expressions evolved from sad to resigned to stern. She looked at me with renewed resolve.

"If I can't take you away...I will find a way to support you here. But, you must do something for me."

"I promise not to get killed," I said, jumping the gun with a smirk.

She scowled, seized my wrist, and shook it. "You must promise to kill! If that's what it takes."

I didn't know how to respond.

"They're bad men, Walter. Doing very bad things. DG can only babysit me for so long. If they kill you, I'm as good as dead, too," she said.

"Thank you for the pep talk, love," I said. "But, I have all the motivation I need."

She continued as if I hadn't said a thing. "You can show no mercy and no pity. Not anymore. Not with these men. Understand?"

I watched the anguish percolate across her face. She wasn't going to look away until I made that dark promise. A promise, which seemed crazy, but rang true.

"You are protecting yourself, your family, and me. You are kicking ass for those who can no longer kick," she said and patted her bum leg. "Even if you hate the idea, remember it doesn't make you a killer. It makes you a hero. And, heroes do what it takes, no matter how ugly."

I did hate the idea. But, she was right.

She folded her arms. "Deal?"

I nodded. "Deal."

She swiped her welling tears a way. A sniffle. She cleared her throat. She looked to me.

"Now, shut the door and make love to me."

She didn't smile. It was an order and I followed it.

Afterwards, she fell asleep fast. The last thing I remembered as I drifted off to sleep was the birth of my first son, Evan, and the first moments I held his soft, warm body in my hands; I understood then and there that because I could create life, I knew it was in me to take a life. I could kill. And, I would do just that, without hesitation, to anyone who tried to hurt my beautiful child. It was a scary thing to realize about myself. No one wanted to admit they could do it. But, in that precious instant, it became an undeniable truth in me. I could and I would kill anyone who messed with my kids. For Ilsa.

My timid husk was gone. With Ilsa's blessing and my own, I was now ready to go after the executioners.

35

I slept sound and woke up rested and refreshed. Ilsa looked the picture of peace as she lay next to me. I couldn't wait to tease about her snoring.

Shower, shave, and fresh clothes and I was back to feeling like myself. All I needed was a few hours to write to feel all the way back to normal. No time for that.

I found DG in his living room holding court with five guys from his gang. He said to give him a minute, so I went to the kitchen and heated up breakfast. He found me there stuffing my mouth.

"I don't think I even ate yesterday," I mumbled through a mouthful of biscuit.

"Eat up. You're gonna need it," he said. "Things are getting too hot with you around."

I looked around at the kitchen we were in. "If you can't take the heat, get out of the...?" I said with a smirk.

He forced a smile but wasn't amused.

"Look, Walt. You know I love you like a brother. And, you can count on me. But, you're bringing the fuzz too close to my operations. It's swarming. And, I can't have 'em sniffin' this hound's butt, you dig?"

"I dig."

"That means you and Ilsa either split for Europe together or don't come back 'til you get things cleared up. However they have to get cleared up."

"You've been great to us. I can take it from here."

"That's a peculiar decision on your part," he said.

"I've thought it through," I said.

He nodded.

"Ilsa can stay. She can't go on her own and you can't have her slowing you down. We'll take care of that fine lady until you're ready to come and get her. Plus, I got guys running her bars."

"How much is that costing?" I said.

"Usual ten percent skim. She's cool with it. And, those boys will shotgun any one who tries to mess with the place," he said.

That was good to hear. Ten percent seemed like a small price to pay to keep everything from falling apart. Wish they could fill in for my writing business. But, that'd be weird. Although, I bet DG's boys could muscle higher rates out of my clients. It was something worth considering.

DG continued, " They came snooping around."

My heart started racing. "Who?"

"I dunno. But, we checked the surveillance cameras and pulled a pic."

He extracted a small black and white photo out of his grubby flannel pocket. It showed the scrawny blonde man who'd tried to stab me at my house. He was standing outside Ilsa's bar, The Brute, in downtown Gainesville. A cigarette dangled from his lips. He looked to be sizing things up.

"He tried to pry info from the bartender. He asked about Ilsa like they were old friends. Said he was supposed to meet the two of you there. My boy told him to get lost and get fucked."

"Your boy's lucky to be alive," I said.

"So is that guy." He flicked the picture.

"Thanks for everything, DG."

"Any time. I'll help however I can. But, for now I need you to pull the cops away from here."

"I'm going back to Union County. That's where they're hiding," I said holding up the photo. "But, the cops were out in force last night. I can only imagine it's worse today."

He nodded, knowing all about it.

"Don't worry about that. I had some of my Miami boys phone in fake sightings, saying they'd seen you. One saw you in West Palm. The next down in Kendall. Then another said he seen you moving south through Marathon Key. I suspect they're already racing down to trap you." "Nice."

"But, just in case they keep a fleet up here, I've booked you some alternate transportation. It leaves in two hours and you can't miss it," he said.

My alternate transportation was an hour and a half away from DG's hideout. That meant I barely had time to bid Ilsa goodbye. Brave faces for both of us. But, there was a heavy silence knowing it could be the last time we see each other. If things went wrong. We kissed and I was whisked into the back of a cargo van made up to look like a cable company truck.

I couldn't see out any windows on the drive down, and no one told me where we were going. When the back of the van opened, I saw we were at a private dock at the end of a winding, mangrove lined inlet. The dock looked out to a wide, stunning view of the Gulf of Mexico. A pair of dirty, brown pelicans bobbed up and down as the greenish water beneath them chopped against the pylons.

It was blazing hot and the glare off the white crushed shell path that lead to the dock made squinting necessary. My drivers lead me aboard a shrimp boat that looked like it had served for thousands of voyages over several decades. Appearances aside, it felt sturdy when I stepped on it. One of DG's boys told me to make myself comfortable, so I sat at the back of the boat on a bench that stored life jackets. I was offered my choice of beer, joints, and an array of fresh seafood that had been prepared on the dockside grill. I took a little of each.

The beer refreshed under the brutal sun and tied in well with the breeze as we motored along. The shrimp and grouper were fresh and stellar. And, the marijuana relaxed me. A precious clarity formed in my mind, allowing it to wander in positive directions as I sized up my situation.

I looked at the picture of the executioner. Young, blonde, and with a defiant face. His features didn't scream redneck. But, his clothes hinted in that direction. He had the same anglo/Euro features as the other attackers I had seen up close. That tied right in with their supposed French history, per the Warden. I memorized every detail of his face so that I would recognize him before he recognized me the next time our paths crossed.

I had a map of Florida, but had no idea where we would dock. So rather than chart a path from the Gulf, I concentrated on Union County, memorizing the main highways, and just trying to absorb as much about the geography of the place as I could. It might come in handy.

It occurred to me that I needed a weapon. I couldn't go up against these guys unarmed. Not anymore. And, I had left the Skull Crusher back in the car in Defuniak Springs. That was okay. As handy as it had been, I'd prefer to have something that fired from a distance or could be thrown, like a blade. Not that I was an expert marksman of any sort. That just felt like the right way to go. Plus, the weight of the Skull Crusher had taken a toll on my arm muscles. My shoulder was killing me from swinging that thing.

I was struck with a substantial realization: Acting like a complete novice – which I was – wouldn't cut it anymore. I need to throw down the gauntlet and do something drastic. In advertising it's called "pattern interrupt." You disrupt the consumer's pattern to stand out and get a sales edge. I knew the only way I could stop these killers was to disrupt their pattern of operation and attack them from an angle they'd never suspect. Instead of worrying about them stalking me, I needed to stalk them. And, when the opportunity presented itself...keep my promise to Ilsa.

Just over five hours later we pulled into another private dock on the west central coast of Florida. It was just north of Steinhatchee, a small coastal town known for their scallops and scallop fest. Scallopalooza, they called it. Ilsa and I had considered going then realized we'd missed it by a week.

DG's guy introduced me to Boris, DG's three hundred plus pound Steinhatchee contact who appeared to sweat professionally. He said he could give me a ride into Cross City as soon as they unloaded the boat, and that's it. I'd be on my own after that.

Fine by me. I leaned against the dock railing as the boat crew unloaded bales of something I presumed was illegal. Fifteen minutes later, I was on the back of Boris' motorcycle holding on to his rotund belly.

His goodbye was brief and I soon found myself standing on a corner in little, bitty Cross City. I was outside a boutique "for sassy, stylish gals" and across from a greasy spoon with a small crowd. A green highway sign indicated the way east to Gainesville, the way I needed to go. That meant I had to cut through the middle of town to get to where cars would be heading my way. Maybe I could hitch a ride. In truth, that was my only hope. Otherwise I'd be stuck on the dark highway and turned into insect or alligator bait. No thanks.

I crossed through the town's main intersection. No one appeared to recognize me. For that, I was thankful. Next problem: I'd have no place to hide once I got out onto the highway. Any police cruiser that passed by would size me up quick, pull over to question me, put me in their computer, and bam, that's that.

But, two blocks down the main drag I stopped worrying about police encounters and found inspiration for my drastic action.

36

He was standing next to a battered Toyota Camry in a dusty parking lot adjacent to the Cross City office of the Dixie County Advocate, the small, hometown newspaper. A camera hung over his shoulder while he jotted notes on a palm-sized notepad. It didn't take a genius to figure out he was a reporter. His fresh face and preppy pink shirt gave him a just outta college vibe. And, the focus with which he wrote made it clear this was but a small stop on his path towards a Pulitzer Prize. Just what I needed.

I waited for a cattle truck to pass and stepped through a cloud of swirling road dust.

"You work for the paper?" I asked as I walked up.

He looked up from his notepad.

I offered a megawatt smile.

"Why, yes," he said, smiling back.

"How would you like a scoop on the biggest story in the State?" By the time I'd finished saying it I had moved around his car and opened the passenger side door.

"Uh, well, yeah! I'd love it."

"Good. Get in and I'll tell you all about it."

"Where are we going?" he asked as he settled into the driver's seat and shut his door.

"Starke. Union County."

"Wait, what? I can't. I have an assignment," he said, stopping short of starting the car.

"For what?" I buckled up and locked my door. He noticed and started to look concerned.

"Mrs. Strother's new petunia blooms. Local interest."

"Sounds boring, uhh…"

"Teddy. Teddy Salters. Hey, if I don't go, I'll get fired."

"I seriously doubt there are many people lining up to get your job, Teddy. Besides…" I reached over and turned the key to start the car. "I have the story that's going to change you from a flunky Teddy to a respected Ted and make your career."

"Holy bones! You're the guy the police are looking for? I've seen your face in the paper. And, on TV."

Teddy couldn't believe it.

We drove east on Highway 26 towards Gainesville.

"That's right. Only what you've heard about me isn't true. Not in the least," I said.

"So, why are they saying those things?"

"Because the guys who really did it want me captured and killed. They're bad men with important connections and if they can't find me themselves, they'll have the cops and media do it for them."

"That sounds pretty incredible. How do I know you're not making it up and you really did do all those bad things they say you did?"

"Because what man on the run from the law asks to be driven to the same city as the Florida State Prison? That's where I'm trying to avoid going," I said.

He thought about it then nodded. "That's a good point."

"I know."

"You must want more from me than a ride, right?"

"Teddy, I can already tell you have a sound journalistic mind. And, that will serve us both."

"How so?"

"I need you to do some things that I can't do with my face plastered all over the place. So, here's the scoop: The guy the paper is saying I killed is actually one of the death row executioners for the State of Florida."

"Why would you kill him?"

"Because he was trying to kill me."

"So, you did kill him," he looked at me, worry growing on his face.

"Watch the road," I said. He obeyed. I continued, "It was accidental and in self defense. For real."

He focused on the road ahead but his brow was furrowed with confusion and questions.

"Teddy, this is where you say, Walt, why did you have to defend yourself from them?"

"Why did you have to—"

"Because they've been trying to kill me. And, they're doing that because I know they killed my good friend Ken Kerenz. At his house, right along the beautiful Rainbow River, where I should be swimming now instead of talking to you."

Teddy thought about it for a minute. He really did have a sharp mind and a budding bullshit detector.

"One of Florida's state executioners killed your friend," he said.

"Yes," I said.

"In his home."

"His backyard."

"Not on Death Row."

"Out of his jurisdiction, wouldn't you say?"

He nodded.

"So, why would one of Florida's state executioners kill people other than on Death Row?" he said.

"That's what I've spent the past several days trying to find out. And, the answer is, they're freelancing," I said.

He looked at me, a grave expression on his face.

"Now, you're getting it," I said. "The only sanctioned killers in the state have expanded their business and are working for the highest bidders."

"Unbelievable," he said. It was a very low-key "a-ha!" moment for him.

"Here's what I know. The executioners are marketed as a service to a select group of politicians who hire them for contract killings. These contract killings could be for themselves or on behalf of their influential donors. Corporations, lobbyists, et cetera."

"Who does the marketing?"

"A middleman. I don't know who that is. If we can find that out, we can find out who the executioners are and stop them."

"You don't even know who's trying to kill you?"

"Scary, huh?"

"Yeah."

He drove a few moments in silence. Pinched expressions on his face indicated a brain working overtime.

Finally, he spoke, "What does this have to do with your friend. Ken?"

"Yes, Ken. He found out about the service from a guy named Ross Chambers, who was working for U.S. Representative Trip Wingart. Chambers overheard Wingart talking about it and Chambers was able to get a list to this guy Duncan, who gave it to Ken. Duncan's expectation was Ken, a prominent activist, might be able to do something with the information."

"Do you have the list?" he asked with growing excitement.

"No," I said. "And now, Ken and Duncan are both dead. Killed."

He looked spooked.

I continued, "Maybe you heard about police storming Wingart's office in Tallahassee yesterday. That was me. I confronted him. He confessed to hiring the executioners for the Innovative Tomorrow Group out of Jacksonville and their CEO, a guy named Doug Tanjeris. But, he didn't give up any names. He only confirmed my suspicions. Now, we need to find the people behind them."

"So, we should talk to Tanjeris," he said.

"His contact was Wingart. I think he was hands off," I said.

A lull in the conversation.

I contemplated the highway passing by. Long fields of weeds and scraggly grass went past. Trees whipped by in a brown blur. Pastures rolling over the hills had centerpiece houses looming in the distance. How nice it must be to have your life and your business out in the middle of a peaceful nowhere. Wake up, work, eat, relax. Then, do it again the next day. I guess I'd had a similar luxury writing from home. But, that seemed like that was a long time ago.

Teddy said, "So, that's everything up to today?"

I snapped back to attention, "Everything."

We had passed through the small town of Trenton. A highway sign indicated we weren't far from Newberry and closing in on Gainesville.

I turned to face him better. "The middleman has political connections and access to the executioners. That's quite a social straddle."

He raised a finger and started to speak. I cut him off.

"It's not the Warden. I've spoken to him. He's either an ace liar or innocent. I suspect the latter."

"Maybe he knew who you were and put on his best performance," he said.

"I used a fake name. Told him I was a reporter," I said.

He gave me a look like that didn't mean anything. And, he was right.

"Good point," I said. "But, it would be odd for you to interview him now since I just interviewed him the other day."

"Who else?"

He pulled himself up in his seat. He looked focused and poised to reel in this story.

"It could be someone else working at the prison. Someone in the Warden's office."

"Did any state politicians ever serve time there?" he said.

"Don't know. We'd have to research."

"I can do that. Research is my specialty. What about Reps and Senators for Union County?"

"It's possible. Don't know who that would be."

"I can find out when we get there. What else?"

He gave me confidence. I could use another ally in this fight.

"I don't know. Maybe the Mayor?"

"There has to be a way to find out who these guys, the executioners, are," he said.

"I have one thing that might help," I said and pulled out the photo of the executioner taken outside The Brute Bar.

He took it and examined it, glancing every few seconds back to the road.

"This one of them?"

"Yes. Taken outside my girlfriend's bar in Gainesville the other night. He went there looking for me," I said.

"Looks young."

"The one I killed looked older, by a generation. But, similar features. The Warden told me the team of executioners came over from France once the death penalty was outlawed there."

"Maybe they're not a team," he said handing the picture back to me. I tucked it in my pocket as he fixed his eyes back on the road.

"Maybe they're a family."

37

We arrived in Lake Butler near three in the afternoon. Our first stop was a grease pit motel on the north side of town. The motel looked like it had once been a fine stop on the long journey down Highway 301. Maybe back in the Fifties. But, like so many highway motels, it took a dive when the interstates arrived. This one probably made its monthly nut off families of convicts locked up nearby in Florida State Prison. We booked a room to serve as our central meeting location later on.

From there, we went downtown. I was driving now and pulled up to a curb just off the main drag. Teddy opened his door to get out. A "March with Arch" flyer caught my eye. It was plastered to the side of a sheet of plywood plugging up a window in an old, abandoned brick building.

I pointed. "There's the guy to talk to right there. He may know something."

"I'll swing by his office and then the library to research French executioners," Teddy said.

"I'll try to get info from the locals."

He climbed out of the car and leaned in with his hand on the doorframe.

"Be careful. I'm gonna need you alive to corroborate my story," he said and smiled.

"Well...if I don't make it, do me justice, eh?" I said.

"You got it. I'll meet you back at the motel," he said.

"See you there," I said.

My plan was simple: blend in and listen. I had three locations in mind. One was a bar and tap just around the corner, which I had seen during my previous visit to the area. The after work crowd would be arriving soon and they'd be focused on their friends, not me. There was another spot east on Highway 100 between here and Starke. I figured that would bring news from both towns. And, there was a country dive bar just west of Lake Butler and not far from the prison. It seemed like the perfect place for guards to blow off steam. And, I needed some talkers.

Monty's Bar and Tap was dead. Just a few faces, most buried in the bottom of their glasses. I tried to get a conversation going with a bartender, but I got the sense she thought I was just the first of a dozen guys who would hit on her tonight. Her answers were short and her only elaboration was a forced smile followed by a sigh as she grabbed a nail file from the back of the bar and set about fixing her nails. I didn't stay long.

"Hey Chuck. Chuck! Check this out! This guy here writes those damn info-commercials that we see on the TV every night."

Those words were spoken by a dumb, drunk Oakie who had his fat calloused finger stuck right in my chest. He had a big smile on his face. I'd struck up a conversation with him earlier and had yet to shake him loose once I realized he didn't have much information I could use.

Chuck said, "Son of a buck! You cost me a lot of money. My wife can't resist those things."

The other guy, Gus, said, "It's like he's seducing your wife, only instead of getting in her panties, he's getting in her pocketbook."

They howled.

I was amused, too. It's kind of a thrill having that kind of power. From thousands of miles away, my words can command you to fork over that hard-earned money. Doesn't matter how much you had to sweat for it or how much bullshit you had to wade through. When I turned the charm meter to 10, your money was mine. Or so, it was nice to think.

Chuck said, "Which ones did you do. You do the one where the noodles spill all over the place?"

"I did," I said.

More howling. It was shaping up to be a good night for them.

"How about the one for the back cushion where the guy stutters and says 'muh...muh...muh...my butt!'?" They leaned in with eager anticipation.

I said, "That was a big hit for me." It was.

More howling.

Chuck put a hand on my shoulder, "Hey, what's the weirdest one you ever did? Cuz some of 'em don't even make no damn sense know what I'm sayin'?"

I nodded. "I've written a lot of bra shows. But, the weirdest product I ever wrote for was a pair of leak control panties—"

He'd stopped listening and turned away before I finished.

"Hey, Wanda! Get your ass over here, I finally found the guy who can solve all your problems," Chuck yelled.

He looked to Gus and they shared a laugh.

Wanda staggered over and settled in between them. She sized me up and I reciprocated. Early fifties and she had a body that meant business. Hard times and good times had aged her face. I suspected more good than bad. She had a devilish smile when she looked me right in the eyes.

"*You* gonna solve *my* problems? Hope you brought some energy drinks," she said.

Chuck shot spittle on her face when he said, " He's a info commercial writer who writes for ladies with wet panties! Can you believe that?"

"Ohh, maybe you are the man for me," she said and took my arm. "My panties are always wet." She led me away from the boys.

We sat down in a booth, her next to me.

"Forget those idiots. They're always a handful," she said.

"I bet."

"What brings you to town?"

"Well, I don't just write 'info commercials'. I also write books. And, I'm doing one on the death penalty," I said. I'd come up with that angle while sitting in the last bar.

"Well, son. You sure came to the right place. We fry 'em and poison 'em up here."

"So, I heard."

"Here to do some research?"

"Exactly. You know, artsy-fartsy things like 'catch the essence of the place' and 'see how it affects the lives of the locals', that kind of garbage."

"I might could help you out."

"Really? How so?"

"My brother's executed a few prisoners."

Everything stopped. My heart started to pound. I caught my breath and looked her dead in the eyes.

She smiled like she was pleased she could do something nice for me.

"Wanna meet him?" she said.

"Yes," I said without even thinking it through. Then, I regretted it. What if he was one of them? What if he recognized me? He'd try to kill me. Without a doubt. And, if the others were there? His family, as Teddy had suggested. I'd be on their turf. That put everything in their favor. This could be bad. But, if Teddy came up dry, it could also be my only approach. I had to take it.

"Let's go," she said and grabbed my hand.

I didn't have a chance to decline.

"I'll drive," I said.

"How 'bout you follow. I ain't leavin' my car here," she said.

Fair enough.

38

We took Highway 100 a few miles west then cut onto a smaller paved road, which lead to an even smaller dirt road. Her pickup truck kicked up dirt that swirled in the red glow of her taillights. It wasn't until her truck parked and the lights turned off that I saw our destination was a run down, dirty house at the end of a neglected cul-de-sac.

I grabbed the nasty fishing knife I'd taken off the boat earlier and pocketed it as I stood out of the car. I scanned the property while she walked over to me – a flimsy, rusty fence ran along the driveway. Assorted all-terrain vehicles in various conditions, automobile and miscellaneous junk were scattered about. A goat butted its horns against an empty, yellow Prestone container. The soft, pale sand around the house led into the dark woods beyond.

"Follow me," she said with a seductive smile.

If I hadn't been so worried about the potential impending deadly encounter I'd have contemplated why this woman I just met was leading me up to the house by the hand. And, why did she smile seductively if we were about to meet her brother? Strange folks.

The screen door creaked on its single working hinge as she opened it and led me into the house. It stunk: old beer, dirty ashtray, and what I guessed to be stale Avon goods.

I stood in the foyer and watched her walk towards a hallway that I presumed led to bedrooms.

"I'll see if he's up," she said.

She disappeared around the corner.

I got spooked and wandered over to the kitchen. I shouldn't have let it get this far on a whim. I checked drawers. My best options for an additional weapon were a pair of pliers from a utility drawer. I also pocketed two books of matches. You never know.

She appeared from the hallway just as I returned to the foyer.

"He's was sleepin'. Be out in a sec," she said. "Get you a drink?"

She walked into the kitchen.

"Sure, whatever you got," I said.

A thump from the back room.

I steadied my legs and put my hand on the knife in my pocket.

"All I got's some Steel Reserve. Work for you?" she said from the kitchen.

"That's fine," I said back. I didn't take my eyes off the hallway.

I flinched at the sound of the door opening down the hallway. Then footsteps. Then a yawn. Then, him. Her brother. He stared at me with disbelief. I start to slide the knife out.

"Wally Grainger, how do you do?" he said. He stepped up, hand outstretched for a shaking.

I hesitated and looked at his thick, stub-fingered hands as if they might be traps. He came closer. And closer. His hand reached towards mine. I didn't want to release the knife, but...I shook his hand. He smiled and studied my face.

Something cold stung my arm and I jumped.

"Easy tiger." Wanda was at my side. The cold came from a can of beer pressed against my arm.

"Wally, Walt. Walt, Wally. There, you've met," she said on her way to plopping on the couch, one leg tucked under her ass in a way that spread the crotch of her tiny jean shorts wide open. She smiled, knowing I'd noticed.

"Good to meet you," I said. He wasn't one of the men who had tried to kill me. But...

He waved me off and fell into an overstuffed recliner that had been reupholstered in well-worn areas with duct tape.

"Wanda says you're writing a book on executions," he said as he picked a half smoked cigarette out of an overflowing ashtray that sat on a television tray table next to his chair. It was now being used as an end table replete with a television remote, pill bottles, and a tattered copy of Skank Magazine.

"Well, yeah. Just up here doing some research," I said.

He studied me to the point that I grew uncomfortable. Like maybe he knew who I was. If so, he was in no hurry to get me. And, if not, why? He'd had time alone in his room after Wanda announced me. He could have made a call. Were the other killers on their way?

"I done quite a few executions. Pulled that lever on Ole Sparky plenty of times," he said while blowing out smoke. "Killing a man's a special thing."

I looked to Wanda and saw her rub the cold can of beer up and down the crotch seam of her jeans. What the...?

Wally's voice pulled my attention back to him. "I mean, what a power trip, right? Yanking that lever and sending them right into the after life. Like a toll keeper between life and death I guess. Best job I ever had. God, did I love to see those fuckers fry."

I looked back at Wanda. No disputing it: She was aroused by his words and sending it in my direction.

"They'd scream and buck. Their pelvis would shoot out..."

Wanda's pelvis shot out in the corner of my eye.

"You could hear their head sizzling, smell that burning hair. Smell the electricity through the room..."

He sniffed the air.

Wanda moaned.

She had lust in her eyes now.

"She loves when I tell that story. Gets her hot every time," said Wally.

I looked over and saw him eyeing her. In *that* way.

Wanda said, "That's when I pull his lever." She followed it with a sultry laugh.

Wally folded down the recliner, stood up, and faced me. It was an abrupt move that made me step back.

Wanda pulled offer her top to reveal a pair of sad breasts.

Wally smiled with excitement. He thumbed back to the bedroom, "I got a life-size perfect replica of Ole Sparky back in the bedroom. Wanna sit in it?"

"Yeah, sit in it. Wally will play executioner and I'll play the prison matron. Won't that be hot?" said Wanda.

I looked over just as her jean shorts dropped to her ankles. No panties.

"Wait. Did you say 'best job you ever *had*'?" I said.

He nodded and started unbuckling his pants.

He said, "They cut me loose a few years back. Said I was too 'enthused' by the killing. That I had an unhealthy interest in the process."

Wanda wrapped her arms around me. Her hand went for my crotch. "But, looks like we got a new dead man walking," she said.

I shoved her off me. She staggered back then reached out to caress me.

"It's all right baby. Gonna be a lot of—"

I smacked her arms away before she could finish.

"Hey, ain't nobody gonna push my older sis around like that," said Wally. He put his hand on my shoulder. On instinct, I punched him square in the mouth and he spilled back over his recliner. I was ready for him to spring up and fight back.

"Why you getting' all hostile for?" said Wanda. She pounded my back with her fist. It didn't hurt. I turned and kicked her right in the gut. She fell back on the couch gasping for air. I took in the scene - the scummy room and the weak, helpless, sleazebags. I ran out of there.

I punched the car into reverse and sent sand shooting into the back of Wanda's truck as I raced backwards out the dirt drive. They stood naked in the doorway imploring me to come back even while Wally checked his lip for blood. Fuck that in the neck. Actually, do *not* fuck that. At all.

I was furious. Angry because I'd been misled. Angry because they had just wasted an hour with time running out. Angry at myself. I should have caught on a lot faster. And, I over-reacted. They were freaks, but harmless and I hammered them. That wasn't cool. I needed to keep myself under control if I was going to get the real bad guys. Now, it was night and I still didn't know the identity of the real executioners.

I didn't recognize my third destination, the country dive bar, until I had almost driven past it. I skidded, turned, and slid across the dusty gravel parking lot. Once parked, I caught my breath and rested my head on the steering wheel. I needed to calm down and re-calibrate.

Progress report: So far, so bad. Two dead-ends. Make that one dead end, one freaky end. Or, a very promising opportunity if I had a capital punishment fetish. Which I don't.

Hunger rumbled in my stomach. I hadn't eaten for several hours. I thought about running into town to grab food. It would make a good foundation for the beer I'd probably have to drink inside the country dive. But, that would set me back another forty minutes, at least. I couldn't decide so I reclined the driver seat back to rest.

Lying there with my eyes shut, I hoped Teddy was doing better than me. Maybe he had made a big discovery. A name from the French execution records, perhaps. Or a lead on a politician. Something. I worried beyond that. What if we both struck out? Then what? I needed to just calm down and focus on the present.

I tried a catnap. They work for me. Just fifteen minutes of sleep and I'm good for another three or four hours.

The crackle crunch of gravel under tires woke me up. I opened my eyes to the glare of headlights. I waited for the truck to pass and park before opening them again. The clock said I had slept for twenty-five minutes. So much for saving time. I rubbed my eyes, yawned, and tried to stretch. But, the car was too small to fully extended my six-foot-one frame. So, I turned the engine off and got out. I reached both hands towards the sky and let the stretching muscles ripple through my body.

That's when I saw the man from the photo.

39

He walked out the dive bar with a young girl on his arm. I squatted down by the side of the car. A glance down at the photo then a glance over the hood to compare faces.

It was him. No doubt.

Young and cocky, strutting his stuff for the girl who appeared naïve and enamored. He guided her over to his car. Same brown Camaro, same white pinstripes. Just like I'd seen outside Ilsa's house. How did I not recognize it when I pulled in to this parking lot?

That poor girl had no idea who she was dealing with.

They got in the car and drove west.

I got in mine and followed.

That's all I was going to do for the time being. I didn't feel ready to take him on. The girl was a problem, too. She'd be a witness. She could help him attack me. I didn't know. I had to wait until I could get him alone. Or, was I just scared and making excuses now that I had my shot?

He continued west to Lake Butler, then cut north on Highway 121. He drove for many miles. We passed Florida State Prison. I could have sworn I saw him point it out to his passenger. Bragging about his job? She'd be young and dumb enough to find it romantic. Maybe he had put a heroic spin on things. A young girl would probably like that.

The highway grew dark and there were no other cars. That made it tough to follow him without being noticed. So, I had to drive casual,

vary the distance between my car and his. But, most importantly –
DON'T LOSE HIM! Not now. This was the break I'd needed and I
had to make the most of it.

His car breezed through the small town of Ellerbee. But then, he
turned off a barely there access road leading into a dark, forested area. I
had to pass it to make sure they didn't see me following. A mile down
the road I pulled onto the soft dirt shoulder and U-turned.

Once I spotted the access road on my return, I stopped the car and
killed my lights. I faced a wall of black forest. No light glow from his
car in the distance. Now what?

I opened the door but the inside dome light turned on, revealing
me. I fumbled to flip it off. Then, I sat still. Waiting and watching. No
movement up ahead.

So, this was it. The encounter I'd been wanting. The one I told Ilsa
had to happen. It could be the first step towards saving us. Or, the last
breath I take.

I got out and shut the door without making a sound.

I stood still and listened. The air was warm, humid. The night talk of
insects and owls was alive and echoing through the trees.

I heard something. A faint thud. Maybe? Too far away and too soft
to indicate which direction it came from.

My eyes adjusted to the dark now that the headlights were off. I
could just about make out the dirt path ahead. I thought about re-
starting the car and driving further down the road. It would save some
time. But, I balked. I didn't want to make any noise. I checked the
highway behind me one last time to make sure no cars were pulling in.
I was alone. I started walking down the dirt road, into the night.

I couldn't tell if my eyes had adjusted more or if the moonlight had
gotten brighter. Either way, I was seeing better and further. The soft
dirt muzzled my footsteps and I picked up the pace.

I reached a sharp bend in the road and stopped to catch my breath.
I looked back at the path I had traveled. With my breath just about
under control I listened for the couple that had traveled ahead of me.
My pounding heart made it difficult to hear much. The insects and
owls didn't help.

But, her scream ripped through the night.

It was terrifying and loud enough to make me jump and get my
adrenaline pumping. Danger was the only interpretation.

I ran as fast as I could along the twisting path, following the fresh
pressed tire tracks in the sand. Gnats and mosquitos crashed into me.

Something bigger whizzed past my ear. I didn't stop. My lungs started to tighten but I pushed on. I needed to get there.

I dead-stopped at seeing his car a hundred feet ahead. My shoe slipped in thick sand causing my leg to buckle and me to tumble to the ground. I pushed myself right up, even though my knee was killing me. Sand coated my sweat soaked skin. I brushed it off, but kept my eyes fixed ahead.

There – a flashlight beam. Beyond his car. I flopped back down and rolled to the side of the road, next to a row of palmetto scrub. The flashlight was shining the opposite direction. I guessed about fifty feet past the car and off the trail, amongst the trees.

I got up and snuck over to the car, slowing about fifteen feet away and watching to see if any one – any life – was in it. All clear. I walked up to the trunk. There was the Union County license plate I had seen before. At that time I had no clue I'd be making a pilgrimage here to save my life. To save Ilsa's.

I touched the trunk. Metal still warm from the day and driving. It sent a shock through my system. Eerie and surreal to touch anything belonging to my enemy. This car drove him to kill me. It was a mind fuck. This guy wanted me dead.

Another scream.

I dropped fast, belly first onto the trail. I could hear the scream echo through the forest. More screaming came. Words I couldn't distinguish. But, a horror I could. It was a plea. A desperate one. I peeked under the car and saw nothing. I rose to a squatting position and checked around both sides of the trunk. Nothing still. I got up and walked around to the driver's side door.

Keys in the ignition. I reached in and grabbed them. I ran in the direction of the flashlight. But, I stopped and ran back to the car. The keys popped open the trunk. The trunk light turned on so I kept it low. A quick survey of contents: rope, dirty boots, gas can, a small hatchet that looked intricately designed. Top quality. Just like the ones they'd attacked me with before.

I grabbed the hatchet and started towards the light in the woods. As loud as the insects and owls had been before, their noise now seemed to disappear as I focused all of my senses on the area of my approach. The flashlight beam was still shining. But, now it was stationary. Someone walked through the beam and their giant shadow cut tall across the trees.

Her voice grew louder. I couldn't understand the words. But, I now understood she was gagged. He didn't care what she had to say.

I tiptoed through the scrub. Taking my time, careful not to snap twigs or crunch leaves too loud. Creeping closer...

The light grew bigger and brighter. I could hear the slink of metal chain links running over each other. I heard bark rubbing off trees. I heard the grunt and groan of a man engaged in focused physical labor.

I got low behind a cluster of palmetto scrub and peered through its fronds into the clearing ahead. The executioner moved around, agile, swift, and intense. His shirt was off. His body glistened with sweat in the humid Florida night. He looked off screen, where I couldn't see. A devilish smile on his face.

Her gagged voice, I could understand her words - "Please, I'll do anything. Just let me...let me go. Please!"

He laughed.

I scooted a few palmettos over to get a new view. He pulled out a large, menacing blade. Like nothing I'd ever seen. Shorter than a sword. Longer that a big hunting knife. With a hard curve to the blade. Like a mini saber, with a diametrically opposed barbed dagger on the end of the handle. This was no knife you'd find at the hunting store. And, it lacked the showy embellishments of gimmicky collector's knives. Like the ones they sell on the home shopping networks. This was a real-deal cutting and killing instrument with a style designed to terrify.

He walked towards me. I skittered back into darkness and pressed my body against the dirt. I stopped breathing and stayed dead still. He came closer. The air in my lungs started to hurt, pinch. I gripped the hatchet, but was in no position to wield it. If he saw me, he'd get a good jump on me.

He leaned down, barely three feet from my face.

Shit!

I tensed and tightened.

He glowed white hot in the light beam.

I started to push my body off the ground.

He reached right at me...

He grabbed the flashlight and turned away from me.

The light beam shining in his face prevented him from seeing me.

Too goddamn close!

But, this was perfect.

His back was too me, I had the hatchet in my hand and an open shot.

Do it! Now!

Kill him!

I got on my knees, then up to a crouching position. I quick-stepped into the small clearing.

My eyes followed the light beam. Hatchet cocked. Ready to strike.

But, I would never be ready for what I saw before me.

40

The flashlight beam made her glow. She was naked and restrained to a tall pine tree. Belly against bark, chains wrapped tight around her neck and lower back. Tears streaked down her cheeks, her pink lips twisted and trembling. Her feet kicked up sand but offered no defense. Red scratches raked across her arms and back made it clear she'd been raped. Her back and bum were fully exposed for the blade.

But, it got worse.

As the flashlight beam swung from side to side with his natural movements, it revealed a forest of rotting corpses chained to the trees behind her. All disemboweled and in various stages of decomposition. At least, six or seven rows deep.

Girls just like her. Innocent, pretty, and fooled. All killed with no chance for escape.

It was the worst thing I'd ever seen. A raccoon nibbled at a dead girl's blood-caked calf.

She saw me over his shoulder and screamed, "Help!"

He caught it.

He spun around and slashed with the blade. He missed. The flashlight blinded me. I kicked without looking and connected. He grabbed his ribs as I blinked vision back into my eyes.

"You!" he said, incredulous.

He ran at me slashing that beast of a blade. I ducked and chopped his wrist as he passed. He screamed as my small blade ripped through his right forearm causing muscle meat to flop away from the bone. He had to put the blade in his other hand.

We circled and sized each other up.

"How did you find me?" he said.

"I followed the stink," I said and took a jab at him. He blocked. We fell apart and circled again.

"Your death warrant's been signed. You're a dead man."

A French accent. It sounded like it had drawn out and slowed down after years of living in the Southern United States.

"I didn't do anything to you," I said. "Why are you guys trying to kill me?"

"I don't have to explain to you."

"Who hired you to kill Ken Kerenz?"

He swung at me. The blade slashed through my shirt, across my pecks. Not deep or painful, but scary close. I stepped back to give myself more room.

He pointed the tip of his blade at me.

"You been a real pain in our ass. Père don't like that."

"Who?"

He slashed and slashed. I jumped back and stumbled, landing hard against the tree. Her tree. She screamed in my ear as he charged with the blade. I dove at his legs and clipped him hard. He dropped the flashlight as he went up and over me.

She screamed again.

I got to my feet, grabbed the light, and shined it in his face. He squinted and stalked towards me.

He tried to project menace by cutting the air with the blade while inching closer.

"Père est le maître bourreau. Vous pourrez soumettre à sa lame," he said. I could tell by his smirk he knew I wouldn't understand it.

"I don't know what you're saying. But, I know you left France when executions were outlawed. And, I know you work at the prison. And, I've told others all about it. Including the press. By that, I mean...you're screwed," I said.

He started to say something else. But, I threw the hatchet at him. He would have only caught a glimpse of it with the flashlight shining in his face. He hit the ground hard.

I ran over. The left side of his forehead was dented in. The back of the hatchet must have hit him. I looked around but couldn't find my blade. So, I grabbed his and raised it to finish him off.

I hesitated.

Then, I remembered: He had wounded Ilsa and killed Ken. And, he tried to kill me.

I brought the blade down hard and fast, slashing his stomach and neck.

I tossed the blade over his body while I watched him start to bleed out. The sand absorbed the blood at first but then it spilled too much too fast and a puddle formed.

A cough.

At the tree. Blood dripped from her lips. The side of her torso had been punctured when he'd launched at me.

I ran over to unchain her. Padlocks held the chains tight.

"Hang on!"

I ran back over to his bleeding body and reached into his pockets. I found a key. And, his wallet. I tucked it in my pocket and ran back to the girl at the tree.

My legs felt weak in the sand. My hands shook and I had to steady myself against the tree to get the key into the lock.

It popped open. I yanked it out and both the chains and the girl slid down the tree into a heap on the ground.

"Come on. I'll get you out of here," I said as I reached under her shoulders to pull her up.

She moaned and resisted. I put too much pressure on her wound. I released that side and pulled her up by the one arm and put it around me.

We staggered back to the killer's car.

"I'm taking you to the hospital. We have a car. We'll get there fast," I said, breathless while setting her in the passenger seat of his car.

I hopped behind the wheel, started the engine, and backed out of there as fast as I could without losing control. At the sharp bend, I ran the car into a cluster of palmetto scrub. I had to stop and pull out and slowly re-work the angle. Then we were flying. Sand and dust kicked up and swirled in the headlight beams. I had my arm around her seat and looked back over my shoulder.

"Shit!"

I stopped too late. I rammed right into the front of Teddy's car—the one I'd been driving. I pulled the car forward.

"Sorry, we have to switch cars," I said.

I ran around and pulled her out of the car. She was heavy and slow to move. Her heels dug deep into the sand as I dragged her over to

Teddy's car. I laid her over the hood while I fished out his keys. Found them, opened the door, got her in, shut the door.

As I walked around the front of the car, I took the dead guy's keys and threw them as far into the rough scrub as I could. On the off chance he did live, I made sure it was a long, miserable walk back to town for him.

I backed Teddy's car out to the main without even looking to see if traffic was coming. We drove off into the night.

The car raced across the quiet, black asphalt. Forest darkness to the left and right. Blue moonlight shimmered on the long road ahead.

She barely moved.

"Hang on. We're almost there. It's not your time to go," I said.

I moved the hair off her face. She looked out of it, fading fast.

I felt the extra wallet under my ass, pulled it out, and flipped it open.

His driver's license. I finally had a name: Clovis Gagnon.

I screamed triumphant.

Son of a bitch, I fucking found you!

I snooped through the rest of the wallet. Nothing of consequence.

No matter. I had what I needed. A name and an address.

It was exhilarating. I survived my first battle. I got one of them. I could fight them, despite what Ilsa and DG believed. Knowing that, and perhaps because my adrenaline was still pumping, I didn't feel any remorse over killing him. Especially not after seeing all those dead girls in the forest.

It wasn't over...but it was a good start. I didn't have to worry about ornery Clovis any more.

That one's for Ilsa. The next one will be for Ken.

41

Back in town. I found the Lake Butler Hospital and pulled up outside the emergency room entrance. I ran in, grabbed a wheelchair, and loaded the girl into it. I wheeled her back up to the reception desk.

"I found this girl being attacked by a man. She needs help, now," I said.

They looked at her battered, naked body and started to ask questions but I dashed out of there. As I ran to the car, I wished the girl well.

I was exhausted but electrified, run down and revitalized. This night had almost done me in. My muscles were feeling the burn of excessive action. But, for the first time in many desperate days I was hopeful.

My mind raced as I drove back to Starke. If Teddy had any kind of breakthrough on the middleman, we'd be golden. We could trace the name Clovis Gagnon. Maybe find his home address and go there. He wouldn't be coming home anytime soon. If he lived alone, we could go in and try to find clues about the men he works with. Maybe I could circle back to the Warden. Tell him I know Gagnon is one of the executioners. Who are the others? Tell me.

The Warden said *they* came from France. Teddy said *they* could be a family. That felt right. That meant find more Gagnon's in the phone book. In search engines. Hunt their French asses down and make them pay.

Find the middleman. Stop them, turn them in, and clear my name. Ilsa's, too. We needed the middleman to call off the press and the cops. He had to be the one with the power and the influence. Maybe it was Wingart. When he learns the executioners and the middleman are dead or headed to jail he might have the juice to clear us. He sure as hell owed me.

I couldn't help but feel it was all coming together. Like we had done the high climbing and were now set to glide down and wrap this up. I slashed a man to death not even forty-five minutes ago and I couldn't help but smile.

I thought about falling into the Rainbow River, letting the cool water wash over me. Sinking down below the surface and floating above the lilting river grass. As I floated, my muscles would untie from their clenched knots. My tendons and veins and arteries would relax back to normal posture. The stress would float out of me and catch the current down river.

I thought of Ilsa. A smile back on her face. Ilsa behind the bar, at the helm of her empire. Only now she'd be hobbling. She could pull it off. For others it might be a handicap. For her, the bum leg just added character on top of character.

I thought of writing again. It had been too long. When extreme circumstances strike, normalcy becomes the ultimate luxury. There is no desire for excess. No striving for more. Just a need for what you had when you had it good. That's where I was now. I just wanted to see my woman, go home, and do normal things.

As I pulled into the motel, I felt that could happen soon.

A light was on in our room. I could hear the television through the door. I knocked.

"Teddy, it's me. Walt."

The door opened and I stepped in excited to tell the news.

Something big and solid smashed me from behind.

I fell onto the corner of one of the double beds and spilled onto the floor. My elbow smashed against the thick, oak leg of the desk. It hurt awful. I grabbed it and turned to get up but a massive boot stomped on my chest and pinned me to the ground.

I looked up and there he was. A big, brawny, brute of a man. Thick fists that looked like they could smash cinderblocks. A barrel chest that stretched the limits of his shirt's cotton. Menacing arms that looked like they'd been cut by lifting raw steel. A dusting of dark hair coated each arm up to the biceps. These weren't mirror jock steroid arms. This dude was the real deal. Thick neck, a grooved, stubbled jaw, and impersonal eyes that gleamed like hot dimes in sunshine.

His facial features resembled Clovis'. But, he was older. Family, for sure. Maybe father?

Brain click.

Clovis has used the word 'père' in the corpse forest. Fourth grade French class snap back reminded me 'père' meant 'father'. Clovis had been saying something about his daddy. And now, daddy was staring down at me while his scuffed work boot crushed my rib cage and forced air from my lungs.

I hadn't seen him before, but I recognized the other one slinking into the room behind him. He was one of the men from Ilsa's house. Same rough exterior, but leaner and meaner. Similar age as Daddy Big Boot. They looked like brothers.

They sneered down at me. Papa put more weight on his foot, on my chest. I grabbed the desk leg with one hand and clutched a bed comforter with the other and waited for my rib cage to crack at any moment.

Where was Teddy?

"Teddy?" I said. It hurt to turn my neck and scan the room.

Papa leaned forward and rested his elbow on his knees. I could barely breathe from the pressure.

"Nous avons quelque chose de spécial pour vous, oiseau insaisissable." He didn't say it so much as the words seethed out through his yellow, crooked teeth. His breath was doused with garlic and brine.

He reached down and wrapped his hand around my face. The thumb pressed my right ear while the web of his hand covered my jaw and his long fingers went past my left ear and up into my hair. Massive hands. He squeezed and I had to tense the muscles in my jaw to keep him from snapping it off.

Then he gave me a hard slap that felt more like a punch. I had to shake it off.

"Remy!" he roared as he stood straight again.

Remy, the brother, stepped forward and held out what looked like a pre-twentieth century axe. I'm no expert. But it, like the blade in Clovis' hand and the tiny hatchet I'd pulled out of his car trunk, looked crafted by a master and deadly beyond belief.

Remy set the business end of the cool blade against my throat. It was so heavy it probably could have decapitated me if he just let go of the handle. No swinging required.

Blade in place, Papa stepped off me and walked towards the door.

Remy spoke in French tinged English, "Rise. You are coming with us." He grabbed my shirt and pulled me up. Papa kept the blade pressed against my throat the entire time we walked out of the room. He didn't seem to mind if anybody outside saw what was happening. In fact, a couple of bystanders did see us and did nothing about it. When I made eye contact with one of them, they just moseyed away as if recalling an oven they'd forgotten to turn off.

Remy pushed me over to the same truck in which they'd tried to lock Ilsa and I in back at Crystal River. I had the depressing feeling there were no bikers coming to save the day this time. They opened the doors.

Teddy lay battered inside.

"Teddy!" I said.

Remy and Papa picked me up by the waist of my pants and threw me in the back of the truck. I fell hard against the metal floor, but didn't dwell on it. Maybe I was used to the beatings. The thick metal doors slammed shut, then locked. A moment later the truck started and began rolling.

"Teddy, you okay? Teddy," I said.

He was out of it. But, not dead. I could hear him breathing.

I felt awful. Just a kid. And, another person I'd put in danger. If I got through this ordeal alive I was going to have some serious I.O.U.s to pay back.

Man.

Just when I thought I was back in control, everything changed. Instead of breaking the case with Teddy, I now felt like we were being transported to death row, where I would see the executioners do what they do best.

Send a man to his grave.

42

I relaxed as much as I could during the drive. Why bother trying to break out of the truck? On the off chance that happened, I'd have to leap onto a road and kiss the pavement at sixty miles an hour. That guaranteed at least a few broken bones and a nightmare case of road rash. I'd also have to leave Teddy behind to fend for himself, which I couldn't do. And, the last thing I wanted to do now that I'd found Remy and Papa was run away from them. No, this was the inevitable conflict we'd spent the last week heading towards. This is what I wanted. And somehow, that emboldened me.

Do or die.

I was either going to stop or kill them.

Or, they were going to...

Let's think positive. Let's presume I still had a chance even though all signs read otherwise. Let's ignore the dire state of my present predicament and think about what survival options may still remain. *Imagine the possibilities.* Pretty sure I had written that saccharine aspirational line a time or two for commercials. Now, it was time to take my own advice.

Features and benefits. That's what I dealt in as infomercial scriptwriter. Let the features reveal the benefits...

Feature: They could have easily killed me at the motel with one of their pretty poison filled glass capsules. But, they didn't. They let me live.

Benefit: I had been given more time. To plan, scheme, rest, and rejuvenate. How any of that would be put to my advantage was still unknown. But, at least I had it. I wasn't done yet.

Feature: By letting me survive, I might see more of their operation.

Benefit: That will be handy if I escape later on and can't stop them right away.

The truck hit a pothole and jostled me into the hard metal bench. Teddy rolled over and groaned.

Question – How did they find Teddy? What hive did he stumble into that sent these killer bees into a frenzy? Unanswerable. He'd have to give me the scoop when he woke up.

Back to features and benefits.

Feature: I knew about Clovis. I could lie to them and say we made a deal. I could tell them Clovis was in jail. And, ready to talk. That didn't seem like much. I'd mention Clovis' corpse forest as proof. But, I had the terrible feeling they approved of it. Like it was a hobby to keep his killing skills sharp. Instead of collecting baseball cards, little Clovis played with dolls. And, he loved to put them on display. Sickening.

If worse came to worse, I could let them know where to find Clovis' body if they would let Teddy go.

Benefit: It wouldn't save my life. But, it would help Teddy. And, my conscience. It was something.

Feature: I had a belt.

Benefit: I could use it to climb, tie someone up, or strangle. Better than nothing.

Feature: My body may be beat to shit, but my mind was still sharp.

Benefit: Sticks and stones may have broken a few of my bones. But, I could still charm and bullshit my way free. Maybe.

It was all about making a connection. They tried to kill me because they were hired to. They didn't know me. They didn't care. It was impersonal. It was business. Unfortunately, their business is killing. But if I could forge a common bond with them, then there was a chance I could persuade them into a different deal.

One that let me live.

Lord knows how I'd bond with a pair of psycho French ex-pat killers. But, we're all human, right? Seemed like a stretch with these guys. But, it was my only chance.

What the hell. I'd spent the last decade plus talking the money out of complete strangers wallets. Maybe I could talk my way out of these strangers murder plans.

The truck slowed, turned, and started to bump around. We had turned off the pavement and onto a dirt road. We were getting close.

No sound from the boys up front. Not surprising. They didn't seem like the chatty type.

I laid flat and stretched my body, head to toe. My injuries nagged at me, but weren't debilitating. The stretching loosened me up for any action to come. I might need to act the second they opened that door. In fact, that might be my best bet.

Feature: The metal truck doors. I could let them unlock the doors and kick that heavy metal into their unsuspecting teeth. It would stun at least one of them. Best if I hit smaller Remy. That could knock him back or out. And, despite Papa's brawn and power, I suspected I could outrun him. That would buy me more time.

Or, would they expect something like that? Sometimes you just gotta go for it.

Teddy started to talk, "Where...what the..."

I crawled over and brought my face close to his.

"Teddy. It's me, Walt," I said. "Do you understand what I'm saying?"

He looked in the direction of my voice. A few slow blinks and we made eye contact. A moment unsure. Then, recognition.

"Walt?'

"Yes."

He took a deep breath, rubbed his face, and ran fingers through his hair.

"Man, I screwed up."

"We're not out of it yet, bud. We're in van being driven by the guys who attacked you. They got me, too, when I returned to the motel."

His clarity returned at an exponential rate. "Did you find anything out?"

"I found the guy in the photo. His name is Clovis Gagnon. And, he's dead," I said.

"You...you killed him?"

"It was him or me. And, if it had been me it also would have been a young girl he'd had strung to a tree," I said.

He tried to process it, but instead looked off to another part of the rumbling truck. His face showed things still weren't making much sense.

I nudged his shoulder. "Teddy."

He looked at me.

"What did you find out? And, how did they find you?" I said.

"I'm trying to remember," he said.

"Did you discover anything at the library? Speak with anyone? Remember, you were going to look for—"

He looked away and said, "What's that smell?"

I smelled it as soon as the words were out of his mouth. Something bitter. Too dark to see...

43

They slapped me awake. Words were spoken. But, emerging to consciousness I couldn't make out what they were saying. Or who was saying it, or...

My eyes fluttered open to blurred vision. A few blinks and it started to clear. I wanted to rub my eyes but couldn't move my arms. More blinking and I could start to make out a few of the surrounding details.

I was in a room. It was brown. Wood beams, wood floors, wood walls. All natural cuts. Nothing looked processed. Nothing smoothed down. It was like a hurricane had whipped a forest into the air, cracked everything apart, and it all landed in the shape of this room.

A cabin vibe but not cabin size. This room was much bigger. Like a mess hall or a church bingo facility. It smelled of wood and faintly of smoke. And, it looked more like a workshop than living quarters, with assorted workstations scattered throughout. Each station appeared to serve a different purpose. A massive wooden workbench sprawled through the middle of the room. Metal tools were laid across it. A pair of heavy duty clamping vices perched on the end of it.

I pinpointed the source of the smoke smell - a blast furnace at the side of the room. It showed signs of being used often and for a long time. Close to it stood a worn and scuffed anvil situated atop a thick tree stump that elevated it up to waist level.

I looked past the anvil and saw its output: The wood walls running out from the furnace were covered with swords, axes, hatchets, and blades of every conceivable variety. And, they all had the same professional flair I had seen on the daggers, knives, and sabers used against me over the past several days. So clean and precise were the sword maker's skills that each gleam was a seductive invitation to butcher. My skin prickled and terror grew inside. Whoever made these was a master.

And the master walked into my line of sight.

It was the one called Remy. As ugly as before, but now clad in a dirty, leather apron and calfskin gloves and holding a large, heavy hammer. He sized me up as he walked over to and then leaned against the big workbench. He rested the hammer on his shoulder and kept staring.

I blinked first. To cover it, I looked around some more. That's when I saw I was sitting in a wooden, straight back chair with flat armrests. Wide metal cuffs restrained my wrists and ankles. And, I felt something on my head.

"Is this...am I in an electric chair?"

I wasn't sure what the unit of measurement was for a laugh. But, whatever it was, Remy emitted one "laugh" without smiling, then nodded and felt the need to say, "Zzzzap," in benign fashion. Like he was sick of his nagging girlfriend and had just said, "whatever."

I snapped to full consciousness at this revelation. My heart rate increased, my breathing accelerated, and sweat beaded on my brow. Worse *had* come to worse and I didn't know how to get out of it. Time to start talking.

"I'm pretty sure there's been a massive misunderstanding between us," I said, grasping.

He shook his head.

"Look, Remy. Right? Your name is Remy?"

No response.

"I like what you've done with the place. You're obviously very good at sword making."

I nodded my head towards the sword wall. He followed my gaze with a casual glance. Like he'd seen it a thousand times before. Big whoop.

"You know, I've actually sold swords before. And, I have an eye for quality craftsmanship. I really do. And, never have I ever seen craftsmanship as good as yours. I mean it. I'm not just saying that. It's truly superb."

"I know this," he said.

"I'm sure you do. My question is why haven't you shared your work with the world," I said. "You know how much money you could make? I could hook you up with the right people, get those things selling all across the country, like that." I snapped my finger and raked my wrist against the jagged edge of the metal cuff.

"You can't do no thing when you are dead," he said in his French accent. "But, you will learn all about my craftsmanship on the way."

What I would have done to wipe that shitty sneer off his face with the very hammer he was holding.

"Does that mean you're not going to electrocute me?" I said, hopeful.

He just shrugged. Then, he walked out of the room through a door to my left.

My eyes glanced around the room for any chance of escape, something to break these cuffs, anything. My perusing stopped when I took a closer look at the large workbench. Not only was it chipped and scuffed from heavy, regular use. It also had crimson stains on it.

A shocking pain ripped through me.

My body convulsed and slammed back against the chair. My arms and legs seized up against the metal cuffs. They dug into my skin. I bit my tongue. The hair on my arms stood up and I could hear the electrical zip-zap as a burning, metallic smell stung my nose.

A second later the shocking stopped, but the pain lingered. I buzzed, numb. In shock from being shocked. And, the only clear thought that passed through my mind was that this was no prop electric chair. It was wired for action. They had me primed to kill. That thought was almost as defeating as the electricity itself.

For the first time, I felt it was over. I had lost. Dread came from knowing I'd never see Ilsa again. I wouldn't be able to protect her. I wouldn't be able to help her with her bum leg. I'd never see my kids' beautiful faces again. Never kiss their soft cheeks or hear their voices. And worse, they'd have to grow up without a father. Without even knowing what happened to me. It wasn't fair. It wasn't fucking fair!

I braced for another jolt of electricity.

But, the death shock didn't come.

Instead, I heard the squeaking of caster wheels rolling from the direction Remy had just exited. I turned as far in that direction as I could. But, I couldn't see much.

The squeaking and rolling sound got louder. Remy backed in through the doorway he'd departed through moments ago. He dragged whatever was squeaking. Something tall and wooden. Two vertical beams situated atop a thick wooden platform. A cross beam connected the vertical beams at the top.

Then, I looked down. Connecting the two vertical beams at their base was a three foot-tall wood panel. But, on the top and in the middle it had a U-shape cut out. The top of the U was about eight inches wide. Wide enough for a man's neck. That entire lower panel was stained brownish crimson and looked well used.

The entire piece looked like a sturdy, made-the-old-way, genuine antique.

Remy smirked when he saw the shock on my face.

The shock of me recognizing the guillotine.

44

He wheeled the guillotine over to the worktable. The guillotine's rolling platform base fit flush between the table's legs, as if by design. Remy extracted a set of thick wooden pegs from inside his leather apron and plugged them into the table legs, securing the guillotine. Then he removed a wide metal sheath and revealed the gleaming, ghastly blade. It was beyond sharp and angled for effortless slicing — through flesh, spine, tendons, and arteries.

Remy twisted to peek at my face, to see what I thought about that. I wanted to vomit I was so scared. But, I tried not to show it.

He set the blade cover down on a nearby bench. He strolled over to the blast furnace and picked up a thick cut of wood that had been sitting on a pile of logs next to the furnace. He brought it back over and set it on the worktable, situating it so the wood hung over the table edge and under the blade.

As if working through a well-rehearsed and choreographed routine, he stepped to the side of the guillotine and extracted a rope out of a groove in the wood. The rope was tied to a metal cleat bolted to one of the vertical beams. He untied it, then let up a bit on the slack.

The blade started to fall down it's grooved path between the beams. Even though it had only dropped three inches it still made that nauseating 'shwink' sound you think of death blades making.

I struggled under my restraints. No luck. I wasn't getting out. Not until they let me out, which I presumed would be once they were ready to take me over to the guillotine and chop my head off.

Remy pulled the rope until the blade reached the top of the wooden arch. Then he threaded it through a series of what looked like gears that lead to a three-foot high metal pull lever. With the rope properly threated, he locked the lever in place. It kept the rope taut. All he'd have to do now was yank that lever to release the rope and drop the blade. I had to agree; This was a much classier approach.

"You know what this is?" he said, allowing his French native tongue to bleed through.

I nodded. "I've seen 'em. Never up close."

"This was the official guillotine of France."

"Charming."

"Is marvelous," he said as he took it in with an admiring glare and caressed it. "This is the only Guillotine ever used for execution in France," he said. "Dating back to the very first execution of Nicholas Jacques Pelletier. Twenty-five Avril 1792."

"So, I'll ask again. Why the hell are you killing people for hire when you could make a mint selling that thing?" I said.

I glanced around the room, "Your lifestyle doesn't appear to be too ostentatious. You could ride that payday for quite a while."

"No, no. You do not understand," he said. "It was used for every execution since 1792. All the way until 1977, when executions were banned in my country."

"You lost your job and that this was your severance package, that it?" I said. I didn't point out the awful pun.

"When one loses any other job they simply go and get another with what skills they have. But, when we lost our job, we lost our place in society."

I wasn't really in the mood to hear his sob story since my current sob story of impending death trumped his. But, I was latched into an electric chair. He had a captive audience.

"When you are an executioner you carry a burden. It is the dirtiest of work. And, no matter how much you accept it or reconcile it with the public good, you are tainted by it. Society needs you, but they do not accept you. They do not want to acknowledge such a person exists. So, you are forced to live on the fringe. So it was for my family for generations. Because a child of the executioner is tainted from conception as well, no? The only business for the child to learn is the family business. Death."

He watched my eyes to see if he'd made a connection...if I was starting to understand the meaning behind his history lesson. Not really.

"Where are you going with this?" I said.

His expression grew stern, "You continue to ask why we kill. We kill because it is simply what we do. You look down on it. But, this..." He gestured to the guillotine. "Is a job the world demands but does not respect. It is a job we sacrifice our lives for. It is our fate."

"Oh. Sounds more to me like you're society's garbage men taking out the human trash."

His face grew dark. He was insulted and simmering.

"We lost everything in France. We are forced to lower ourselves working in your grimy prison. And now, you insult me for doing your dirty work!"

"You kill people for money. You're soulless whores. You killed my friend. You almost killed my girlfriend—"

"Will," he inserted.

"Listen, jerk. You better not slip up. Because if I get the chance – just one fucking chance – I'm going to kill you better than you've ever killed anyone in your long, goddamned illustrious career."

"This will not happen. You will not escape. You will not 'get lucky'," he said. "The only reason you are still alive is because we respect your tenacity and determination. You are a capable adversary. It is the French way to respect such from an enemy."

"Well, isn't that evolved thinking."

He nodded, thinking I agreed with him.

"That doesn't mean much when you have me strapped into an electric chair."

He leaned back on the table, crossed his hands in front of his crotch, and looked at me. A curious smile worked cross his face.

"You will appreciate this guillotine more once Luther returns. My brother."

"I would appreciate you guys fucking off, letting me go, and laying your own heads under that blade."

He looked up at the guillotine blade and shrugged.

"It would be a good blade to die by," he said.

The double doors at the far end of the room kicked open. And, there was brother Luther of the big boots. He stared me down as he entered. I only broke the stare to see what he lugged in.

Teddy.

He was hogtied, hands to ankles behind his back. Luther held a handle rope that looped around Teddy's shoulders and crotch. He carried him like a heavy duffle bag full of human.

Luther walked and, with one hand, lifted Teddy up and set him belly first onto the worktable. He grabbed Teddy's ropes and dragged him to the edge of the table, until his neck rested in the guillotine slot.

Teddy looked at me. Little boy scared.

Guilt punched me in the heart.

I jerked in the chair. "No!"

Luther stared at me as he walked over and took hold of the guillotine lever.

"He didn't do anything and he doesn't know anything. He just gave me a ride to town. That's it! I swear! Please don't!" I said.

Teddy let out a sob. I heard Luther yank the large, wooden lever. I heard the rope hiss through the channel and the blade start to drop.

I saw Teddy's tear hit the floor.

I saw his head splash into it.

45

I squeezed my eyes shut, as tight as I could. I was shaking, trembling. I couldn't look. I couldn't look. I couldn't see what I knew lay on the floor in front of me. I couldn't *not* look.

But, there it was. Teddy's head – eyes closed, face expressionless while blood from the body above poured on top of it. His face and hair were soaked and glistening like he had been swimming in a red lake.

It was the worst thing ever.

And, I had caused it.

Teddy was dead and headless because I didn't stop snooping. Because I didn't go to Holland. Because I tried to avenge Ken. Who would avenge Teddy?

Grief, guilt, rage, and fear. I felt them all. I wanted to cower and hide. I wanted to snap my arms off so I could get out of this damn chair and run. I wanted to pick the chair up with my broken bleeding arms and smash it down on their faces and drive the sharp corners of metal brackets into their eyes and wipe their stupid faces across the sharp edge of the guillotine blade and shove their battered, shredded bodies into the blast furnace. Nothing was too much for them. Nothing would ever be enough payback for what they had done.

But, I could do nothing. Just look and fester and hate. The worst thing they could do to me at that moment was simply let me sit and look at Teddy. See what they'd done. See what I had caused. No torture existed that would hurt worse than what they had already done to my mind.

But, Luther spoke as he and Remy walked over to my chair.

"You will not be so lucky. You get something even more special."

They unbuckled my restraints, starting at my ankles. I screamed in their faces.

Luther cold-cocked me in the face, stunning me, neutralizing me, shutting me up. Then they unbuckled my handcuffs and dragged me out of there.

Each killer had one of my arms. My feet dragged behind as they lead me through a maze of hallways in the house. Parts of it seemed perfectly normal – a quaint, French-inspired kitchen, past a tidy bathroom, past a row of bedrooms, each with a different decorating twist. We walked down hallways lined with family photos. I caught glimpses of Luther, Remy, and Clovis. Different ages, different stages of life. Pictures of them posing in brick paved public squares.

They stood next to bleeding corpses in black execution hoods. Were they smiling under them?

Pictures showed them leading prisoners to their fate. Pictures of Remy making swords. Pictures of the family in their poor countryside home, the only home around. Pictures of them with a political type. Pictures of them with their old, toothless mother. Pictures of them as boys with their corncob pipe smoking father. Each holding up an executed prisoner's head. They were smiling.

Luther kicked open a back porch door. A trio of ragged, filthy poodles ran up, sniffed, and licked blood splatter off Luther's pant leg. He kicked them away. They yipped and fell in line behind us.

Luther and Remy dragged me down wooden patio steps and across a dead leaf covered yard. They dragged me down a well-worn trail that lead into the woods. A lizard darted past.

My senses amplified. I felt the humid air on my skin. I could smell the minerals in the dirt, the piney aroma of the trees. I could hear the insects buzzing, the owls hooting, frogs croaking, Luther and Remy's feet stomping through leaves, and my feet dragging across them.

We arrived at a wide, circular clearing. The setting sun shot golden beams between trees. Magic hour sunlight. The kind that made it possible to look at someone and clearly see all the details and imperfections in their eyes. And, see all the beauty, too.

At any other house this cleared space would serve well as a meditation garden. But, this was different. The lone stump in the very middle of the circle told me so. So, did the giant double-bladed battle-axe leaning against it.

It was massive. Bigger than any axe I'd ever seen.

The handle seemed as thick as a two-by-four and was wrapped in X-crossed leather strap. The blades were shaped like back-to-back Ds with curvature down the spines that created piercing tips at the top and bottom. An ornate, medieval looking design had been smelted onto the blades.

And, of course, the angled edge of the blades gleamed showing how just sharp a blade could be.

Luther and Remy dragged me over to the stump. Luther picked the axe up by the handle as if it was as light as a baseball bat, then he and Remy slammed me down belly first on the stump. It knocked the wind out of me. A poodle pranced over and licked my nose.

I couldn't move. My arms were numb from being dragged for so long. I could feel the blood rushing back into the parts where their vice-like hands had been squeezing. My legs were still weak from the electrocution.

Luther set the top tip of the battle-axe down on my back. It felt like it weighed a hundred pounds. At least.

"Vous n'êtes pas un homme ... vous êtes la viande!" said Luther.

Remy laughed, "Would you like a translation, Monsieur Asher?"

"Huh?"

"My brother stated, with total accuracy, that you are not a man...you are meat," he said. "What do you think of that?"

Insult to injury.

I said, "Why don't you just get it over with. I'm sure you have clients eagerly awaiting your services."

Remy nodded, "A fine idea."

Remy took hold of the axe handle.

With a snicker he said, "We must take care of you so we can return to our previously scheduled assignment."

Jerk.

I peeked out the corner of my eye as Luther stood over me pulling a black executioner's hood over his head.

Everything inside me sunk. I didn't feel so tough or mouthy anymore.

He pulled a long, leather strap from his pocket. He knelt down and attached it to a metal stake hammered into the ground a few feet from the stump.

I knew he intended to wrap my neck and secure the loose end of the strap to another stake on the opposite side of the stump. Once that happened, I was done. They'd cut my head clean off and my blood would soak down into the earth never to be spoken of again. The rest of my body? I'm sure they had a place in the woods where they could dump it.

Ilsa was right. DG was right. This wasn't a fight I would win. I wished I had listened to her.

46

Remy spun the axe on my back. I could see through peripheral vision when the sharp, wide blades would windmill past my head.

He said something to his brother in French. I got a sense it was about their next assignment. Luther's response sounded impatient, with curt talk and a gesture to me like they gotta get this shit over with first.

The blades spun past my head.

Luther approached with the strap. Time was running out.

Remy looked off into the horizon. His hand held the spinning axe up right.

Luther stepped over, his knees aligned with my shoulders. I felt the warm leather from the strap loop around my neck.

I saw the huge axe blade swing behind my head, running parallel with my spine.

Now!

I rolled hard and fast towards Remy and used my shoulder blade and elbow to shove the heavy axe his way.

I caught him off guard. The blade split his shin wide open.

He screamed and fell over.

I yanked the strap off my neck just as Luther made a grab at me. He missed.

I grabbed for the axe. It was too heavy to swing. I could only pick it up to my waist before dropping it – blade first into Remy's sternum.

His scream stopped short as his sternum cracked and blood pooled into his throat and mouth. His panic convulsions shook the axe deeper into his body.

Luther stopped, stunned to see Remy dying on the ground. He looked to me with rage in his eyes. *Did you just kill my brother?*

Who knows and who cares, I thought.

Luther steeled his nerves then pulled the axe out of his dead, cleaved brother. He cocked it back and stalked towards me, ready to swing.

I staggered backwards, almost falling but keeping my balance.

There was hate in his eyes behind the black mask.

I looked around for a weapon, anything. There was nothing.

Luther roared as he brought down the massive axe. I jumped back, just avoiding the blade. The axe chopped so deep into the stump Luther needed a second to wiggle it out.

That bought me time. So, I ran deeper into the woods. I never would have made it past him had I gone for the house.

I stopped to look back. He marched towards me, ready to straight up slay me.

I found a few large rocks buried in the soil. I dug two out and kept moving into the forest. I had to keep space between us. If he caught up to me, there was no way I'd be able to fight him. He was all muscle and hate.

I threw a rock at him. He swatted it away with the axe and charged forth.

I leaped over a small brook, which cut through the trail I had been following. The grass had been pressed down due to regular traffic. Unless the French brothers just enjoyed nature hikes, that meant I was going somewhere specific. And, only he knew what was ahead. Maybe he knew there was no way out. What would I do then?

I kept moving. I put enough distance between the two of us, maybe about thirty feet, where I could slow down to look for more rocks or some sort of weapon.

I reached down for a rock and--

The tree right next to me cracked and split, shooting splinters against my face and body. The axe had flow mere inches from my head.

I looked back. He ran towards me.

If he could throw that massive blade with that much precision, I was in more trouble than I thought. I ran full speed further into the woods.

The ground turned swampy. My shoes stuck microseconds longer and longer the further I ran into the muck. I hoped my shoe wouldn't come off and slow me down.

My shoe got stuck in the mud and pulled right off. A glance over my shoulder - he was approaching fast. Despite his massive size, he was able to leap over logs and duck under branches with agile ease. The big battle-axe swung in his hands.

I left the shoe and boogied further into the woods. Next thing I knew, I was up to my knees slogging through swamp water. I used the hard, upright knobs of nearby cypress trees to keep my balance and propel myself forward. The swamp seemed to sprawl forever in every direction. Options were running out.

With the water slowing me down he started to catch up. He charged into the deeper water without hesitation. I pressed on. I threw my last rock. He dodged it. He held the axe up out of the water. It was cocked back on his shoulder and ready to swing at the perfect moment.

Up to my waist now. I debated giving up running and switching to swimming. But, just as I was about to dive I saw the gory remnants of a human corpse floating in the water.

Headless, missing an entire shoulder and top of a rib cage, and recently plucked by vultures.

So, this is what they do with the bodies.

It was nauseating.

It also stopped my forward progress.

But, not Luther's. He closed in, ready to strike.

I stepped forward and sunk down to my neck. Either I'd stepped off an underwater ledge or the silty muck could no longer hold my weight. I was going down.

I spun myself in the water and looked back. Luther was twenty feet away and charging. The water wasn't slowing him down. And, he wasn't sinking.

Fifteen feet away.

I looked around for options. Nothing.

Ten feet.

Luther lifted the battle-axe with both hands over his head. He charged forward.

Five feet.

I ducked down into the dark water.

Three feet.

Luther shot forward, axe first. The deadly blade flew right at my head.

I submerged down to my chin...my mouth...my nose...

Something massive shot out of the water between Luther and me.

An alligator. Big, green, and with a jaw full of razor sharp teeth. It's jagged, leathery back was covered in algae slop and dripping with mud.

I froze.

The alligator's teeth sunk into Luther's massive torso. Geysers of blood squirted in several directions. Some even splashed near me. I knew it more than I saw it. I couldn't take my eyes off the dueling beasts.

Luther smashed his axe blade into the gator's back forcing a deep croak from its throat. The blade was sharp enough to cut through the tough exterior, but didn't go deep.   The gator flopped and rolled Luther under the water. The tip of its tail splashed mere inches from my half submerged face.

They were rolling my way!

I dove under the water and swam out of the way. When I came up they had moved several feet in the opposite direction. Luther pulled the gator out of the water and hacked off one of its hind legs. Blood poured out of the wound and turned the tail crimson. When the tail flicked, it shot blood in every direction.

Luther swung the blade in between the top and bottom of the gator's jaw. The hard, heavy metal sent gator teeth flying.

The gator roared as it attempted to clamp down on Luther. They both fell back under the water.

Silence.

Long enough for me to look around and see...

More gators. Their beady eyes just above the water's surface. They smelled blood and were heading my way.

Being neck deep in a body of water with a gator nearby is its own special kind of terror. One that makes you get the hell out of there, everything else be damned.

Run!

I splashed and ran and grabbed my way through the swamp, away from the gators, away from Luther and the gator thrashing a short distance away. My heart felt ready to burst. I'd never been this scared in my life.

A loud gator croak echoed across the water. I didn't look back. Just run, crawl, fight, GO!

I reached higher ground and fell flat in the mud. I crawled and kicked my way to drier soil, pushed myself up on a log, flailed over it, desperate to put something – anything! - between me and the gators and...

Luther screamed.

I got up fast and looked back. Luther ripped the battle-axe through the gator he'd been wrestling. It flopped dead in the water. But, by that point the gators that had been after me were nearly on him. He started smashing the battle-axe into the water.

A gator sunk its teeth into his thigh and dragged him down.

One more executioner about dead and done for.

I'll take it.

Now, get me the hell away from these beasts.

I ran through the woods, the way I'd come earlier. The sun was close to setting, leaving a dark blue sky with clouds tinged pink. When I arrived at the clearing, Remy was still dead on the ground. Good. I ran towards the house.

Another cry echoed from deep in the swamp. I didn't look back, didn't acknowledge it, didn't care. All I wanted was more distance between me and those gators and this hellhole. Even though I'd won the battle, I felt like I was sinking into a rotten quicksand of sleaze and death. I was desperate to wash off me. But, I knew I wouldn't be able to cleanse my mind of these horrors for a long, long time.

47

I ran into the house and down the hallways through which they'd dragged me. As anxious as I was to flee, curiosity stopped me. I studied the photos on the walls: The executioners, smiling. Happier times? I suppose they'd had them. One picture in particular caught my eye. I pulled it off the wall and examined it. It was the four executioners – Clovis, Remy, Luther, and the man I had killed on the street near Ilsa's, "Barry Wilson". They were standing with another man. He looked familiar. His face had similar features to the other four men. They were related. Luther and Remy was the older pair. Clovis, Barry Wilson, and this other man were younger. I ripped off the back panel of the frame and pulled the picture out. There, on the back, written in finely detailed cursive – *Pere Luther, Uncle Remy, et fils Clovis & Adolphe et Archibald.*

Wait a minute.

I looked at the photo.

I'd seen that face before.

But, this picture had to be at least fifteen years old. I couldn't place it. I moved on.

I ran into the weapon room. Teddy's body was dead on the worktable and appeared to have completely drained of blood, which was everywhere. I had to steel myself from vomiting. It was horrible. I ran towards the door on the other side of the room as fast as I could.

But, I stopped. There was something I had to do.

I turned around to the worktable. The worst of Teddy was at the far end. I needed to check his pockets. To see. Just, to see. If there was a clue. A note. Something.

I walked over to the table. The willies sent chills down my back. I didn't want to touch a dead body. Let alone one I felt I'd been responsible for. But, I had to do it.

Teddy's blood had spilled under and around the table. That meant I'd have to walk through it. More willies. Bad ones. Some things you can't un-see. I would never forget this nightmare.

I couldn't do it. Besides being beyond gross, somehow it felt disrespectful to walk my muddy shoes onto this man's blood. The very thing that had kept him alive.

So, I climbed up onto the table, which was not bloody, and crawled across it My arms and legs were shaky – from fear, from shock, from a mental hex I put on myself that made me think I would slip and fall any moment now.

But, that didn't happen. Instead, I reached Teddy and crawled up to his pockets. I placed my knees between his legs and did my best not to touch any part of him.

I dug my fingers in his pockets. Back left pocket, nothing. Back right pocket, nothing. I had to check the front pockets. Eww.

I took a big breath then wiggled my hand under his body. His dead weight made him difficult to lift. But, my fingers crawled inside his pocket. Nothing. Damn.

I shifted weight to my other leg and reached under his left side, wiggled my hand under his torso, and guided my crawling fingers into his pocket. Slow. Easy. *Don't think about the fact that you're basically fondling a headless corpse, Walt.*

My fingertips hit something. Paper. Folded.

I pushed the body with my free hand, tipping it to make more room to reach. My hand sunk inside the pocket. I paused.

Ugh...it was wet.

I snatched the paper out fast, as if something inside the pocket was going to bite me.

The paper was damp soft and red. No time to sit around. I scrambled off the table, making a point not to step or splash in any of the blood.

Once clear, I unfolded the paper. At first all I saw was the bloody Rorschach print formed by Teddy's blood. Then, I saw his notes. A checklist with names and ideas. Some scratched off, some not. One name jumped out – Arch Gagnon. The politician. Circled and starred. Urgency in the writing. This was important. Did he meet with Arch?

Did he learn something? Did Arch know something?

Arch Gagnon meant something to Teddy. And, then Luther found him. That wouldn't happen doing research at the library. They wouldn't have recognized Teddy or been on the lookout for him.

So, how did Luther find Teddy and know Teddy would lead them to me?

Arch.

Dot connect.

The picture on the wall.

The politician with the executioners. *Fils?*

Fourth grade French class comes through again. *Fils* means...Jesus...

Arch Gagnon is *Archibald*, Luther the executioner's son.

"March with Arch!"

Arch Gagnon is a Union County politician. A politician with clout and reach up to Tallahassee. A politician who could run in elite circles. A politician who would know Rep Wingart. A politician who intimately knew the State of Florida's death row executioners. A politician perfectly poised to bring the two parties together for profit.

"March with" Arch Gagnon is the middleman.

And, he was the last of these bastards alive. He didn't know his brothers were dead. He couldn't. He'd be thinking they'd gotten Teddy and were waiting for me or had me. They could have called him from the truck. They could have done it from the house while Teddy and I were gassed.   Safe assumption – Arch knew Luther and Remy had me and were ready to kill me.

And, what did Remy say? About another job to do? Who? When? Right after they killed my ass dead.

But, that didn't happen. Last Arch heard, I was going to die and Luther and Remy were going to leave for their next job.

Perfect. Arch couldn't know I was alive. And, he was who I needed to see next.

A nearby phone rang.

I froze in place. Two, three, four rings. An old-fashioned sounding landline. That you Arch? Calling to see if your brothers got the job done? Wanting to know if you're in the clear? So, you can put all the blame on me? So, you can get back to business?

Bad news, Arch. Business was about to get brutal.

I snatched a savage looking buck knife off the wall and got out of there.

48

I took the only vehicle around – the truck they'd brought me in. It was a growler; it shook, rumbled, and roared down the road. The soft cloth bench seat bounced me with every bump in the road. My body ached so much, part of me just wanted to pull over and lay down. There'd be time for rest later.

I wasn't a cop or a reporter or a spy...or anyone you'd think could stop three executioners. But, I'd done it. This mild-mannered infomercial writer fought them and beat them. They'd tried to kill me but couldn't. The executioners were dead. I won. That put wind in my sails for the tasks that lay ahead.

First, I had to find Arch Gagnon. He was just as guilty as Luther, Remy, Barry, Clovis...and Wingart. He had to pay, but, how? I'd get him alive. Alive to fill in facts for the cops and prove my innocence. Alive to turn off the phony media witch-hunt that portrayed me as a mass murderer on the loose. I needed him to clear my name. I also wanted to know what he knew – when did the executioners start? How many were there? Who were the victims? Who were the clients? I wanted to know all of it.

I wanted to know how much money he made per execution—a disgusting statistic to be sure. But, I had to know. I had to know what amount of money he thought justified wiping a person off the planet. And, I wanted to know why he felt he had the authority to make that happen.

I wanted a clean slate. That meant throwing light on all the dirty details. Not just the execution ring, but the other stuff. The perks and privileges Wingart hinted about. The stuff Arch Gagnon held over Wingart. Let's get it all out. Show the world and let the motherfuckers burn in the sunlight. I'll be happy to hold the magnifying glass.

Exposure. That was my job now.

As soon as I could make that happen I could go back to my life, to Ilsa, to my kids. And with a little luck, that would happen tonight.

Arch Gagnon dead wouldn't do me much good. I wouldn't get the details I needed. I needed to pin him down and get a confession. On paper and signed. I felt the buck knife at my side. That would provoke the direct response I was looking for. My guess: Gagnon the politician didn't have the stones to stand up to a deadly blade like that. Not like his brothers had.

Speaking of which, I'd need to let the cops know where Clovis' body – and his bodies – were. The gory garden. And, I'd have to tip them off to Luther and Remy's place. A quick look around there and they'd know exactly what those boys had been up to. They'd find weapons, bodies, and maybe even victim details to lock down the case against them.

A regret: Luther, Remy, and Clovis wouldn't get to stew on their very own death row. They wouldn't get to sit in the electric chair they'd once controlled. Wouldn't get to feel the lethal injection push poison into their veins. That's the poetic justice the world deserved.

Rage drove my thinking. I'd need to get that under control. Let the shell shock have its way with me later. That was inevitable. Too much had happened; too much trauma, too much fear, too much death. My mental fabric had been ripped. My previous identity shredded. Like anything, it could be mended back together. But, it would never be the same.

My time in the hospital a few years back had proven this true. In good health otherwise, I had gone in for a routine appendectomy. It was anything but. I aspirated. My lungs collapsed. And, I went into a sedative induced coma. The first doctor gave up on me. A second opinion doc made all the difference and got me on the road to recovery.

However, the sedatives made me freak. I was a raging madman every time they tried to bring me out of the coma. So, they put me back under. It went on for eight long days. And, I knew nothing about it. When I finally woke up a week and a day later I had double vision. My muscles had atrophied so much I couldn't walk, sit up, or even hold a fork.

I improved day by day, but it was terrifying. I dreaded knowing I'd been in good health and still came so close to dying. Just like that...I was almost gone. My parents wouldn't have a son. My kids wouldn't have a father. Ilsa wouldn't have her partner. Despite a quick recovery, it was heavy stuff.

That first week at home alone was scary. I had to keep my mind occupied in order to keep the black thoughts out. I experienced that dire dose of mortality that makes the bravest men cower. Death was inevitable. You just didn't think it was coming for you, right then and there. After a close brush with it, the specter of death became a shadowy template you lay over all the different aspects of your life. It made you wonder how many years you had left with your parents...what you could do for your kids to prepare for when you were gone. Have you lived a full life? Have you made a difference? Questions like these leave you flattened on the couch with tears streaked down your face.

Once the shock of the past several days wore off, and my wounds started to heal, I would again be left alone to contemplate all that had happened – all that was lost and all that was saved. I'd find myself flattened again on the couch wondering *what if*. My hospital shell shock would pale compared to what I psychic trauma I could expect after this.

Arch Gagnon had a big bill to pay. And, I was coming to collect.

The motel where Teddy and I had almost stayed was on the way back into town. I swung into the parking lot and tried the motel room door. Locked. I didn't have the key. So, I ran over to the front desk and was greeted with a very suspicious look from the Indian desk manager. I told him I'd lost the key, could I have another. He relented. I ran back to the room and did a quick search. No notes, no nothing.

I hopped back in the truck and headed for Arch's office. A quick stop at a nearby gas station to get directions was required. As I climbed back into the truck I realized I was no longer worried about being identified as a criminal. The situation had changed enough in my favor.

Ten minutes later I pulled up to a modest strip plaza that housed a hair salon, a pawnshop, and Arch Gagnon's office. I parked away from the building and just watched it for a few moments. A gaggle of country women with big asses, tight t-shirts, and wedged, bleach blonde hair cuts waddled out of the hair salon. They talked their way over to a cluster of SUVs, appeared to make future plans, then drove off in different directions. Meanwhile, a skinny black man exited the pawnshop with a weed whacker. He looked very pleased with his purchase.

I was procrastinating. Not sure why. I was out of energy. The week, the fighting, the battle with Luther and Remy had taken it out of me. A physical confrontation wasn't my top concern with Arch. But, I would need enough gusto to add force to my delivery and make clear his loss was inevitable. Time to get it over with, even if I had to wing it.

The truck door creaked open as I stepped out. I scanned the parking lot – still paranoid, perhaps – as I walked up to the front of Arch's office.

It had an all glass façade with white vinyl lettering across the door and a white vinyl Seal of the State of Florida along with his title. Campaign posters were taped across the windows. You couldn't miss them.

A deep breath and I yanked the door open.

It was quiet and still inside. No movement, no sound except the hum of the air conditioning. No one greeted me.

I stopped short and caught my breath. The secretary greeted me. She was blood red and dead on the floor next to her desk. Brain and bone chunks drizzled down the filing cabinet. Papers she had been carrying were scattered and splattered. A red bullet hole glistened between her eyebrows. She was young and innocent. Bastards.

I pulled out the knife and peered deeper into the office. There was no sign of life.

My feet made no sound as I walked further into the space.

A phone rang and I jumped. Then, I ducked behind a cubicle divider and waited. No one answered. Eight rings, then silence. I got the feeling no one else was in the office. No one alive.

I hesitated. What horrible mess would I find next? It's not like I wasn't used to seeing dead bodies at this point. Nothing could have been worse than Teddy's dead head looking up from the floor at his own decapitated corpse. The notion nagging at me was disappointment—disappointment that I might not get my confrontation with Arch. That this silly hunt would go on.

It's like when you're in grade school and you dread having to speak in front of the class. But, then the class runs out of time and you have to sweat through an entire weekend before you can get the presentation over with that next Monday. I didn't know how much fight I had left in me. And, I was just ready for it to be fucking over already. Please.

Deeper into the office. I recalled the hours posted on the glass door behind me. Business hours had ended for the day. There weren't going to be many people in here. Or bodies. Most of the office appeared in order. An older couple smiled at me from a framed photo atop one of the desks.

I reached Arch's office. The door was open, but I didn't go in. I scanned the room first. The person who killed the secretary may not have left. It could have been Arch. I nudged the door open with my shoe. It squeaked on its hinges until it knocked against the wall. I looked through the gap. No one was hiding behind the door.

Five steps into the room and I knew I was alone. Any spot where someone could hide was exposed for viewing. And, they couldn't be waiting for me under the desk. That spot was already occupied.

By Arch Gagnon's dead body.

49

Arch had been shot in the head. It was a big mess. His bloody face was pressed against brown carpet growing browner with the absorption of his blood.

His butter yellow suit vibed no taste and no shame. He looked like a bigmouth who loved attention, but with a pay grade that couldn't afford much respect. He represented the smallest county in the state, after all. That didn't seem to be a prestigious position. No wonder he was so happy to promote his brothers' bloody work. One could make a lot of money delivering taboo favors. And, once someone enlisted his services, that person – like Wingart – could be blackmailed for more. And, that's what gave Arch Gagnon serious skin in the game. I suspected he played that card every chance he had. Power and ambition. It had been within his reach. All it took was a little bit of murder.

Blood was splattered on the wall behind his desk. I shut the office door and started rifling thorough his papers. Too much to read now and I didn't want to be found hanging around a crime scene. I grabbed a cardboard filing box and tossed them in along with everything on his desk and everything on the table behind it. I was careful to touch as little as possible.

Frisking this corpse, I grabbed his wallet and searched the pockets. I checked his desk drawers. Locked. Keys from Arch worked. More files inside. I stuck them upright at the end of the box so they'd stand out. Locked drawer equals important info. I hoped it was the important info I needed.

I grabbed the box and stepped towards the door. As I exited, I glanced back and saw a briefcase sitting on the floor next to a shelving unit. I went back and grabbed that, too. Then, I looked down at poor, old dead Arch Gagnon. French Archibald. I was relieved knowing the four men I had needed to stop were all as stopped as any man could be. I hoped that meant the end of this nightmare was near.

Then again...who killed Arch? And, why? And were they going to come after me? What if Arch and the boys worked for a larger power? What if they had been compelled to kill? That seemed unlikely. Luther, Remy, and Clovis clearly relished killing. And, Arch was from the same psychotic gene pool.

Had they wronged someone who'd caught up to them before I could? Were there more people in the same fix as me? My gut wasn't buying it. But, I had no other clear answers.

What I did know was that I needed to get out of Arch's office fast.

Arch's phone rang. But, none of the other phones in the office did. Someone was calling Arch's private line. I stopped, waited, and listened. The answering machine clicked on and played aloud.

"You've reached my hot line. Can't answer or assist you at the moment, but please do call my cell phone if it's of great importance..." said the pre-recorded message.

I set the box of files down, ran over to Arch, and double-checked his jacket pockets. There...cell phone. I tossed it in the box. For the third time I started to exit his office.

A male voice came on the answering machine. It sounded haggard, like the caller was struggling to get the words out. "Archibald..." he said.

I knew that voice. I knew that accent.

Luther wasn't dead.

50

So, the fight wasn't over. I ignored the depression rolling over me
and focused on Luther's message. He spoke in angry French. I had no
idea what he was talking about. But, I did catch a name.
Wingart.
What did he want with him?
I couldn't stick around to find out.

I threw the box of files into the truck. Next, I took Arch's keys,
matched the make on the key fob with the only Lexus I could find in
the parking lot, and opened it up. Front seat, back seat, trunk. Just a
few small slips of paper. They didn't tell me much. I got out of there.
No one at the hair salon knew there were dead bodies next door. They
would soon enough.
I drove Highway 100 East to Starke then broke north up 301 to
Highway 16 towards Camp Blanding. I had no destination in mind.
But, I was taking back roads to throw anyone who might be looking
for me of my tail. That included Luther.

A gas station convenience store offered more to eat than candy bars
and pork rinds. I paid with cash from Arch's wallet. He wouldn't need
it. After stocking up, I took my food back to the truck where I ate and
perused Arch's files. Much of it was political business. Despite his dirty
work, he did seem to have his constituents best interests in mind.
Memos about farming, highway renovations, money for an extreme
power sports arena the city fathers expected would turn Lake Butler

into a mecca for such enthusiasts.

But, there was nothing on his father, brothers, Wingart, or the execution scheme. He knew the deal. In this business, the only thing his team executed were people, not contracts. It was strictly whispers and handshakes.

Once I had the notion the rest of the paper files weren't going to shed light I tossed them back in the box. I skimmed through Arch's black contact book. Plenty of names and numbers. Some numbers without names. Just initials. That could be important. I set the book on the dash opened to those pages.

Arch's phone rang.

It startled me, even though his ringtone was a bland new country song.

I didn't answer.

The phone stopped ringing. I waited and watched to see if a voice mail notification would pop up. Two minutes later, it did. But, when I tried to access it I couldn't get through the password protection. I tossed the phone on the seat.

A small key on Arch's key ring got me into his briefcase. First grab was a couple of folders filled with memos regarding upcoming legislation. Next grab, a small leather change purse. It was filled with condoms. You're a dirty dog, Arch.

A loose scrap of paper in the bottom of the briefcase caught my eye. An address was written on it: 860 Centurion Drive, Jacksonville Beach, FL 32250

Jacksonville was Wingart's turf.

Presuming Arch had written the address down, it meant he was either going there or sending someone there. That made it a place I needed to be.

I bypassed the interstate to Jacksonville, which meant taking smaller roads and more time to get to The River City. I arrived from the southwest and drove up through the Five Points district then into the heart of downtown, which always seemed to be deserted.

Jacksonville is weird. It had a ton of potential despite what I perceived as a complete lack of municipal personality. But, I never disliked going there. The massive St. John's River chugged along right next to it leading out to the east coast beaches and then the Atlantic Ocean. It was unlike any other part of Florida.

After weaving through a string of gentrified neighborhoods, I cut east towards the beach. Zip code 32250. Executiveland. Exactly where I'd expect to find a politician.

Large, stately houses. Golf cart lanes. Signs pointing the way to a private country club. I hated the neighborhood the second I rolled into it. It was predictable and boring. Oh, well. I assumed its occupants hated me for driving this obnoxious truck past their manicured lawns. I didn't stick around to get their thoughts.

I pulled up to the address on Centurion Drive. There it was, just like all the other houses. The lawn team had done their work well. No hedge looked overgrown. No sign it housed a murderer.

51

A new model Mercedes sat in the driveway next to its golf cart equivalent. I wondered if Wingart had splurged with money he made off the ITG execution deal. I noted the golf clubs on the back of the cart. They'd be great for smashing in the car windows.

I crossed the street and walked up to the house. I didn't even bother concealing the big buck knife. Instead of knocking on the front door I walked in through the open garage. A beep signaled my entrance and a dog started barking. A moment later a scrappy Shih Tzu ran over and sniffed my shoes. I let it do what it liked and kept my eyes on the kitchen before me.

"What'd you forget, Carol? I told you stay gone until..." Wingart stopped when he saw me. "What are you doing here?"

I took in the vast kitchen, which led to a sprawling, sunken living room. The walls were lined with a menagerie of taxidermied big game heads. In the far corner stood a stuffed and posed grizzly bear next to an elephant foot stool. I pictured many "guy's nights" here, playing poker, drinking fine scotch, and comparing mistresses while looking out at the water.

"Bet you're damned surprised to see me again," I said.

He nodded.

"Don't do it," I said. He stopped moving towards the alarm box on the wall. "We don't need to invite anyone else."

He glanced down at my knife. It spooked him.

"Well, I don't know what you want with me. I gave you a head start in Tallahassee, just like I promised," he said. He leaned casually against the island kitchen counter and folded his arms.

"But, then you told Arch and the boys I'd escaped," I said.

Fascination flashed across his face. He hadn't expected this. "I told you I would. I had to make sure they didn't come after me," he said.

"You don't need to worry about that," I said.

"I'd say. They know none of this is my fault and I did everything to keep the operation quiet. I even went a step further to remind them that their sloppy work is what caused the exposure. But, as long as you were taken care of there would be no more problems," he said.

"Well, they tried."

"What do you mean?"

"I mean they tried. And, failed."

He frowned, not quite getting it. "Well, that would explain why you're here."

"And, why they're dead."

That one hit him. His jaw dropped with surprise. But, he forced a smile.

"Really?"

"Well, all but one. Luther," I said.

"You really did find out a lot. Congratulations," he said. "I am very impressed. To track them down while there's a manhunt on for you, that takes skill. And, some balls."

"That would mean something if it wasn't coming from trash like you," I said. My blood boiled. I swung the blade down into the wooden edge of the counter causing damage.

He glared at it but stifled his irritation. I knew he was wondering if I knew how much a countertop like that cost. I didn't and I didn't care.

Excitement from a sudden brainstorm whisked him back onto his feet, his hands on his hips.

"Well, hot damn! This is good news for both of us," he said. He saw that I wasn't understanding him so he elaborated. "If they're dead, they can't kill you and you can pin all the murders on them. You're gonna be a free man! And, so am I because those heathens won't be able to strong arm me anymore, and I can get back to serving my constituents!" He was thrilled with this turn of events. Who the hell uses the word 'heathen' these days?

"That's how this whole mess started. You serving Tanjeris," I said.

He nodded, yeah, well okay.

"You know what I mean. The people. I work for the people. Frankly, I am very relieved this nightmare has ended," he paused then looked at me as if a magnificent idea had just been born from a tiny golden acorn inside his mind. "And you...you helped end it."

He approached me. I twirled the knife as a reminder. He stopped approaching.

"You know what this means, don't you?"

I shook my head.

"You're no criminal. You're a hero! And, I'm going to make sure the governor knows all about it. You're not going to have to worry about a thing," he said in triumphant fashion.

After years of selling on television, there's one thing I know: People aren't dumb. They like to buy, but they don't like to be sold to. I was being sold to.

"Bullshit," I said.

"Not bullshit! Not at all," he said.

"You're covering your ass. Your money was on them. Now, it's on me."

"From what you've said, it sounds like the game is over. You've won."

"What about Luther? He's the most dangerous. And, he's still alive."

He started pacing around the island counter.

"Him. I met him once. A brute. Barely speaks English. Can't hardly form an expression on his face let alone articulate. Not very friendly," he said. "Arch was the brains. The others, just helpers. I think the brother, Remy? He made all the weapons." He continued pacing, his body language getting into the story now.

"Arch approached me with the whole set up. He was just a nobody state rep in the smallest county in Florida. When you're that small, you need to make a lot of deals to get any kind of power up at the capital. Fortunately for him, he had one powerful bargaining chip – his brothers. The state executioners. And, he knew it. Cocky son of a buck."

"Were you the first one he approached?" I said. I needed the full story.

"No. He'd worked with a few others. By the time he got to me he had his pitch down. And, a mutual acquaintance referred him. He came in knowing I had a problem," he said.

"Tanjeris."

"Tanjeris," he nodded.

"And, you liked the solution he offered."

"Well, no. Of course not. I do not like that kind of dirty business."

"But..."

"I mentioned it casually to Tanjeris and he liked the idea. A lot. In fact, when I tried to brush it off he wouldn't let it go. And, he let me know just what it would mean to me if I didn't take his interests to heart," he said.

"Okay, skip ahead. I already know you're a greedy fuck. What I need to know is who else hired the Gagnons to kill?" I said, waving off the rest of his story.

"The who?"

"The Gagnons. That was their last name."

"Oh, Arch. Okay, yes. Well, I don't know all their business. I just had the one deal with them," he said.

"The guy who referred Arch to you. What's his name?"

Wingart looked a little queasy.

"I don't think I can tell you that," he said. "The Gagnons..." he smiled and gestured wanting me to recognize and be impressed that he'd remembered their name. "...are gone. There's not going to be anymore killing. I don't think we need to throw anyone else to the wolves."

"Because you're worried they'll rat you out," I said.

His hesitation told me I was right.

"But, look...you can find out from Luther who they killed then you can pin those murders on them without exposing me," he offered.

Turn on a dime. Complete self-interest. Protecting his cronies. This guy was redefining how sleazy a politician could be. It was sickening.

"We can't just ask Luther to tell us who he killed. Not without getting an axe to the face," I said.

"Sure, we can! He doesn't know I'm with you. I'll act like I'm still on his side and we'll get it out of him. And, then we'll have him arrested," he said.

"What the hell are you talking about? That guy's a monster. And, who knows where he is. His brother said they had more people to kill once they were through with me. We need to stop him before he goes through with it," I said.

"Well, he can't do that until he gets the information from me. That's why he's on his way here now," he said.

I almost choked on my heart.

"Here?!"

"He called just a short while ago," he said. "He's on his way."

"Why didn't you just give him the target address over the phone?"

"Never know who could be listening in. And, with Arch dead, and me not knowing if you were alive, we were improvising. Until you showed up," he said. Then he waved his hand between his chest and mine. "But now, *we* have a plan. And, a damned good one!"

He smiled, so proud of himself.

I paused a moment to think.

"Would you like a drink? Snack?" he asked moving towards the pantry.

I held out the knife, "Stay right there."

He froze.

"I'm fine."

"Just offering."

I had more questions.

"Why did you tell your wife to stay gone?" I said.

He looked at me confused then stitched it together. "Carol knows nothing about this business, nor should she. Plus, I don't want her anywhere near Luther. No telling what could happen," he said.

"No telling," I said.

"We'll need to be ready for him. I have a gun in my den."

"I'll take it," I said. He looked disappointed.

"Hey boss," he said. "You're in control. And, I'm gonna go along with whatever you say. You've proven you can handle a situation, and I respect— "

"Shut up. Just shut your dumb mouth for five seconds," I said.

He clammed up.

Something wasn't right. There was nothing stopping him from selling me out to Luther when he arrived. Then, it would be two against one and my chances would be slim to nothing, especially without the gun in the den.

"Let's get the gun. Now!" I said.

"Sure thing. It's in the--," he said.

I waved the knife indicating he needed to lead the way. We walked through the mansion, across tile floors, past built-in bookshelves filled with self-help books and military thrillers, and down hallways that lead to room after room.

His den décor was just as dull as the rest of the house. Lots of brown tones, a few plaques, pictures of him with various somebodies. It'd make for a boring estate sale.

"Get it," I said and prompted him with a wave of the knife.

He nodded and removed a picture from the wall, revealing a wall safe. He spun the dial and opened it. Before he had a chance to reach in, I knocked him on the back of the skull with the butt of the knife. He grabbed his head and cowered. I grabbed the gun and the few papers inside.

"Damn, what'd you do that for?" he said, irritated. But, he caught himself and tried to cover up his rage. That told me a lot.

The gun was loaded. I tucked it in the back of my waistband and waved him out of the den.

"You know, this whole hostage routine is really unnecessary. We're on the same side," he said as we walked back towards the kitchen.

"Until it's convenient for you not to be," I said.

"Luther has no chance."

"Why is that? Because you have the same guy who killed Arch ready to kill Luther?"

A ghost of shock and worry flashed across his face.

"I'm not an idiot," I said. "Keep walking."

He walked in silence. No doubt he was calculating his odds. I just waited to see how he would play it. But, he didn't say anything. Perhaps he was worried the more he talked the more he would reveal.

"The way I see it, you thought Luther would wipe me out. So, you had Arch killed and invited Luther up so you could kill him. Cutting the head off of the snake. That leaves Clovis and Remy. Only I took care of them for you," I said.

He just glared at me. That was encouraging.

"With the Gagnons out of the way, this whole deal disappears...except for me."

I watched him close. He kept walking and looking ahead. He'd gone from not wanting to talk to not even wanting to look at me.

"And, you've already stated how you feel about someone knowing your dirty secrets."

We arrived in the kitchen. He turned to me and leaned against the kitchen island. His expression was matter of fact.

"So where is he?" I said.

"Who?" he said.

"Your new executioner."

He vibed defiance and just shrugged. That meant he felt confident and I may have lost control of the situation.

"You were going to have him kill Luther. And, then when I showed up, you decided to have him kill me," I said.

He shrugged again. A beat later he said, "If you think you can take us all, have at it commercial boy."

I flipped the buck knife in my hand and moved in to stab him. He flinched and staggered back, tripping over the legs of a barstool. He held his hands up. I dropped down on top of him.

The door beeped. Someone walked in.

52

I crawled off Wingart. He got up fast and straightened out his clothes, ever the professional.

Footsteps approaching down the hallway. Clicking across the tiles. Heavy and slow.

"I'm in the kitchen, Luther," Wingart said.

It startled me and I looked at him like *you asshole.*

The steps continued in unsteady fashion. Almost as if one of his legs was dragging, maybe limping.

I watched the hallway that led to the garage – the same one I'd entered through – waiting to see how much of the big French behemoth remained intact. How much damage could he do after being mauled by alligators? How much of him was left?

Luther appeared around the corner and my heart sank.

He looked bigger than I'd remembered. And now, he looked meaner. He wasn't half a person liked I'd hoped. His skin was shredded around his neck. He was muddy, with a milky-way pattern of blood crust across his brawny, bare chest. A flap of torn skin dangled from his bicep. His leg wasn't dragging, his battle-axe was. And, his eyes – one white, one dark red with broken blood vessels – looked menacing under the black executioner hood, which had been frayed along the bottom and torn around the eyes. Even through the hood he looked meaner, angrier. He wasn't here to do the job he'd been hired for.

He was here for revenge.

Wingart pointed at me.

"Luther, we lucked out. I don't know how he got away from you.

But, he was dumb enough to come here, and I kept him from leaving till you arrived," said Wingart.

Luther didn't look at Wingart. He projected pure hate my way.

"He's setting you up, Luther," I said. "He wants you and me dead so he can tie up all his loose ends and skate back to Tallahassee."

"He killed Arch! Shot him!" said Wingart with his hands outstretched and pleading desperately.

"I did not. He murdered Arch. I killed Remy in self defense," I said. "And, I wouldn't have had to if he hadn't started all this."

Luther looked over at Wingart, who went sheet white under his evil gaze.

"Now, listen, Luther. Don't be dumb. A) He's just an infomercial writer, he's worthless!" said Wingart. "I'm a well-known politician who *will be noticed* if I am dead or missing. And B) I can get your ass out of this jam. I can cover it all up and you can go back to your simple life killing people at the prison."

Luther lifted his axe into striking posture. Me and Wingart, we both stiffened up in anticipation.

"Isn't it the same old problem? The politicians shut you down in France. And, now they're trying to do it to you here. After everything you lost, now this jerk's gonna make you lose it again," I said. "Same thing's happened to me. I've lost my house, my friends. You've crippled my girlfriend. Life will never be the same for me either. Meanwhile, the slick politician is sitting pretty. He still has his nice house, his job, his family. He's been making a big mess, but his hands aren't even dirty. Not like ours."

I wasn't sure how much English Luther could even understand. But, it was just like with writing a sales prospect – I had to make that connection. It was my only chance. And, if he had any sense of justice, he'd know I wasn't the man he wanted.

Wingart stepped up, "Luther we had a deal. And, a deal is a deal. And, on our deal that man right there was listed as one of the targets. It's time for you to finish the work you've been contracted to do so you can get paid in full."

Luther roared and slammed the battle-axe down on the island kitchen. It shattered the glass stovetop and sent black shards flying. Wingart and I ducked. Luther swung again and about chopped the refrigerator freezer in half horizontally. When he ripped out the blade the vertical doors pulled open and half the cooled contents spilled out.

I stepped back but didn't want to go too far. That would mean descending the stairs into the sunken living room. And, as little as I know about fighting and warfare, I do know it's better to have the higher ground.

Luther stopped swinging the axe and looked to Wingart. But, he pointed at me. In his best broken English he said, "My brother was shot! In ze head. Archibald was a fighter. Zees man could not have shot him like zat!"

Wingart looked uneasy, then glanced at me with a sly glare.

"Do you know how many men Mr. Asher has killed over the past several days?" he said. "He killed your brother and *both* your sons — that's right, he got Clovis, too."

Wingart paused to let that sink in.

Luther stood emotionless.

"If he could take all of them, why couldn't he take Arch?" Wingart said.

Luther stepped forward and looked at me.

"I trust nobody. I kill you both, zen my problems go away," he said. "You both deserve to die."

I said, "Hey, at least I was a worthy adversary. Remy said that himself. That has to count for something." I thumbed to Wingart. "He's just playing you for a fool."

"I am not a fool. I am the final word," said Luther.

Another smash of the blade, this time shattering the glass dining room table Wingart had been standing next to. He quick-stepped back and down into the living room.

"If you kill me and let him live, the moment you walk out of here, he's going to have you killed. And, after he's gotten away with it, every time he thinks about how he fooled you, the dumb French oakie, he's going to laugh and laugh and laugh," I said.

"Shut your mouth, goddammit!" Wingart hissed as he stepped further back into the living room. "That sumbitch is looking you right in the eyes and lying to your face!"

He flushed red. The real Wingart was on now on display, the one who eviscerated his staff when he looked bad, the one who wouldn't accept defeat and who wouldn't take the blame.

"Luther, I'm gonna tell you one more time. You need to kill his ass dead right now before this turns into a mess that even I can't get you out of. It's that simple. Do your job!" said Wingart.

I couldn't tell if his arrogance was genuine or a portrayal of authority that didn't truly exist.

Luther looked to me, like I was a nuisance. As if maybe he should just get rid of me. That way he'd be free to concentrate on disemboweling the bossy son of a bitch in the living room.

I pulled out the gun and pointed it at Luther.

"Now, I know this looks bad, like I'm the one who has something to defend. But, this is just to get things wrapped up," I said and shook the gun. "I'm quite fine with not shooting you, Luther, as long as you keep cool and swing that thing away from me." I pointed to the axe with the gun.

He didn't budge. He looked at the gun with about as much fear as if I was pointing a feather at him and threatening to tickle.

"Personally, I don't care what you do to him," I said and nodded my head at Wingart. "I suspect the world would be better off without him."

He leered at Wingart, who pursed his lips and looked like he was both mad and surprised for losing control of the conversation.

I continued, "But, no matter what you do, I'm calling the cops. Because I didn't start any of this and I didn't cause any of this. The two of you did. If you can talk your way out of it, fine. But, I've had enough. It's time for me to get back to the life I loved and have you deviants out of my hair. So, what you do is up to—"

"Son of a bitch!"

It was Wingart, charging up the stairs with a sharp, iron fire poker aimed at me. I jumped back, but tripped and fell hard against the pantry door. I dropped the gun and it tumbled away from me.

Wingart launched himself from the second step. He gripped the poker with two hands above his head. The pointed tip flew at my chest. I could have kicked my legs up but he could still jab the poker into me. If I rolled he could slam it into the side of my rib cage. Nothing to throw. Damn.

I rolled.

From the corner of my eye I could see Wingart redirect the poker to follow for my movement.

I pushed off the dining table, rolled the opposite direction and brought kicked wide. It was enough to hit his shoulder and change his trajectory. The spike shattered the kitchen tile. Wingart fell on top of me and knocked out my wind. I was stunned.

He crawled off me, grabbed the poker, raised it over his head, and slammed it hard across my chest. It hurt as bad as you would expect.

I tried to roll away. He kicked me and whacked me again with the hard iron. He smashed my ribs. Excruciating pain.

I hustled and flailed to get away. But, I moved just a few yards...

And, landed at Luther's feet.

I didn't realize it until something cold and metal touched my cheek. I peeked over and saw it was his axe. My shoulder was pressed against his muck-covered boot. He kicked me away. I rolled onto my back and slid head first down the trio of steps to the living room. My head hit the living room floor and stopped the rest of my body from sliding down the steps. I could barely move.

Wingart moved into view at the top of the steps. He raised the poker, rage on his face and hate in his eyes.

"Allow me to finish the job you couldn't, Luther!" said Wingart.

I wanted to kick but I couldn't. I wanted to roll but the incline of the steps made it too difficult.

I couldn't move.

And, Wingart had the high ground. He had the spike. He had me pinned.

He cocked the poker back. He was ready to stab me with full force.

I had tried. But, now...what could I do?

I saw my kids, my parents, Ilsa...their smiling faces. I sent my love.

I flinched my eyes closed.

I said 'goodbye'.

53

Heavy metal landed on me.
Then a scream.
My eyes opened.
They stung. Everything was red.
The scream turned into a crying howl.
I rubbed my eyes with my forearm.
A voice:
"Nooool!"
I blinked partial vision into my eyes. I had to spit. Something warm and wet spilled into it. My blood?
No.
Wingart's blood.
Through squinting eyes I saw why:
Wingart's arms, from the elbow down, were missing. Completely gone. His upper arms flailed as if reaching out to take hold of something, to brace himself, but he had no way to grab on. He was stunned by the sheer horror of his disfigurement, no longer a sane man.

But, he didn't have to worry long.

Movement caught my eye and I turned just in time to see Luther swing his giant, bloody battle-axe at Wingart. It was laid out flat, like he was swinging a baseball bat, and moved in a semi-circle level with his hips. The axe sliced right through Wingart's back, severing his spine with little resistance, and sending the upper half of his doomed body tumbling into the living room.

I covered my head to avoid getting hit by the torso. It spritzed me with blood as it slammed hard against the living room floor and tumbled into the side of the leather couch where it came to a rest.

It was so horrible *I couldn't not look.*

From my position on the floor, he was above me and everything was flipped upside down. Wingart's eyes were closed, his head cockeyed between his shoulder and the couch. A puddle of blood rose as he bled out.

My ankle.

Something grabbed it.

Strong and tight, squeezing my Achilles tendon.

I buckled with the pain and tried to kick loose.

Luther had it wrapped tight in his meaty fist and was pulling me up.

I couldn't shake free. My butt, then my back lifted off the stairs. Luther's hand raised me up until I was dangling upside down with only my forearms touching the ground. Then he lifted the axe with the other hand and looked down at me.

"I...", he said, then pounded the axe against his chest in self reference. "...am the executioner!"

If a demon dog from hell could speak English, that's what his voice sounded like. But, with a French accent. The only thing missing was brimstone smoke puffing out between each word. Despite all that had just happened, my heart started pounding with a new level of fear.

He continued, "You are guilty of the crimes for which you have been accused. The judgment has been made by those with the power to decide, and..." Luther pointed the head of the axe at me. It was dripping with blood. "Your sentence has been handed down," he said.

I tried kicking harder but his grip wouldn't budge. I was now a chicken heading towards the chopping block. Luther squeezed my ankle harder and the pain was stunning. I stopped kicking. I felt the blood rushing into my face, the sweat on my brow.

"You...are condemned to die!" Luther said.

He raised the axe.

Then, a loud 'ping.'

Something invisible sparked and smoked against axe blade metal.

It distracted him.

He lowered me.

He looked at the axe then spun the opposite side of the blade towards his face. What he saw alerted him because he moved the axe from his field of view and gazed through the open sliding glass doors and into the yard.

I coughed.

He looked down.

Mighty Luther shook and grunted as a third hole appeared in his black mask. Left side of his forehead. Blood started gushing into his eye.

Smoke wafted out the end of the pistol in my hand.

The one I grabbed when he lowered me.

Luther's powerful arms dropped. He released my ankle and I tumbled down the steps. The axe dropped from his other hand and nearly shattered my eardrums as its steel clanged against the tile.

The executioner fell down dead. No staggering, no grabbing to hold himself up. No drama. Just a flat flesh smack and thump against the ground.

54

Luther looked at me from inside the executioner's mask as his last breath seethed out.

I wiggled my toes to get the blood flowing back into my leg. Otherwise, I didn't budge. I was in shock. There were too many dead people and I'd had too many close calls. Very close calls. I was beyond exhaustion, physical and mental, and my energy and adrenaline were zapped. It was too much. I felt nauseous, needed air. I inhaled deep, and when I did my body shivered in ripples that washed down to my toes.

I screamed cathartic. My eyes welled up. I was overcome. I'd been ripped from my life and force to fight. I'd had to leap blind into a dangerous world, and my body was still intact. I'd faced pitch-black death and survived. Was it skill? Luck? Divine intervention? Why did I beat the odds and keep my skin?

Click.

The barrel of a high-powered rifle hung inches from my eye.

I gazed up the barrel...to the arms that lead to the familiar face of the man holding it.

Warden Durfee.

"Not a reporter, are you?" said the Warden.

I shook my head. Blood tingled as it rushed back into my legs.

He surveyed the damage and carnage. He looked down at his shoes then checked for footprints back to the sliding glass door. There were none. The gun stayed pointed at my face.

He turned to me. "Quite a mess."

I nodded.

"You weren't working for Wingart were you?" he said.

I inhaled deep and steadied my breath before speaking. "Wasn't working for anyone. Just trying to save my ass," I said.

"That either did or did not work depending on who I'm working for."

The Southern charm he'd presented in his living room days ago was absent. This was his no bullshit side—the same disposition he used to keep inmates in line.

He said nothing. The silence was brutal. If he shot me, I'd be dead before realizing what had happened. That could come at any second. If he was gonna kill me, he'd kill me no matter what I said.

"You shot Luther. Means you're working for Wingart," I said.

"If I'm working for Wingart then maybe I'm supposed to kill you," he said.

"But, he's dead," I said.

A long pause. No response.

He re-directed the gun and held out his hand. I took it and he pulled me up. I had to lean on him for a moment. My legs still weren't right.

"Did you know who I was at your house?" I said.

He pushed the dusty Stetson back on his head.

"No clue." He smirked. His charm returned.

"Then, I'm lost."

"It's simple," he said. "I know..." he looked at Wingart's legs at the top of the steps. "Knew Wingart. And, he knew a few things about me. Things I would rather not have discussed. From a long time ago."

"Did you know what he was up to? With the Gagnons?" I said.

"Had no idea. But, he called me when it got out of sorts. Needed me to tidy up. He...compelled me to do it."

"Blackmail?"

He nodded and looked out the window, perhaps contemplating his past.

"He thought I was the perfect man for the job since I already dealt with Luther and the boys at the prison. I knew what a fearsome son of a bitch he was. How crazy they all were. Not insane crazy, but crazy in their view of the world, in their place in the world. He knew I would realize there'd be no negotiating with 'em. So, he spelled it out real plain: Kill 'em quick or else."

"Did he explain why he wanted them killed?" I said.

"In roundabout terms. But, I didn't question it much. I was too busy bristling at the fix I'd gotten myself into. And, this wasn't the first time I'd had to clean up one of his messes."

Flies were already starting to land on the bodies. I couldn't fathom the depth of Wingart's evil.

"He just gave me his list of targets and said get going," he said.

"And, you did. Starting with Arch Gagnon," I said.

He nodded.   "Then Wingart called you up here because Luther was on his way to get the information for his next target."

"That's right."

"What about Remy and Clovis?"

"I found Remy at the house. That your work?"

I nodded.

"Impressive. That's a lot of man to get the best of."

Remy's bloody death flashed in and out of my mind.

"Where's Clovis," he said.

"Dead. The woods just north of Lake Butler," I said.

"Where they found them girls?"

I nodded.

He continued, "I heard a report on my way up here. Didn't say they'd found him."

"He'd been taking them there for a while. I couldn't count them all."

He looked disgusted.

"Bad people doing rotten things," he said.

"No wonder they got on with Wingart," I said.

He looked to me. "How do you fit in?"

I explained how I got sucked into Wingart's world. And, that I'd been fighting to get out ever since, including when I went to the Warden's house.

"That explains all your prison questions. You had a hunch it was our executioners," he said.

"It was more than a hunch. I knew it was them. I just needed to find out who they were and trace back from there."

"That's damn impressive."

"Why did you shoot Luther? Wingart was already dead."

"He was a bad man."

He held up the gun. "Don't suppose I'm much better. But, it felt like the right thing to do."

We sat in silence for a moment. Then, I broke it.

"So, now what?"

He considered my question, then looked at me and asked, "Can you keep a secret?"

I took a moment to figure his angle. I nodded.

"Then, I see no need to kill you," he said.

"I'd appreciate that," I said.

I stood up and walked towards the glass doors. I took in a big breath of fresh air. He walked over next to me.

"We both stepped in a trick of shit that wasn't neither of our fault. It's time to put it to rest," he said.

"I have to clear my name. Right now, I'm a wanted man. But, I'm innocent."

"I'm a prison warden. I know plenty of cops. I'll set 'em straight. And, you'll never speak a word of this."

I nodded.

"With Wingart dead, I'm not even gonna bother with the other two. Not my problem anymore," he said.

I thought about whom that might be.

"Tanjeris?" I said.

He gave me a sly glance. "You may not be a reporter, but you're pretty sharp."

"I'm just an infomercial writer."

"You mean those ridiculous things on TV?"

I shrugged.

"Guilty."

55

The Warden told me not to worry about the mess. He'd stay behind and arrange things so it would be a quick case closed. But, I had to do a good job getting rid of Luther's truck. I told him I knew the perfect guy to help me with that. But, I didn't give him DG's name.

I was headed that way anyway. To see Ilsa. And then, we could finally return home to Gainesville. It seemed safe enough now.

The Warden and I shook hands and I left the house out the backyard. When I got into the truck I scanned the neighborhood. Still quiet and peaceful. Everyone existing in their personal orbit with their own worries.

To the observer, the reunion would have been underwhelming. There was no explosive greeting. No gasps of relief, surprise, or delight. No words even. It was simple. Ilsa saw me the same time I saw her. I walked over and we hugged for a very long time. Long enough for her to start and stop sobbing.

"They're dead," I said.

That relaxed her. But, I could tell by her expression she had questions about what went down, what I had to do.

"No more?" she said.

I shook my head.

She frowned and grabbed my chin.

"No more." Her question became a command.

"No more than necessary."

"Is it over or not, Walt?"

"It's over. We are free to go home," I said. She saw I meant it and smiled.

"I love you, Walt."

"I love you right back."

She wiped the wet from her eyes. "I'm very proud of you. And, I wasn't doubting you."

"There was a little doubt, but I understand."

She nodded, taking her lumps. "Maybe it was better to fight," she said.

"Not fighting was the bigger risk. Even if I'm a writer, not a fighter." I said.

"Apparently you fight as well as you write."

She smiled. We kissed.

Despite some deep bruising that continued to throw off my gait when I walked, my body healed up well. I had my share of scars, but I dug them. To me, they were less mutilation and more mementos of a hard battle fought and won. It may not have been a pleasant experience, but it was my experience. It made me who I am today.

When something changes or defines your life as much as Wingart and his French executioners had mine, you become attached to all people and elements involved. They were dead. But, we will be forever linked. Alumni of the assault.

I hadn't given them much thought over the past several weeks. The business of day-to-day life had returned to distract. I had to get Ilsa set up at her place, where I had moved in for the time being. She started her physical therapy rehab, but it would be a while before she could return to work. So, I relieved DG's men from running the bars and took over for Ilsa. That would save her ten percent.

That also meant I found myself writing behind the bar more nights than not. I had to scramble to build back my infomercial writing business. When clients don't hear from you for a couple weeks and deadlines are looming, they tend to not call you back. Especially, the ones who had heard the bogus news stories about me. But, I cleared everything up, plied them with reassurances, and business boomed again.

It was a relief. I could live with the scars of battle, but not with having to go back to the nine-to-five corporate life. Crisis averted.

The Warden lived up to his word and got the heat off my back. I was cleared as a suspect. And, by the time Ilsa and I were ready to leave DG's place in Defuniak Springs, reports were starting to break about the horrific slaughter in the woods north of Lake Butler and the deranged French family behind them. There was also mention of Wingart going missing. But, he was not connected to the Gagnons.

With the heat off me, the heat was off DG. He and his gang were able to return to normal operations, whatever that meant. He apologized for having to shove me out on my own. But, business came first. Too many people depended on him. I told him I understood and I would only resent him periodically, when I would remind him how he threw me to the slaughter.

We made plans to meet back in Dunnellon, back at the river. He'd be down there in a few weeks to see how the re-build of his house was progressing. DG also hinted at some wild new features. The boyish gleam in his eye hinted at trouble—ridiculous, fun trouble.

Things were getting back to normal. And, normal felt fantastic. My bond with Ilsa had grown deeper, our love richer. That's what mattered most. We were still a 'we'. I was grateful for that.

56

But, there was unfinished business. And, that's what had me standing in that dark alley on a dusky Florida night. The air was cool with a crisp edge you rarely felt down in the tropical, southern part of the state. Fall had arrived and it felt good.

No one in the alley. No movement amongst the trash bins and parked cars. Those cars would belong to the help. Most were parked just outside the back gate entrances that lead to opposing blocks of massive homes. The kind of homes owned by titans of industry. Odds were, everyone here owned something similar in Aspen. You know, that type.

I pushed a rolling trash bin on its side, steadied it, then used it to launch myself up to the top of the privacy wall. I swung my legs over and sat for a moment. No guard dogs. No signs referring to guard dogs. One alarm system sign. One loooong yard leading up to a robust pool retreat, with the big house dwarfing the skyline behind it. I dropped into the yard and walked up to the house.

Just like at Wingart's, the sliding glass doors were open. Only here, two sets of glass doors met to form a corner off the house. With them open, it was like an entire wall was missing. I walked right in.

Bland, contemporary music played down the hallway. I followed the sound, my sneakers making minor squeaks along the tile. If someone were paying attention they'd have heard my footsteps.

When I reached the main foyer at the front of the house I was able to pinpoint the music as coming from an office den straight ahead. The music lowered and a male voice called out.

"Stop teasing, love. I'm super ready."

A female voice called from upstairs. I ducked back down the hall.

"Don't worry, lover. It will be worth the wait," she said.

I peeked up at the top of the staircase. The landing was empty. I had time and used it to cross the foyer and walk towards the music den.

And, there he was. Sipping a cocktail, dancing to the music, wearing an open robe, ready to party. But, first checking for updates on his phone. A sip, a wiggle, a thumb scroll. Doug Tanjeris, the king in his castle.

I slipped into the den and shut the heavy oak door behind me. The thud of the wood got his attention.

"Who the fuck are you?" he said.

"Nice dick, Doug," I said and gestured towards his open robe.

He spilled his drink on the plush carpet as he cinched and tied his robe shut. He groaned at the mess and looked around for something to sop it up. Then, he remembered me.

"You need to get out of here. Now." he said.

"How's business at ITG?" I said as I strolled further into the modern-retro styled room. It was a sweet pad.

Sensing a business angle he went from looking incredulous to sizing me up with a sly glare. "What's this about?"

"Still shitting on everyone in the name of profits? I mean, progress," I said.

His expression softened with realization.

"You're one of those damn activists, aren't you? Here to help your cause," he said.

I made a face letting him know I hadn't thought about it that way, "Yeah, guess you could say so."

"Okay, I have a few moments. Which defenseless animal or natural resource are you here to protect? Perhaps you can tug at my heartstrings before my date arrives."

What a prick.

"The species that needed defending was Ken Kerenz," I said.

His cocky smile vanished.

"I'm afraid I don't know that breed," he said. It was poor cover. He grabbed his drink and sipped. The glass covered his face.

"You're a bad liar. You and Trip Wingart had him killed."

He spit out his drink, "The hell you say."

"Okay, look. Just stop. I'm not an idiot. You and Wingart hired the executioners through Arch Gagnon. You had them kill Ken Kerenz because he was hassling you and ITG. And, you're a real piece of shit for it."

His face went white as I unraveled those juicy details.

"Don't look so surprised. Business that messy is hard to contain."

He didn't speak. Just watched me, gears in his mind working.

I continued:

"Okay, I'll do the talking. You're a rich and powerful douchebag who thinks he can get away with anything, anything at all. That's how you conduct personal business. And, that philosophy trickles down through your company. You're a bad person making what I presume are mostly good people do bad things for your obnoxious personal gain. Fair characterization so far?"

"No," he said.

"Tough shit. That's because you lie to yourself. Every time you look in the mirror. You're huffing the fumes of your own corporate aspirational bullshit. And, you're as high as the drag lines you use to rip this state apart."

He pursed his lips. Tough to tell if he felt insulted or was growing impatient.

"You know what you do is lousy. That's why you had Wingart. He was your fixer at the Capitol. Or, wherever fixing was needed. Such as Ken's backyard, where I found his dead body."

My anger rose.

"Oh, you're the guy who found him. That's how you fit in. Well, I've heard enough. You need to get the hell out now or you're going to jail," he said as he started to dial his phone.

I grabbed a nearby decorative glass orb he likely paid way too much for and threw it at him. He missed blocking it with his phone and yelped when it hit him in the sternum. I yanked the phone out of his hand. A quick throw against the side of the bar and it smashed to pieces.

I grabbed him by the robe lapels and pulled his face close to mine. "You're going to shut up and listen, Doug. You almost got me and my lovely lady killed. I'm a very angry man," I shoved him down to the ground and stood over him.

"By all means, continue," he said with a wave of his hand indicating what choice did he have? It was smarmy and I should have smashed the lamp on his face. "I'm sure this is leading somewhere. You want me to say I'm sorry? I'm not."

"I wouldn't expect you to be," I said.

He glared at me like I had crossed a line one simply does not cross. And, I could tell he was waiting to strike. As soon as he could figure out how.

"So, ITG did something to piss off Ken and his friends. And, Ken had the power to damage you and ITG. Not bad PR damage. Real, stock dropping kind of damage. And, he worked at doing just that. He went after you and he went after Wingart, who had publicly defended your company and brought deals to the Governor on your behalf. I did my research, see?"

He wasn't amused. And, he didn't deny it.

I continued, "What neither of you banked on was Ken meeting Ross Chambers, the flunky in Wingart's office who caught wind of the execution for hire services. Now, Ken had you and Wingart by the balls."

"Not exactly, Walt."

It was the female voice. In the doorway stood the last person I ever expected to see.

57

"Karen..." I said in complete disbelief.

Karen Kerenz pushed the door aside and walked into the room. She wore garters, stockings, and a sheer negligee top. And, she was stunning. Enough to confound my anger and propel my confusion.

"But..."

I looked down at Tanjeris. He was admiring her.

I looked back to her. This time she wasn't so stunning. She had a small pistol pointed at me.

"Don't move, Walt," she said.

All I could think to say was, "Where are the kids?"

"In West Palm. They're fine."

"Oh." I nodded at least pleased to hear that. But, still flummoxed by it all. I had not expected this. And by that I don't mean seeing Karen. I definitely didn't expect that and really wanted to know what it meant. But, I hadn't expected to be in such a vulnerable position. I figured I'd have the upper hand with Tanjeris. If I had thought otherwise, I never would have bothered to come here. I could have gone on living my life undisturbed.

Maybe.

Truth was I couldn't be sure if I would have been left alone. Tanjeris had hired someone to come after me once before. If he thought I could cause problems down the road, there was no reason to believe he wouldn't have had someone come after me again. My being here tonight proved him right. Damn, I should have stayed home.

I said to Karen, "Mind telling me what's up?"

"Your time," said Tanjeris, now off the floor, straightening his robe, his cocky smirk back in place.

"That's hilarious," I said.

He walked over and stood next to Karen.

"Are you two, you know....together?" I wasn't sure if I was confused, shocked, or just disgusted.

She nodded, "Yes."

"That was fast."

She gave me an unimpressed look meant to tell me to stop being sarcastic.

"It started some time ago," she said.

"Before Ken died."

She nodded again.

"Before you killed him," I said.

"She didn't kill him," said Tanjeris. "Luther and those guys did it."

"For you."

"We've been through that. Yes, for me, all right? And before you ask why, I'll just tell you."

Tanjeris was worked up. I had trespassed, humiliated him in his own house, in front of the woman who was now his woman, and found out sordid details that were none of my business.

He continued, "Here's what someone like you will never understand. It's different for people like me. Captains of industry. Politicians. Insiders. It just is. Lower class dopes like you suspect it, but don't want to believe it. But, yes...we, and by that I mean the elite, have all kinds of privileges that you don't. It's not something that's advertised. But, it's well known within the circuit, you could say. So, all I did was make the most of those privileges. I'm not dumb. You would, too, if you had access to what I do"

"Which privilege are you referring to, murdering people or having sex with another man's wife. Both are pretty shady," I said.

It was then I noticed a ring on his pinky finger. I presumed platinum, with symbols I couldn't decipher from this distance.

"It's maximum freedom. But, like I said, you just don't get it. So, there's no point in explaining." He shrugged. "You won't be able to do anything with the information anyway."

He paused for a moment. But, something compelled him to continue.

"But, you know, I can't resist. Let me just give you a rundown of some of the secret privileges men like me are afforded. As if my fortune didn't give me enough already."

He was a first class prick. He knew it and he relished it. With Karen's gun pointed at me, I had to take it.

"Of course there are the parties. There's the inside information and priority position on investments. Illegal? Maybe. But, we get away with it."

Tanjeris separated from Karen and started walking the room. Neither she nor her gun budged.

"There's the influence. At the capital, in Washington, around the world. We make the decisions that make the laws that *you* have to follow. But, not me. I'm too important to be tripped up in that red tape. But, let's dig deeper. I can have any woman I want..."

I checked Karen to see how she'd take knowing she was expendable. She looked a bit put off.

"That's why I am with Karen. And, why she's no longer with her pain in the ass ex," he said.

Nice recovery, jerk.

She had no reaction to that blunt assessment.

"Take the most amazing sports car you can think of. They're not just making it. They're making it for me. I can have the best medical care in the world. If the doctor I want is performing surgery on you, I can take him straight out of your operating room and bring him to mine. Maybe you'll die. Who cares? My life matters more than yours. That's how the world works. I'm sure to you I sound like a stereotypical, rich bastard. I can afford to. Doesn't make me heartless. I don't try to be cruel to everyone. Just ask Karen how considerate and caring I can be. Her kids love me. And, I love them."

Her admiring smile confirmed it.

"I mean, despite all these privileges I'm a live and let live kind of guy. Unless you got what I want. Then, well, you know...sucks for you."

I didn't want to take anything he said seriously. But, there was an underlying truth to it all. It was something everyone knew, deep down, but avoided admitting; that there are two different worlds for two very different types of people—the haves and the have-nots as they're most often called. The more he talked, the more this subconscious universal truth gnawed at my defenses and depressed me. And, the more it made me want to kill him. This was a first. I was ready to kill not in self-defense.

By this point, he had wandered over to the bar. He walked around to the serving side of it and pulled something out of a drawer. It was a

German Luger. He admired it for a moment then walked towards me.

He said, "When there's a drought, I'll have water. When there's famine, I'll have food. When the earth falls apart I'll be riding first class into outer space. And, I'll have a swank place to stay there, too," he said as he approached me. "Count on it." He put the Luger up to my head and got right in my face.

"So, if I want you dead, I will have you killed without consequence. And, there's nothing you or anyone else can do about it. Got it?"

Beads of sweat started rolling down into my eyebrows. I nodded. "Understood," was all I could say.

He cocked the hammer.

"Look, I don't blame you for your predicament," he said. "You were born into it. That's life. What pairs perfectly with life? Death. And, that's where we are now."

I swallowed and got my voice working again. "Care to intervene, Karen?" I said.

She walked around me and stood a few feet behind Tanjeris.

"I'm sorry, Walt. I know you tried to help. But, nobody asked for it," she said. Very little regret on her face.

It was business. And, business was cold. No wonder she and Tanjeris got along so well. They were more than willing to make the hard, bloody decisions to get what they wanted. And, there was no shortage to their appetite.

I looked to Tanjeris. Nothing would have given me greater pleasure than seeing a horse kick his smug face.

"Would you have killed me had I not come here tonight? Were you still looking to tie up loose ends?" I said.

"Yes. We'd been planning for that," he said.

"So, there's more than one execution team?"

"Power and privilege. I can get *anything* I want. And, I'd just lined up your hit man this afternoon." He smiled, "You showing up just saved me ten thousand dollars."

My anger showed.

He said, "I know what you're thinking. Too steep a price for trash like you."

"There's no price too steep to take out a creep like you," I said.

He laughed.

Karen said, "Let's finish it up."

Her voice was cold.

Tanjeris glanced at her then looked back at me. "Somebody's hot to trot."

"In more ways than one," I said.

No way out. I had considered knocking the luger from his hand when he glanced at Karen. But, she still had her gun pointed at me. The odds were too dicey. But, now that we appeared to be wrapping up our conversation, maybe it was worth taking the chance. It could be my last chance, my only chance.

I turned to Karen. "I have to know. Did Ken go after Doug because of the shady stuff he and ITG are doing?" I looked to Doug. "Or, because he found out you were fucking his wife?"

He smiled. "That's the punch line. All this stems from a bit of infidelity. Seems cliché. Two people having sex who shouldn't be. And believe me, there's going to be lots of sex—"

I hit his wrist with the back of my hand. The Luger fired, but away from my head. The bulled ricocheted off the wall and shattered a sculpture. I moved with the momentum of my swing and brought my right fist around to Tanjeris' face. He went down hard, smashing his cheek on the marble steps. He screamed and clutched his face. I ripped the Luger out of his hand.

"Too late, Walt." she said.

Her pistol was aimed at my chest and she looked like she knew how to use it. "Drop it."

I tossed the Luger. It slid across the stone floor far away so no one could reach it.

"I don't understand, Karen. You're a mom. And, now you're trying to make sure I never see my kids again. How can you do that?" I said.

"I don't need to answer to you," she said.

"True. You've already killed your kids' father. Seems like a natural move for you to do the same to mine."

"Stop the guilt trip. I'll be able to give my kids everything they'll ever need."

"A beneficial afterthought."

"They'll still thank me for it."

"Oh, my god! My face!" Tanjeris pulled his hand from his bloody cheek. The crash had jacked up his facial structure—his right cheekbone had crumbled and the skin that had been stretched tight over it now sagged lower on his face. The area between his right eye and temple was discolored and swollen, too.

"Relax. You can get any doctor you want," I said without looking at him. That one hit a nerve.

He took a swing at me. But, in his condition he wasn't a threat. And, he got in the way of Karen's shot.

I jumped fast and pounded his broken cheek with the inside of my fist. He howled and clutched his face. That exposed his torso. I grabbed his robe, held him shield-like, and shoved him at Karen. His back slammed into her front and they both spilled onto the ground. He howled as her gun dug into his spine, both hands over his face. She scrambled to get out from under him.

"Lookout, Doug!" she said.

I went for the gun, but she fired. Too close. I felt the breeze of the bullet on my face.

Another shot fired. Shattered light fixture glass rained down on my head and inside my shirt collar. I ran out of the room. Another bullet hit the door, missing me by inches as I dove into the hallway.

58

I scrambled up and ran.

Her footsteps behind me.

I hurried through a large, catalog-white living room into a dining area that led to a kitchen. A large knife in the cutting block. I snatched it. A mental map of the house – or at least what I had seen of it—formed in my head. I needed to get to the front door. Which way next? The direction I had been moving seemed to take me away from the front door. But, reversing direction moved me towards the scantily clad milf wearing garters and carrying a gun. Great in a pulp novel, but not here.

I ran out of the kitchen and down another branch of hallways; How could a house have so many different rooms? Home gym, small office, servants' quarters...then down a staircase to...a sex dungeon? You crazy rich people.

The room was tripped out in padded mats, a worktable, and fixtures, all covered in leather. Chains hung from the ceiling, ropes were coiled up on a table, and a large St. Andrew's cross, complete with leather cuffs bolted at the top and bottom, leaned against the back wall. A naked, sobbing Mexican girl, maybe eighteen years old, was strapped to it, her cheeks streaked with tears.

I looked back. No one was behind me. I needed to run. But, I couldn't leave her.

The girl startled when I stepped in, as if I was there for her.

"It's okay," I said.

I searched the room. On a nearby table was a key to the cuffs. While I hurried to unlock them, I noticed a brand on the inside of her wrist. It matched the design on Tanjeris' ring. The hell?

CNBC played on a television mounted in a top corner of the room.

Stock reports ticked across the screen. A leather studded pig face mask hung below. It demonstrated just how worthless this girl was to Tanjeris. And Karen.

A bullet shattered the mirror behind the cross. I ducked and rolled. The girl screamed and flailed her one free arm. I could see a figure charging forth in a shard of mirror. It was a short Mexican in a servant's outfit carrying a rifle. Another shot. More mirror shattered.

I vaulted over the worktable and smashed into him. Another blast as he dropped the rifle. I kicked it away and pounced. Two quick punches to the neck, then I grabbed a rope and hurried to tie his arm against his neck to where he couldn't put it down or move it. I wrapped the rest of the rope around his legs. He wasn't going anywhere.

I grabbed the keys off the floor and ran over to the girl. She was dead. Blood dripped from the hole in her shredded neck. You poor thing. In my mind, I vowed vengeance.

I grabbed the rifle and raced up the stairs, slowing at the top to make sure no one was waiting for me. I sighted the rifle down the hallway. No movement. There were three doors on each side of the corridor, rooms I had passed earlier. They could be waiting in any of them. But, they'd have to react fast. I ran fast as I could down the hall, whisking past the doors.

Door four, a gunshot. Too late, but enough to send me stumbling forward. I clawed at the wall to hold myself up. A glance over my shoulder and Karen stepped out of the room I had just passed. She fired twice, the last shot splintering a doorframe just before I dashed through it.

I heard her coming after me as I blazed through the kitchen, the dining room, the living room. The door to the den was open, but I didn't see Tanjeris.

No hesitation. Down the hall, the front door was clear. I ran. My shoes squeaked along the marble flooring. I reached the front door, flipped the lock, and grabbed the handle.

"No!"

I stopped and looked.

Tanjeris. He had the Luger. His face was a bloody, swollen mess.

Karen, in her sexy heels, came clopping up the hallway behind me. She was winded, but she still had her gun.

Tanjeris spoke first, to her. "Think you can make him behave in the car?"

She nodded.

BAM!

Marble floor tile shattered as the shot echoed through the foyer.

She pressed the hot barrel against my neck. I screamed as my skin sizzled.

"Next time, I don't miss. So, be good. Got it?" she said.

I nodded.

She pulled the barrel off my throat.

Tanjeris' voice was calm, like she'd just shown him a strong investment portfolio. "Impressive."

"Let's get do it quick," said Karen.

"The Jasper dig site is fifteen minutes away. We can dump him there," Tanjeris said before glancing at her outfit, "Don't bother changing." He flashed a smirk then gave me a menacing look as he opened the front door.

He grabbed my arm and prodded me out the door.

"Don't be dumb. Walk out slow," he said.

I stepped over the threshold and they followed close behind.

"I'll be more than happy to shoot you Walt, so don't..."

The rumble came from just beyond the property gates.

Karen went silent.

Tanjeris' jaw dropped.

They saw what I saw. What I had arranged for and hoped would arrive in time:

DG and the boys rode their rumbling cycles onto the driveway and parked at the base of the steps. To a man, they were armed and aiming at Doug and Karen.

Karen caught her breath.

Oater showed a lascivious smile when he saw her outfit. A catcall whistle squealed out from the pack.

Karen dropped her aim and crossed her arms to cover up.

"Who the fuck are they?" yelped Tanjeris in a pinched, desperate voice.

59

DG dismounted his bike and walked up the steps, shotgun in hand. "Step aside, Walt," said DG.

I did just that, as DG got face to face with Tanjeris.

DG took the guns from Tanjeris' and Karen's hands and tossed them on the lawn. "Good kids," he said.

It was a great pleasure seeing this simple, dirty biker intimidating a man of such power and privilege, to use Tanjeris' phrase.

"Now as I understand it, you're the pieces of shit that got some of my crew killed. We don't let that slide," said DG.

"How much do you want?" said Tanjeris. He was so scared he couldn't control his blinking.

"We'll pay. Whatever you want," said Karen. Tanjeris nodded, eager to confirm what she'd said.

"That's exactly what I expected," said DG.

He made a hand signal. In a flash, two of his bikers were off their choppers and up the steps. A moment later they had chains wrapped and locked around Tanjeris and Karen's necks. Karen's biker made sure to pull her negligee to the side and take in an eye full. She didn't dare move.

DG turned to me. "You've done your part. Now, we do ours. Don't stick around,"

"Got it. And, thanks," I said.

He smiled and patted my chest with his heavy, fingerless-gloved fist.

One last look at Karen and Tanjeris. They looked pathetic. He wiped sweat from his brow. I saw that ring again. With the weird symbol on it. I grabbed his wrist and started to pull the ring off. He made a fist to prevent it. DG pushed the barrel of his shotgun against

Tanjeris' nose. He relaxed his hands and the ring slid off.

I looked at it, checked inside the band, but there was no inscription. Tanjeris looked defeated. And, it was satisfying. I pocketed the ring and looked to DG.

"See you at the river," I said.

I turned and started walking down the steps.

"Wait!" said Karen.

I stopped and looked back.

"What about my kids?" she said.

I contemplated.

"I'll tell them how great their father was," I said.

I walked out through the heavy iron front gate, which DG's crew had dismantled to get their choppers through. As I stepped over the threshold, the choppers roared to life behind me, their engines grunting and snorting in anticipation of action. I turned back for one last look.

DG signaled his crew. The bikers turned their choppers away from the house. To my surprise, DG and the two bikers who had been guarding Tanjeris and Karen trotted down the steps and hopped on their cycles.

That left the couple up there alone and struggling to get loose of the heavy metal chains still wrapped tight around their necks. Chains that were secured on the opposite end to the backs of motorcycles. Chains that would tighten as the choppers pulled away. Chains that would rip them off the steps like rag dolls and drag their bodies across the pavement until they were shredded, powerless, and thoroughly unprivileged.

I turned away before the chains tightened.

The chopper engines revved and roared.

Karen and Doug screamed.

Despite the cooling temperatures, it was time to drive home and take a much-needed dip in the river.

The Excitement Continues in…

When infomercial writer Walt Asher heard the news about a truck full of dead bodies abandoned on the interstate, he knew The Kith had returned. When he finds the corpse on his couch with a note pinned to its lips, it's clear they're coming for him.

Walt's in the cross hairs – hunted by elusive killers…battling brutal human traffickers…and desperate to destroy the sleazy secret cabal that's spreading its cancerous influence into the highest reaches of power. Are Walt's wits, fists, and powers of persuasion enough to smash it all before more innocent people die? Or, will he be the next sacrifice for a gruesome conspiracy that relishes the darkest rituals of the past?

Simmering with tension, bubbling with menace…experience the explosive new thriller that hurls you over the edge of excitement. BODIES, BLADES & RITUALS is the long-awaited second book in the exciting Walt Asher Florida Thriller series.

ABOUT THE AUTHOR

Yes, it's true. Andrew Allan really is a top infomercial writer and director. But wait, there's more! He also makes wild cult movies, runs DailyGrindhouse.com, and lives with his wife and three children in Clearwater, Florida. He also loves to hear from readers at AndrewAllanBooks.com. You'll probably find a free book by Andrew while you're there.